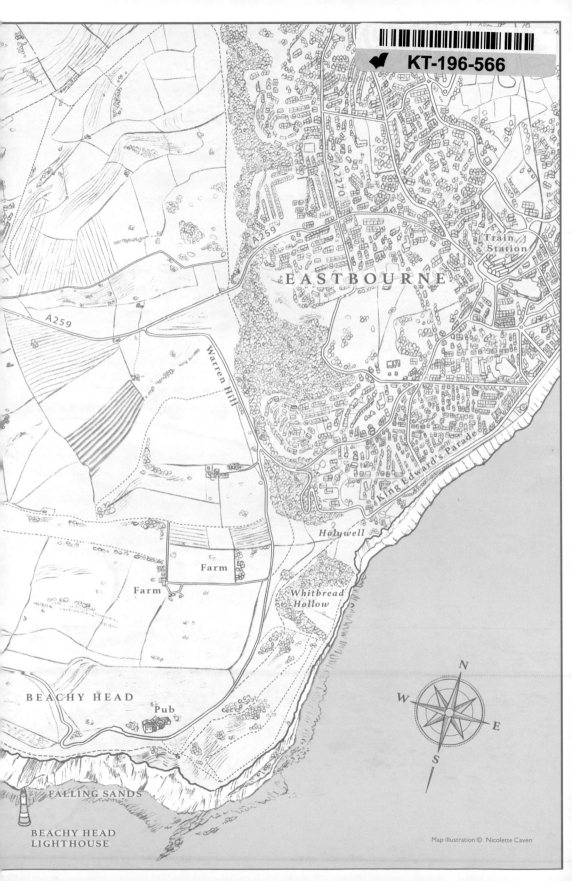

EASTBOURNE

Train Station

A2270

A259

A259

Warren Hill

King Edward's Parade

Holywell

Farm

Farm

Whitbread Hollow

BEACHY HEAD

Pub

FALLING SANDS

BEACHY HEAD LIGHTHOUSE

N
W E
S

Map illustration © Nicolette Caven

'Cole writes with human warmth and bittersweet emotion. I loved this.'
Matt Haig

'Wonderfully written. This is a book that will stay with you.'
Anthony Horowitz

'An absolute thing of beauty. Not like anything else I've read. Really involving and emotional. Fabulous.'
Jane Fallon

'Cole Moreton writes with a poetic beauty and a very sharp eye. Mesmerizing and lyrical, his words create atmosphere you can breathe and emotion that can shred your heart.'
Peter James

'A beautifully haunting read. Evocative, spiritual and deeply immersive.'
Rev Kate Bottley

'Tremendous speed and pace. The ending took me completely by surprise.'
Jeffrey Archer

'*The Light Keeper* is as compelling and ambitious as it is deeply moving. In the interchange of landscape, characters, the here and now and the "Other", this novel brilliantly captures the real spiritual debate of the twenty-first century.'
Peter Stanford

'Beautifully tense and atmospheric. It feels as if the characters are at the edge of the world and could fall off at any time. A page-turner.'
Marianne Power

The Light Keeper

COLE MORETON

First published in Great Britain in 2019

Marylebone House
36 Causton Street
London SW1P 4ST
www.marylebonehousebooks.co.uk

British Library Cataloguing-in-Publication Data
A catalogue record for this book is available from the British
Library

ISBN 978–1–910674–57–4
eBook ISBN 978–1–910674–58–1

1 3 5 7 9 10 8 6 4 2

Typeset by Manila Typesetting Company
Printed in Great Britain by TJ International

eBook by Manila Typesetting Company

Produced on paper from sustainable forests

One

You don't jump, you just keep walking. One step, then another. The edge of the cliff is close now, she can feel the drop but dares not look down. Her eyes fix on a shimmering, far out to sea. Fingers of light reaching down through the clouds to stir the waters, like a scene from one of the stories her father used to tell when she was still a girl and still believed in miracles. She stares at the dazzling light until her eyes go funny, but even when she closes them it is still there, burning. She feels sick, dizzy. Her feet will not move, they will not walk. Her legs shake. Her arms ache, wide open like wings to fly or to plead for mercy. The wind comes from behind, lifting her arms as if to carry her away . . .

Two

'Sarah?' He calls but he knows. Even as Jack turns the key and pushes the door with his shoulder, he knows. The worry that was there all morning and on the street and in his head is louder now as he runs up the stairs, turns another key and falls into the flat. Where's the cat? She's always here at this time, but not now. Sarah's coat isn't on the peg, her bag isn't on the bench.

'Sarah?'

Her laptop is still on the table in the kitchen, the little green sleep-light pulsing.

'You home?'

There's no sign of movement through the half-open bedroom door, no sound from the bathroom. No cat. Only the traffic, like waves breaking. The sleep-light pulsing. Jack runs his finger over the touch pad and the screen wakes with an image: the sky, the sea, the sun on the water. He knows the place immediately. She told him about it the day they first met, in the park. She was golden. Her skin shone under a white summer dress. He didn't know what to say. Jack had to force himself to look away from her body and into her face, into eyes that were laughing at his voice.

'You sound like the movies. I like it,' she said, and he felt so weird and far from himself that he could only grin back at her. Sarah took him to the palace to see the guards. She took him home with her like a lost hound and Jack was found. And in the weeks that followed they went everywhere a boy from New Jersey could possibly want to go in England, including this place, the one she loved the most. The South Downs, landscape of her childhood, where the hills lined up to face the sea. The sky was so vast and the water so wide, they could see the earth curve on the horizon. They walked on chalk and grass and looked out across the English Channel and she said wait – wait, wait, here it comes – then he saw, in front of them, the sudden, shocking drop. The land just fell away. Five hundred feet, she said. Five seconds to the rocks. He counted, moving closer. Five, four, three, two, one. He leaned right over to see and she got scared. 'Come back! You idiot! You always go too far.'

She was furious with him when he jumped back and laughed, and she walked away from the edge fast, right away and hid behind her camera and would not speak to him for a while. But it was already on her camera, the picture he sees now on her laptop screen. The sky, the sea, the sun on the water, as if she was hanging in the air somehow when she took it, suspended in mid-air – and he knows, really knows, where she has gone and what is wrong and what she might do. He shouts for her, knowing she is a hundred miles away. A roar; not a name but a sound.

'Sarah! Say-raah!'

And Jack is away down the stairs, past the bike, fast outside and into the car, stamping down on the gas, making the engine howl, yanking the handbrake up and off hard so that the slow, rusty old wreck moves off into the stream of traffic without a signal. Let them blare. Let them swear. Let them all get out of the way. He's coming for her.

'Wait, Sarah, wait! Hold on!'

Three

And the gull that has been hovering in the air in front of the woman – only a swoop away, but out over the edge in the void – turns as if it cannot bear to watch what happens next. The wind lifts its wings and the seabird slides, riding the rise and fall of the cliffs, away to the west. First a long, slow glide down into a dip, then the land swells again into another half-cut hill. This one has an old granite tower at the summit, a lighthouse whose light was put out a long time ago. It used to be safe, but time has passed and chalk has fallen away and now the ground is almost gone from under the feet of the tower, which stands hard by the side of a very long, white drop.

This is a lonely place in winter, but on spring days like this there is no more beautiful place in the world. The ripped clouds reveal a deep blue sky, the sunlight spills over everything, glittering on the sea or flashing on the bright face of the cliff, and the air is alive with brilliant energy. You are gorgeous, thinks a man who wishes he could do justice to the glory of it all, as he stands at the base of his tower. There's a low flint wall that was built to enclose the lighthouse garden, but bits of it have gone skittering and scattering out into space and down into the sea far below at some point, and where he's standing the chalk, grass and gravel just disappear. The man is scared of the edge and there's nothing irrational in that. Most of the time he keeps away, but today there is a task to perform.

So this tall, slender man with hair whipping into his wearily handsome face stamps the ground beneath him and kneels down carefully, palms against the chalk and grass. This is the man who lives in the lighthouse, who is trying to make it a home even though his stomach turns every time he thinks of the drop. So he lays on the floor and wriggles like a snake with his belly in the dirt and the dust, slowly moving forward, a few inches at a time, arms stretched out ahead of him. His legs are spread, his back arched, his pelvis is pressed into the earth as they taught him during hostile environment training a long time ago, in another life. His neck hurts as he looks past his arms and hands to a small wooden stake, just beyond the broken wall but before the empty space. He is as flat as he can be in this wind, spreading his weight as widely as possible to keep safe, but shaking anyway. The sweat blurs his vision, or maybe it is not sweat, as he offers a fistful of yellow flowers to the stake and ties them, clumsily – failing and trying again – with a twist of green garden twine. There. They are tied to the wood, tightly, so the wind cannot snatch them, at least for now, and he wriggles back, breathing hard.

'This would be so much easier with your help,' he says to nobody but the wind or a wisp of a memory, a face and a scent and a feeling of skin on skin that can never be again. Resting by the wall with his back against the stones and his feet towards France, he thinks of her inky fingers moving quickly over a page, making marks, creating a world out of nothing. The stuff of the sea, the sky, the wind, the waves, the light, was caught in her head as in a refracting glass and spilled out transformed on to canvas and paper in remarkable drawings and paintings. Her name was Maria but she signed her work Rí, the Irish word for king. A male word. She was stealing the power, because names matter, and she told him how to say it properly.

'Ree. Like free.'

The name is strange in his mouth now. Love brought him to this place, but she is gone and there is no freedom. He wants to stay but he can hardly bear it. He wants to leave but she is here. His eyes are closed by the rub of grief. A weary man, so dog-damn weary. Lighter, much lighter than he used to be, with a fluttering heart. Every meal is a struggle with matches and gas and a turning, churning stomach. It's easier to light a cigarette and suck down smoke than finish a Fray Bentos pie from the tin. He will become smoke himself one day soon and be glad of it, disappearing into the air as she did.

You're wasting away, she would say, but he smiles at the thought that she might also like the way he looks. He's back to the man he once was, running through the streets in war zones, dodging the bullets and the bombs, seeking out the stories that needed telling, living on adrenaline, coffee and cigarettes but knowing it was right to be there. Not the man he became, working from an office, walking the streets of a sick city, sucking it all up as a crime reporter, sitting with people whose sons and daughters, lovers and friends had been hurt or murdered, helping them to cry on camera, all those grieving people. Making money from misery. He could never turn away or turn it off until Rí, as in free. The girl who cut off all her raven hair and shaved her head and whose bright blue eyes could be as calm as a tropical sea one moment, as wild as the waves in a storm the next. Now, thanks to her, he's a crazy, broke bloke living in an old lighthouse without a light, on the edge of everything.

'Thanks, love. At least it's quiet.' People come up here on good days to see the staggering views and they are surprised to see him moving about in or near the tower, but they keep their distance and they don't know his name. He likes that. They must wonder at his life, but then so does he. His surfer-long hair is tangled and bleached by the salt and sun. The little blue lucky stone she gave him with the hole right through it is tied on a thin leather around his neck.

'I've got my cheekbones back now,' he says with a hand up to his sandpaper face. 'That's a win, then.' Somewhere at the bottom of everything is the ghost of a laugh. Be kind to yourself, she used to say. Be mindful. 'Live it, breathe it, be here, be present,' he recites. 'See it. Wake up and be thankful. I know. I know . . .'

He breathes deeply, coughs, then begins again.

'Come on. Where are you?'

He's trying to keep a record of his thoughts. Talk it all out, get it all down, as he was told to do by a counsellor he no longer wants to see. He no longer wants to talk to anyone but her, and yes he does know that she is not here. No, he does not care. The dictaphone tucked into a breast pocket, little red light showing, is just a prop really. It makes him feel less awkward about talking.

'What do I say about today?'

There's no answer. Of course not.

'The eighteenth of April. A blustery day. The wind pokes you. "Get up, boy; don't get comfortable, get on with it." The wind is a woman. A proper nag . . .'

6

What a clout he would have got for that. The wind sighs. She sighs all the time up here. All day long and all through the night, whispering or wistful, in agony or ecstasy, gasping and moaning, murmuring, sighing. Nuzzling the tower, never letting him forget.

'I'm sitting on my coat here, because of these . . . I don't know what they are. How bad is that? I should know.' He ruffles the grass and moss and heather or whatever it is at the base of the wall, but pulls away quickly with a tiny black thorn stinging in his thumb. 'I should know the names of these things. Not the sheep droppings; I know them, they look edible. Things are not what they seem here.' The wind thickens, roughs him up, steals his breath. 'I am not what I seem either. Not a tourist, not passing through any more, thanks to you. This is my place. Our place. This is our home.'

That is strange to say and stranger to live. This is the brim of England, right down at the bottom, the last place to be before you fall into the sea. 'So. I spend the nights awake with the wind around me. I sleep-walk through the days. The hours are shortening. I'd rather be out here with you than back in there, however much there is to do. Look at this view. How do I describe it? You were always better than me at that . . .'

He forces himself to look again, squinting into bright light.

Say what you see.

'Ah, hello.'

Silence again.

'Okay, so. Say what you see? The sun coming through again, over there. Picking out that fishing boat. The storm on the horizon, above that freighter. A cloud like a fist. The ship must be massive.'

Tell me the colours.

'The colours? Okay. Dark on the skyline, almost purple. Coming closer, the sea is a wine-bottle green; then a duller, flatter jungle green, maybe, with slashes of black from the deep water. Or the fish, or the shadows of the cloud, I don't know. I should know. The sunlight is silvery today, not glittering but still slippery with traces of the winter; silver draped on the water, rippling with the waves. Papery white at the edges. How could you get that look in a painting? I don't know. Maybe with a splash of mercury?'

7

Yeah, mercury.

'I knew you'd laugh. I love that sound.'

Loved.

'No. Love.' He closes his eyes, hearing the shush of the waves far below. Breathing out. Breathing in.

Good. That's enough for now.

'That's enough.'

Four

Jack drives fast through the city, as fast as he can. The traffic is heavy but he overtakes, undertakes, ignoring the horns, refusing to acknowledge the drivers he knows are shouting at him. Down under the river, through the tunnel and out into the last light of day, the dying light that shows up all the smears on the windscreen, and he's slipping left and right with the speed cameras popping, and thinking, rambling, letting his thoughts run. 'Why now? Why can't you just wait? It might be okay, it might work out . . .'

He doesn't really believe that any more than she does. They have three more nights to get through, then she will wake up early in the morning and take a test like all the ones she has taken before. Padding downstairs with the pen-shaped thing in the pocket of those tartan pyjamas she got from her dad, the big, baggy ones she wears for comfort. Cuddle Jams. He'll be outside, by the closed door, listening and waiting.

The first time she took the test was the only time she let him in the room, and he felt so unwelcome, trying to give her space and not react to what he was hearing, smelling, seeing. The sound of her water. The yeasty scent rising, mingling with toilet damp and lemon freshness. Sarah counting down from thirty, under her breath. 'Twenty-seven, twenty-six . . .' Jack was ambushed at that moment – as he waited in the shadow of her warmth – by the thought of a life just starting. A whole life of living and loving. A boy or maybe a girl, laughing and smiling, cuddling and tumbling, learning to walk, kicking leaves in the forest, playing football in the park, holding and being held, knowing they were loved. Daddy would always be there.

But there was no life starting at all. No damn blue line. Then came the tears, the shouting. The lashing out. Then the silence.

Such a long silence, longer every time.

But all the silences so far were just leading up to this one that is coming. The last time. The last chance. They have no money left. No more strength. No hope. No expectation at all that it will work. He knows he has lost her and he fears what she will do. Wouldn't she wait, though, for the result? Wouldn't she just want to hold out for this one last chance?

'Come on . . .'

Shadows are filling the car. They're up to his waist, up to his neck and he's drowning in them. They're over his head now. He's under the surface and the red tail-lamps glowing all around him in the slow-moving motorway traffic are the lights of an undersea procession, the people of the depths all calling for their queen. The indicator clicks and he drifts left, into the deeper darkness of the countryside, following the signs and road numbers and the memory of the numbers. Twenty-one. Two-six-seven. Like Sarah counting down the seconds of the test, to the moment when she knows.

'Fifteen. Fourteen.'

Faster. Too fast.

The tyres hiss. The car slides. Leaves splatter the glass, branches lash the windscreen. A flash of white and an explosion. 'Shit!' The wing mirror has gone. He jerks the wheel one way then the other, wrestling to keep her straight as he brakes, pumping the pedal, and the car slides and shudders and slows to walking pace. And stops. 'Sweet mother . . .' Jack flicks on the wipers, and through the muddle of mulch and muddy water sees a churchyard, a stone angel. Not much of a guardian angel right now. This is a dark road, someone will come up fast behind him soon. The key turns, the engine coughs and coughs but then starts again and he is moving, creeping past a pub with lights all aglow.

Jack crunches the gears and accelerates into the blackness. Rolling his shoulders like she taught him, to ease the tension. Feeling sick. Where is she? Please God she watched the sunset, as she loves to do, got some peace from it then turned away, back from the edge, to find some pub or a bed for the night. Or home, even. Please let that be true and not the other. How did she get there anyway, without the car? Why hasn't she called? Has she

10

called? He fumbles on the seat where the phone was but isn't now; it's down the side or somewhere and it's too dark to see and he would have heard it anyway.

The half-blind headlamps peer at grasping branches and sudden level crossings as Jack slows and speeds, slows and speeds, until the land rises, to say here we are, this is the Downs at last. The wind quickens against the side of the car as it climbs on a winding road and the door trembles against his thigh. He forgets to change gear and the elderly engine rises in pitch to meet the song in the speakers: the shimmering, enchanted Jeff Buckley version of 'Hallelujah'. And the world is only the music and the arc of light beyond the bonnet, white lines streaming through it, the empty eyes of a hare quickly gone and the orange numbers on the dashboard. A sign looms out of the darkness, saying 'You Are Not Alone'. There's a number for the Samaritans. He remembers it from when they came before, together, in much happier times. They made a joke. This is it then. Gravel under the tyres. Right. He will get out of the car, and cross this car park, and walk in the moonlight over to the edge of the cliff and she will be there and he will hold her and she will be glad and he will take her home. Now. Go.

The wind and the waves and the blood all rush in his ears in a monster roar. It's cold out here and the rain stings and he's shoulder to shoulder with the blasts coming over the edge as he climbs, beyond the car park, up a steep slope on a path that cheats his feet and has him stumbling, tripping, down on one knee. Agony. Maybe a stone has sliced through his jeans to the ligament, it hurts that much . . . But no, he can get up. Get up there, Jack. Find her.

'Sarah?'

The moon is bright in a halo of cloud, and the night is not as dark as it was just now. He can see the glitter on the sea far away and the lantern of a fishing boat flashing and dying who knows how far out. The edge is hard to see and he could walk right over it. Stay away, he tells himself. Keep your eye on the glitter but look up too, look ahead, for a movement in the dark, for a sign.

'Sarah!'

She's here, she must be. Why would she be here in the dark? She must be though. There! A shift in the shadows, a long shape forming into a body, gliding, merging with the ground, getting closer to where the glitter starts.

'Sarah! Babe!'

The head turns. The shape shifts again and the whites of her eyes come to him through the darkness, and it's her and he's found her and . . .

'Get lost!'

It's a stranger, weird and angry, turning his back and walking into the black, gone. And in that moment, the moon succumbs to the cloud. The stars fade, the glitter goes. The cliff is the edge is the sea is the sky, and Jack stumbles again. He's on his knees on the sodden sodding grass with sheep shit oozing between his fingers, and he can't get up this time. He wants to lay down and hug the earth and say, 'Keep her, keep her close, will you? Don't let her go. Don't let her fall. Love her. Sarah. My Sarah . . .'

But Sarah is lost. And so is he.

Five

The nights were black and impenetrable when they first came to live in the tower. She would stand in the doorway talking ten to the dozen about the view but he could see nothing, as if there was a hand over his face. Tight. It was that dark. Rí was frightened by the darkness – that was why she burbled away – but he was frightened of it too in this place, for the first time in his life. He knew that about her, she knew it about him. They knew each other. Now there is nothing to know but a man on the same step in the same broken-down fairytale tower, in the absence of a princess. A lighthouse keeper without a light.

At least his eyes have become accustomed now, so he can see the night sky as she did: rich in billowing shades of blue, cut through with black. Ahead are the blinking lights of freighters in the Channel. Far away to his right, down the long slope for a mile or more, is the little settlement of Birling Gap, with a coastguard hut, a telephone, a few cottages and a very tired pub. Beyond that there is a gate opening on to a path that leads over the backs of the Seven Sisters: seven hills rising and falling with their flat white faces to the sea. There are no roads that way; you can only walk over them or not go at all. And way beyond the line of darkness is an orange glow, low in the sky. The city of Brighton.

That's what the Great Fire of London must have looked like.

'Maria . . .'

Rí, like free.

Is he making it up, her voice? He hopes not, but then he doesn't really care, as long as she is there. The voice comes and goes like the French radio stations that blow over the Channel and fade away again. Down in the sweep of the valley where the sheep wait out the night in folds of downland, there used to be a secret listening post. An underground bunker, where some poor soul had to sit in darkness through the Battle of Britain, listening to the crackle of words as men high above him were dancing, diving, spiralling for their lives in the bright blue sky. Roger that, Tango Charlie.

You should eat better.

He looks down into the gloom. Sausages and beans glowing faintly, melted cheese reforming into a lump. 'At least it's not out of the tin this time.' There's a hunk of crusty bread in the crook of his spoon hand, a mug of tea chilling fast on the step in the dark with the frost coming. 'It's not bad.' He can see her sceptical smile, the tilt of her head, as if she is there. 'I didn't say it was good.'

Be kind to yourself.

He gives up and puts the bowl down. The mess is cold. There's a sound beyond the wind, beyond the sea, and it's growing louder.

'Really? Again?'

Now it's loud: not the sing-song sound of a Spitfire but the ugly, insistent chukka-chukka of a helicopter flying low overhead – too low, it will take out the lantern room. He braces himself, but does not duck any more. There have been six searches like this in just the last week; there seems to be more people going over than before. The searchlight is blinding for a moment then sweeps away, falling down through the dark. The chopper turns over the sea and comes back, blind red eyes blinking, downdraught whipping up an invisible spiral of dust, dirt and gravel, and he throws his filthy bread away and covers his face and curses, then it's gone.

The coastguards are looking for someone. The helicopter is off to his left, a couple of miles away, hovering over the next great hulking headland. That's the place they all go, the lost and the lonely, the despondent and the suicidal. Beachy Head. The place where lives are ended. That's where the drop is highest. You can be sure of death there, or so they say. He has heard of one young man who survived somehow and who is completely paralysed now, his mind in more torment than before he jumped. That is a kind of hell. He prefers not to think about it and to keep his distance from the Head, stay up here on his own hill where jumpers seldom come. The old lighthouse puts them off, they don't want to be watched by anyone, and he is glad of that. He came here for the beauty, not the misery. For a new life, together in their tower. Just the two of them under the huge sky, with the sea

14

spread out before them as a feast for the eyes and the dark earth at their backs. Elemental. They loved the landscape and she felt a powerful sense of belonging, so strong that it moved him to be here too. They had no desire to disturb the life or even death of anyone else; this was to be their sanctuary.

Now it feels like his prison tower sometimes, as if the light-house is keeping him and not the other way round. It's a strange thing to be, a lighthouse keeper, when nobody is paying you and there is no light to shine. It's so hard to be here without her, but he can't leave, because she is still here, at least in his head. His heart. Her things in the tower, the art she made. Her voice on the wind. Soon the helicopter will be back, with a searchlight and a device that can spot the heat of a body that is still alive, or at least has not been dead for too long.

'Lord have mercy,' he says, a remembered prayer. The last one he has left, for a god he has never trusted. 'Christ have mercy.' It's what he used to say, back in the day, in those moments before the medics came in their Chinooks. 'Lord have mercy. Be with them, whoever they are.'

The first room he has tried to make his own in this mighty, empty building is the kitchen. There's a good, solid pine table bearing the marks of life and a wood-burning stove, which should be warmer than it is. A pair of half-spent church candles, waiting to be lit. Copper pans that might glow like a page in *Country Life*, if he could be bothered to polish them. A big fridge with hardly anything in it, and no booze. He will never drink at home again. If this is home. It has to be home. God though, he needs a drink. On a good night, with the moon lighting the way, he can walk down towards the Gap for a pint. The back of the hill is broad and flat with a carpet of grass; it's an easy walk if you avoid the rabbit holes, but this is not a good night. There is no moon, and no stars now the clouds have closed over, and no way of knowing how far you are from the edge. It would be safer to stay indoors, but he needs that drink, he needs some company more like, so he finds the car keys and walks out over the gravel to his old red sports car, the Triumph Spitfire with the soft top that lets in the rain, and the suspension that sends every bump and shudder through the base of his spine. She starts at the second attempt and noses out through the gate and down the hill. There's a metal track half buried in the grass, then he finds the road at the bottom and turns, accelerating past the copse at the back of the hill. The road winds round to the Gap and what he knows beyond a shadow of a doubt, after exhaustive research, to be the worst pub in the world.

Six

'Pint of best, please, Magda.'

'Good evening to you, too! How are you?' He doesn't answer, but she doesn't expect him to.

The beer tastes of mulchy leaves and bonfires and nothing much else at all, really. They have watered it down again, or else he has a cold coming on. The sad, cracked voice of Bob Dylan is singing about being on the dark side of the road, and not for the first time he wonders where the speakers in this place are hidden. The keeper of a lighthouse without a light picks up his change from a puddle of beer and nods to the only other customer, a very old man sitting close to the window, taking his time between sips, fingers twisted like wildwood around an almost-empty pint glass. For more than seventy years, apparently, this lobsterman has woken to the same view of the sea and the sky and nothing more. Except, of course, that he sees everything. He knows every tide, can name every bird, has met the skipper of every inshore boat that passes. His name is Tommy Quick and in his day there was nothing ironic about that. He tells his tales when he drinks too much, but otherwise says little. So Magda fills the silence, standing there at the bar.

'Tomorrow is the day I came to this country. Ten years ago.'

This much the lighthouse owner knows. He listens anyway, taking sips from his pint. He's a good listener – that was always his gift. Listen, let them speak. He already knows there is a man who climbs a tower in the church in the main square of the city of Krakow, where Magda was born, to play a trumpet every hour. He knows the tune is never finished, in honour of some lost watch-man of the past who blew his horn to warn of invaders on the plain. He knows the watchman was stopped by an arrow in the throat, so even now, on the hour, the tune is always strangled to com-memorate that loss. Except on the night that Poland joined the European Union, when the trumpeter did not stop. Instead of strangling the note, he played Beethoven's 'Ode to Joy'. Teenagers hugged each other with tears in their eyes. 'Hello, European!' It was a lovely thing to see. He knows all this because he was actually there, on assignment. But he has never told Magda that.

'History begins again! The next morning, I am on the plane.'

She could have gone anywhere in pursuit of the European Dream. She came first to Redhill, to wipe old people's arses. A man in Krakow who brokered the job said it was the way to the new life. Then on to London, which she was supposed to love but hated.

'I think the men will look like James Bond,' she says, puffing out her cheeks at the obvious idiocy of that thought. Fate brought her under the protection of Chopper Tony, who ran the Eagle pub on the City Road and was no Bond. More like Oddjob. He'd take troublemakers into the yard and give them a beating with his great big hands, chopping away. He bought this place at the Gap for peanuts because of the risk it would fall over the cliff, and came here to hide, to ride out the storm of a failed marriage, cheating the till, drinking the stock. Offering Magda escape, or so it seemed to her then. They'll get him one day.

'I know who you are,' Tony said to his customer one night in the bar, and Magda took a silent interest as she arranged the crisps. 'Seen you around. Back then.'

The man from the lighthouse said nothing, but he reached out for his pint in a slow, deliberate motion that looked very much like a karate chop. Tony thought about that for a long while, before the edges of his mouth twitched into what might have been a grin. 'I get you. Keep it to ourselves. Keep schtum, Mr Lighthouse Keeper.' He looked very pleased with himself. 'You'd say he was a keeper, wouldn't you, Mags? A right keeper. I bet you would.' She turned her back to him, keeping very still over the crisps. 'All right, fella. No names, no pack drill. Keeper. That's what we'll call you.'

The stories we tell about each other are what define us, but the stories change depending on where you tell them from. Tony told the walking guides who came into the pub that the man who kept the lighthouse was a mysterious figure known only as the Keeper; they liked that and they passed it on to their groups, and the lighthouse man heard them talking by the wall, up by the tower, saying that name on the wind. The Keeper. Nice and anonymous. Tony finds comfort in their shared secret too. He thinks it protects him from the unwanted questions of a reporter who already knows too much. But the Keeper has no further questions for anyone. Those days are gone. Listening to Magda's stories is a way of not having to talk. There is something about him he has never dared analyse – a look, perhaps, the sound of his voice – that makes people want to talk. So she tells him that her name means 'high tower' in Polish.

'Like your tower. It is the place for me, maybe?'

She likes him, this lean man with the hair like straw and the face that is both battered and kind, but his pale eyes are elsewhere, always. His woman has gone. Magda does not ask where, because she knows he would not answer. He is restoring the lighthouse on his own, she assumes for bed and breakfast, which is fine by her because there is only one room at the pub and it is not advertised. She keeps it for people in need, of which there are many.

Magda is one of the Guardians, a group of volunteers who patrol the coastline from Beachy Head to the Gap three miles away, where she is standing now. They wear bright red fleeces with the word 'Guardian' written on the chest in gold, looking out for people who seem suicidal. They have torches, drive around in customized Land Rovers with powerful searchlights and work with the police and the Coastguard. They patrol because they are good people who want to help. That is what Magda says and she is right. They save lives.

She would like to know when the lighthouse will be ready for guests, and when they will start to come down the hill to eat and drink at her pub – or when the Keeper will look up and see how she feels and invite her to live with him in the tower, away from Tony – but she will not put those questions today. Poor man.

'So there we are. How are you?'

'Fine. Thank you,' he says.

Her eyes follow as he takes his pint and a small packet of peanuts over to a table in the corner by the fire. He has a book to read. This is how it often is at the Gap: Magda behind the bar, Tony out the back watching football, Tommy on one side of the room, the Keeper on the other. And sometimes, in winter, not another living soul.

'We've got to find her, you've got to help me find her, come on!' There's a boy in the open doorway, shouting as if the place is full, with the night whirling behind him. The draught blows over a lamp that rolls around loudly on the slab stone floor, alarming Magda.

'Close the door, please!'

The boy isn't listening. 'Please. Help me.'

He's shivering. A scraggly boy with black hair, wet through. He looks drowned. The Keeper assesses him quickly, as old habits die hard. Cheap leather jacket, bought in a market. Black shirt with big white polka dots, retro rock and roll, probably second-hand. Vintage, they call it now. Brighton or maybe Camden. Skinny black jeans and pointed boots. Nose like a beak. The boy's a crow. He's from the States, the accent is East Coast but he's been in this country a while, dropping his aitches like that. London then. What's up? Is he mad? No. Desperate.

'What is it, darling? Are you okay?'

Magda is out from behind the bar, her arm around the boy, sitting him down, closer to the fire. 'You need a drink. What do you want?' She glances across at the landlord, who has come out from the back room and shakes his head at her. 'Tea, maybe, yes? I can make you a cuppa. Or coffee?' She knows what to do, because desperate people have turned up after dark here before. Tony has gone again; he will be phoning the police.

'She came here, I think she must have done. Have you seen her? My age. Hair. God, I don't know. Ringlets, copper. Dimples. Sarah is her name. Sarah, okay? Sarah. She must be here . . .' He's getting confused, words tumbling; his hands are rubbing his face, forming a fist, banging his forehead.

'It's okay. Come on, darling, come here,' says Magda, catching his hands and pulling them down, holding them still, inside hers. 'Look at me. We'll help you.'

She's doing a good job, the lighthouse keeper notes instinctively. Lots of eye contact. Speaking quietly but firmly. Calming the boy. He's quieter now. Still talking urgently, but in a voice that can't be heard from the other side of the room, with Magda leaning into him as if they are conspirators.

The police enter like warriors in their bulky black stab vests and high-visibility jackets, radios hissing. They take control. A female officer with blonde hair tied up loosely takes the boy's name, address, phone number. The male officer, black-haired and boyish, directs Magda to one side. They know each other – there's a familiarity about the way she touches his arm as he talks, before her hand flutters up to her chest. He speaks quietly, she nods her understanding. When the police and the boy have gone, Magda closes the door, mutters something to herself in Polish, then says it again more loudly, in English, for the Keeper and Tommy to hear.

'That poor girl.'

Seven

Okay, so this is good, the cops are good, they will help. They will find Sarah. That's great, they have all the resources. Cars, people, dogs. Jack eases back against the head-rest on the rear seat of the police car and exhales. They've got helicopters. He's shivering. Now he's shaking, and pulls his arms around himself to try and stop it but it won't stop.

'You all right, sir?' The female cop sitting next to him is turned half away and looking out of the window. She sounds distracted.

Jack's fingers drum on his arm, tapping out a rhythm. 'Yeah,' he says. 'Yes, fine. Yeah.'

'We're going to the station, then we'll get you dry and warm and have a chat, try to establish what has happened. Do you understand, sir?'

'Okay, yeah.' Anything. Just find Sarah, that's all. There's nothing to see outside, looking past her. Only the rain on the glass as the patrol car glides into town. The lights offend him. Sarah's missing, she's gone, life can't just continue like this. At the station he is given a foil blanket, filthy instant coffee in a cardboard cup and a couple of slices of toast with sickly white margarine. They make him feel a little bit better, warmer at least.

'Can I ask you, sir, when did you last see your wife?'

Now there's another woman, presumably a detective, asking a question straight out of a comic book. Northern accent, he has no idea where from. Flat and sceptical. Jack didn't catch her name. She's older, forties maybe. The roots show in her ash-blonde crop. Her glasses have FCUK on the side – is that even allowed?

'Okay,' he says. 'Okay. Yeah. So. It was this morning. Hang on, yesterday, maybe. What's the time? Doesn't matter. Before work. She goes before I do.'

'What is it you do, Mr Bramer?'

'Drummer.' He looks down at his fingers, tapping on the table. Tapping on. 'I'm a drummer. And percussion.'

'I see, sir.' She smiles weakly, as if to suggest that's not really a proper job at all but she'll go along with it. 'What sort of music do you play?'

'Anything. Jazz. Latin. Rock. Whatever.'

'I see. I like a dance. Is there a good living in that then, sir?'

She can't help herself, can she? Smirking at him. 'Ha! No. I wouldn't say so. Not a good living. Not a living, as a matter of actual fact, as it so happens. A lot of work but not a lot of money. I make websites for people as well, in the daytime. Afternoons.'

'What sort of sites would they be then?'

'I don't know. Music. Companies. Individuals. Whatever, you know? Whoever wants it. I make people look good online. Great, sometimes.'

'And you work from home?'

'Mostly. It's easier. A couple of clients are back in the States, so the hours are a little strange to some people.'

'And your wife?'

'She doesn't mind. Oh, I see what you mean. She's a teacher. High school. Day and night, always working. Marking. It's not like people think.'

'I understand.' The detective looks unconvinced and very tired. 'I just have a few other questions. Could you describe how your wife was, the last time you saw her? What was her demeanour? What mood would you say she was in?'

'Angry,' says Jack quickly, and regrets it.

'Angry?'

'Angry.'

She waits for him to say more.

And waits.

The tapping starts again.

'She was pissed at me, right? She's always pissed at me. That's how it is. Have you got kids?' The detective says nothing, but winces. Jack doesn't notice. 'Okay. So. I said all this in the car to the other . . . we've been trying to have a baby. Trying a long time. Upsides, downsides, sideways, in a pot, in a test tube, any way you like. Nothing works. We've spent a lot of money and a lot of time

23

and eaten a lot of shit over this . . . I'm sorry . . . and we're all done, let me say that. Did I say that? Last chance.'

'What do you mean, Mr Bramer? A last chance for who? Your wife?'

'No. Jeez. Don't put words in my mouth. Do I need a lawyer here? No, that's not what I mean. Not at all. One last chance means us – we've got one more go. At the treatment. The money has run out. This is it. When it doesn't work—'

'You mean "if" it doesn't work, surely? The treatment.'

'I have no expectation of that. Anyway, we have one more chance,' says Jack, lips twitching, fingers rippling. 'So she's tense, Sarah. As tense as . . . tense.'

'And how would you say she is when she is tense?'

'Explosive,' he says, tapping out a soft little galloping rhythm on the table top with his fingertips now. 'Look, Sarah is a beautiful woman. Inside and out. Caring, clever, funny when she wants to be. Used to be. All those things. The best. The drugs they put her on do bad things. They make her mad.'

'Mr Bramer, let me be clear.' She says it right this time. 'Are you suggesting that your wife has mental health issues?'

'Seriously? Don't we all? Don't you? Doesn't he?' He catches the eye of the officer in uniform by the door, who glances away. 'I mean mad as in angry. That's not just a Stateside thing, right? But she does get very, very angry at the smallest things, and then . . .'

'And then?'

'She lashes out.'

The detective leans forward, alert now. 'Mr Bramer, I want you to think carefully about how you answer this next question. Are you with me? Does your relationship with your wife ever involve violence?'

'You mean when she throws knives at me?'

She stares at him.

A dry sound comes from the back of his throat. It was a joke. A dry, bitter joke. 'When Sarah swings on the chandeliers and kicks me in the face? When she smashes a bottle over my head? No. That's the movies. *War of the Roses*. Can I smoke? Look, where is this getting us? Sarah's missing. I need to find

24

her. I need you to find her for me. Can't we just go and look or something?'

'Does she hit you?'

'No, she does not.'

'Then what did you mean when you said she lashes out?'

'I meant it verbally. Obviously. She lashes out verbally.'

'Do you ever hit her?'

How dare she? Jack tries to stare right back, angry now. Tappety-tap, tappety-tap. Then he blows out his breath like a punctured balloon and slumps backwards into his chair, shaking his head. 'No. No, no, no. I do not. Never, ever. I do not hit Sarah. I love Sarah. I need to find her right now, wherever she is, and take her home with me. Do you get it? Can you help me or not here? If not, I'd like to go.'

He stands up and goes to leave but the detective moves to block him. The officer by the door also takes a step forward.

'Just a minute.'

'What?'

'Sit down, would you, please? There's something we need to let you know.' The two police officers exchange a glance. 'Look. We've had a report from the Guardians – they patrol up there, you may have seen them. One of their people saw a woman. A youngish woman. They were some distance away at the time.'

Jack wonders what that means.

'They reported a possible casualty, and both the Coastguard and the RNLI have attended the scene, to attempt a rescue. Or . . . well, a recovery.'

The word is a punch in the face. She means a body. Suddenly Jack can't see or hear or think as his blood pressure soars and he's dizzy. He doesn't know he's staggering towards the back of the room, putting his hand out on the wall. He can't breathe.

'I'm sorry, sir. I am sorry. From what you have told us, there are reasons to believe the female they saw may be your wife.'

Jack refuses to leave. The detective offers to find him a room in a hotel somewhere but he doesn't want to know, doesn't want to leave the station. He demands to see the body, and doesn't hear them when they say it's not possible, not yet. It takes time, they say. They've got to recover the person first; the helicopter is bringing the individual to the hospital, where the coroner's officer will attempt to make an identification. There are records to check, distinguishing marks. Please understand, sir, please be patient, please try to calm down, please, sir. He hears none of that, only the rush of noise in his head, the shouts and abuse of drunks and crackheads as they are brought into the station and slammed into the cells one by one, each slam hurting him.

Frustration builds to rage as the hours pass and he waits in a side room and nobody tells him anything. The plastic chair is uncomfortable, his bum goes numb, so he sits on the floor with his back against the wall. He lies down and tries to rest but there is no rest to be had and he is up again and out of the door, down to the duty desk, saying, 'What is the hold-up? Why can't I see her?' He doesn't hear the explanation or the caution they give him – after a warning, because they have to – when his language goes too far, because he is powerless and therefore in a rage. He doesn't feel the force of his flailing, grieving panic when they try to move him back into the room. Jack doesn't appreciate that they understand, they get it, mate; they just want him to calm down, yeah? Get some rest, here. He doesn't feel the connection his fist makes with a policeman's face or see the blood all over his shirt as he clutches his nose, cursing. Jack doesn't even hear the door of the cell slam and lock. For his own safety. He's oblivious, in a mist. He can't follow what they're saying outside, with his head splitting and his mouth arid and his eyes closing all the time. Closing. He's in a daze, in a daze lying down, when the officers come again for him and he does as they say and he follows them out into the corridor, out of the door, into another car, to another place that looks like a hospital, with high ceilings, halftone walls, green doors and a kindly looking middle-aged man with a helmet of white hair.

'I realize that this is hard for you, Mr Bramer, but what I need you to do is to say whether this is your wife. Sarah. Do you understand?'

Jack indicates that he does, yes, and the door to the next room is opened. The curtains have been drawn against the daylight, the room lit by a light that flickers dimly. There's a bad painting of a mountain, some flowers on a table.

'We will go slowly. I'm afraid there has been some . . . damage.'

It's not real, this. It can't be. Feels like a dream, like he's high, like he's floating, with no control over his feet, moving closer to the body. Standing there. Almost touching the white cloth that covers her body. The man is folding down the cloth. The face is revealed. She was so beautiful.

'Oh no. Sarah. Oh God, no . . .'

Eight

Half a dozen miles away – out of town and way up on the Downs – the man they call the Keeper is running hard. Running into the day, following a wide grass path a good, safe distance from the edge of the cliff. There's a hard frost some mornings that can crack the chalk, so that shards of white fall away without warning. If you happen to be standing on the grass on top of one of them admiring the view, then God help you. Hundreds of feet to fall, with tons of chalk and rock and earth falling around your ears. There's no surviving that. He has walked the beach far below at low tide and seen huge half-pyramids of rubble and ruin, leaning against the foot of the cliffs where they fell. So he stays well away as he comes to the last mile of his run, a long loop of the Downs ending in the place he always stops. A bench with a view.

'Morning,' he says lightly but she doesn't answer. There is nobody else here either yet, this early. The sun is hiding behind a flat, white cover of cloud. The wind-chill is fierce. It hurts his ears, so he pulls a hood over his beanie hat and slides himself along the bench, to where there is a little shelter. His love used to sit here with her sketchbook, surrounded on three sides by trees no taller than women, a congregation wind-bent into swaying, pentecostal forms.

'I said, "Morning."'

He's not mad. He knows she's gone but he still feels her here. It's like when you know you've lost a hand but can still feel the fingers. The white noise of his grief has never stopped, only become part of the music of his life. A drone, a constant note. But it helps to talk. When she's in the mood, which is obviously not today.

'Suit yourself.'

This bench was put here a long time ago, in memory of someone. It's on a slope, just where the hill begins to swell.

'Like a breast,' she said when she brought him here.

'Like a birthday cake in the shape of a breast,' he said, to make her smile. 'A birthday cake for a teenage boy obsessed with breasts. Loves Page Three. Collects pictures of tits and sticks them on his wall. His dad is a bit sheepish about it. Mum hates it but doesn't feel she can say anything, and she's so used to putting up with it that when he says he wants a boob cake she doesn't bat an eyelid.'

'She would!' said Rí, protesting. When she raised her voice, the Irish sharpened her London accent. 'I'd tell the little jerk where to get off. And his dad.'

'Yes, but you're not her. And anyway, I think the boy knows exactly where to get off. That's the point.'

'You're gross.'

'I'm not! He is.'

'He doesn't exist,' she said, laughing.

'Yes, he does. His name is Derek.'

'Derek the teenager?'

'Yes.'

'No wonder he's odd. That's no name for a teenager.'

'He's not odd. He's obsessed with breasts. That's not odd for a teenage boy.'

'Nor an old one, eh? A filthy old boy like yerself?' And she snuggled into him. They were sitting together on the bench, on a summer's evening, with the remains of bread and cheese and an empty bottle of wine at their feet. She smelt of sweat and lemons. It had been a long day, a long walk, a gorgeous time. Gorgeous. She also smelt of the grass and the sea, the wind and the salt spray, just like now.

'Why is it green?'

'What?'

'This cake. This hill cake here.' She gestured up the slope towards the lighthouse. He thought for a moment.

'Because Derek is a fan of Plymouth Argyle.'

'Pardon me?'

'They play in green shirts.'

'Can't you do better than that?'

He couldn't. He had to admit it. He could make up crazy nonsense at the drop of a hat – they both could, it was their game – but she always won.

'I can do better,' she said. 'Derek the teenager with a breast obsession – I hate the word "boob", by the way, dunno if I've told you that, please never use it in my company again – also happens to be a pagan. It's a pagan family.'

'Derek is not a pagan. He supports Plymouth Argyle. That's his religion.'

'Okay, so the mother is a pagan. That's it! She deals with all this breast stuff by making him a birthday cake that is secretly in the shape of the left breast of the earth goddess, so that when teenage Derek and his useless dad – let's call him Clive—'

'Why?'

'Because that's his name.' They both laughed. 'When they eat the cake they are actually worshipping the goddess. Unbeknownst to them.'

'Unbeknownst? Great word.'

'I do my best. So there we are. This hill like a green birthday cake for Derek in the shape of the earth mother's breast, only cut in half to show the cream.'

She thrilled him. The quickness of her mind. The mischief. He looks up at the hill now and smiles, because she was so right. And there at the top of it is the nipple. The lighthouse. Not the most beautiful construction in the world, perhaps – a simple tower of granite, although it sparkles in sunlight and wears a lantern room as a glass crown – but she loved it from the moment she saw it. Even with that ugly three-storey building pushed up hard against it, the keeper's quarters they were making into bed and breakfast rooms, cut into the slope of the hill so that the top floor meets the bottom floor of the tower. Still, it is the view from that soft peak that draws people and makes them gasp.

'The hill and the tower are both called Belle Tout,' she said. 'People say it like Bell Too. They think it means "good view".'

'Surely the French would be "good all"?'

'If you want to be a smart arse about it. I can see France.'

'Rubbish. Where?'

30

'Where d'you think? Over there on the horizon.' He looked along the line of her arm to where she was pointing out at sea and she laughed at him doing so and kissed him. 'You are loveably gullible, do you know that? As a matter of fact, the curvature of the earth makes it impossible to see the coast of France from here, although many people still swear blind that you can. Anyway, you don't say it like that. You say "toot" or even "towt". I'm giving you the good stuff here. It's from the old English for a look-out. Belle is from Belen, the Celtic god of light. They used to sacrifice people up here.'

'When?'

'The olden days.'

'Which was when exactly?'

'The sunset is to die for . . .'

To die for. That hurts.

Run. Get moving. Get away from here. Think of something else.

So the Keeper runs downhill into the dip, where a narrow road comes almost alongside the edge of the cliff. There's just a strip of grass between the tarmac and the drop. People like to get out of coaches in the lay-by and walk as near as they dare. They can look back along the line towards Beachy Head and follow the sheer chalk face down and down and down to the rocks at the bottom, where the other lighthouse – the newer, more famous one with its red and white stripes – looks tiny in the landscape, revealing just how huge these cliffs are.

This morning there is just one car, a big silver Mercedes. The driver is still in the car, both hands on the wheel, looking straight ahead. That's not a good sign, but the Keeper tells himself it's none of his business what state the driver is in. He is not here to keep people from harm; the Guardians have put themselves in charge of that. He doesn't want to talk to anyone. So he runs, but as he does a black coach comes gliding down the coast road towards him, indicating to turn into the lay-by. Suddenly there is another coming up from behind him, a white coach, also indicating. There is only room for one in that narrow space in addition to the Mercedes. The white coach gets there first. The black coach carries on, the driver giving an irritated wave. Bad luck, mate.

The white coach stops, sighs and starts to spill out students. Dozens of them, raggedy silhouettes with bobble hats and hoods and long, skinny legs. They will be told to walk up over his hill and past his tower and down the broad South Downs Way to the Gap, to be picked up again a few miles on. They don't really want to do this, as is obvious from all the slouching and shrugging. It's part of a schedule that will see them take in Brighton, the Tower of London and Stonehenge before supper, or something like that. Students come to the hill every day and he does everything he can to avoid them, but this time he is caught beside the group and feels conspicuous. What will they make of a bloke twice their age in a woolly hat and black wind-cheater, muttering to himself as he runs?

Half a dozen students in a clump are looking at something very near the edge. Very near. The idiots. Two girls even have their legs over the edge of the cliff. His gut tightens at the thought of being where they are. A couple of boys are jostling, as if preparing to push the girls. His shout may as well be a whisper. Even if they hear him, they might be startled into slipping. This place is a hungry tiger if you show no respect. Beautiful, yes, staggeringly so, but it can bite if you do something stupid like hang your legs over. He looks away, unable to watch, deeply fearful of what is about to happen, but there are no screams and his eyes are drawn back to the girls. They've got up. They're walking away. Oh Lord. He gulps in air, suddenly aware that he'd stopped breathing. He runs, and they see him and laugh like demented gulls.

The Mercedes is still there. The door is open. There is nobody inside now. The car driver is out on the grass, staggering about on uncertain legs. He's not in good shape. Hunched, barely able to stand in the wind. One rabbit hole, one gust and he's gone. The Keeper sprints up the slope to him, skidding on the mud, wondering what on earth he's going to say to get him to come away from the edge, when he hears a voice calling.

'Hello?'

A hiker. A pair of them. A bearded man in a light blue mac, a woman in red. 'We're here!' They're coming downhill, calling to the man from the Mercedes, who sees them and puts up a hand to say yes, okay, got you. He's a taxi driver, of course, the old guy with eyes weeping from the wind. There's a flash of gold as the clouds break, a splash of sunshine on the grass, and the lighthouse keeper soaks it up and feels his face warm and tighten with a grin. A bloody taxi driver. What a beautiful, bizarre place this is.

And it's where we're meant to be.

Nine

Jack wakes up grieving, twisting, moaning, banging out a rhythm on his chest. 'No, *no*!' The woman in the coffin – bloated, bruised, her face shiny with broken blood vessels, her nose smashed – can't be Sarah. Say it isn't her. 'It's not her! Listen to me!' Why won't they listen? Where are they? His eyes open slowly, painfully, to take in a bare floor, an open toilet, a heating pipe, a blistered wall. A cell. A door opening.

'Well then,' says a tall policeman in the doorway, his muscles stretching the fabric of an open-necked white shirt. 'You got some sleep. Good. We're not going to have any more trouble, are we? Tea will be here in a minute. Get yourself together, yeah? Back in a mo.'

The door closes and Jack looks at the ceiling, trying to focus, then uncoils himself from the thin mattress, which might as well have been the floor for all the comfort it gave him. He feels as if he has been beaten all over, but he has a scrambled memory of lashing out, thrashing about, before passing out. His hands are trembling.

'Tea?' The policeman offers him a cardboard cup and it shakes as Jack takes it and cradles it close. 'We've got some things to talk about, you and me.'

The giant officer sits down next to him on the bed, which means Jack shifting along. He's got a long, flat face like an Easter Island statue, but there's a mark just under his eye that looks fresh.

'I'm Sergeant Ravi. I'm running the place this morning. I don't want to charge you for what happened last night, because frankly I don't need the paperwork any more than I needed a slap from you, but I might have to do that. In the meantime, I have some news for you. They've found a wallet and credit cards on the woman who went over last night. How should I put this? The body they found, it's not your wife.'

Jack shudders. He hugs himself, eyes closing. Seeing her face again, half destroyed. It's not true, not true. Not real. A dream. A nightmare, in his sleep. She's not dead. She must be alive.

'You all right? Did you hear me? It's not her. They've identified the body; it's someone else. Poor woman. Not your wife. Sir?'

It felt so real. Jack's body shakes until the sobs burst out.

'Well. Okay. I'll leave you be for a moment, yeah? Let you have some privacy.' The sergeant moves away, not closing the door. Jack hears his voice in the corridor, faintly. 'Keep an eye on him.'

Jack sobs because he feels guilty, sobs because he's exhausted, sobs because he sobs and doesn't know why, and while he sobs they watch him and wait and wait. When they're sure he has run dry and calmed down, and when the threat of violence towards a serving officer seems to have passed, they let him go. The sergeant gives him a paper to sign at the custody desk. Just a caution. 'You're under stress. I get that. Just cool it though, eh? We're doing our best. As your wife went missing from your home address, we are handing the details over to the Metropolitan Police, who will no doubt investigate and decide whether to take the matter further.'

'Is that it?'

'Sir?'

'You know what I'm asking. Are you giving up on this?'

'Sir, as I have explained, our colleagues at the Met will take over. They have your details. I'm sure they'll be in touch. My advice would be to go home. You never know, your wife may have left a message. She may even be there. Let's hope so.'

'She came here.'

'Sir, we have looked for her. We'll keep looking, I promise you. A patrol has been out that way several times, the Guardians have been informed. They are out there all the time, all the way from Beachy Head along to Belle Tout and down to the Gap. If she is there at all they will see her and let us know.'

'What about beyond that, the Seven Sisters? There are no roads. You can't just send a car to have a quick look around. What are you doing there?'

'We do have a helicopter, sir. We are doing all we can. With respect, if people do have intentions we usually find them at Beachy Head. She came down by train, so there is no vehicle to trace, but we have spoken to the local taxi firms, who have not picked her up. We're talking to the bus company. We've also put the word out to the hotels, and there are no guests of that name.'

'What about her maiden name: Sarah Jones?'

'One, at the Grand. But it isn't her.'

'How do you know?'

'Various things,' says the sergeant, irritated at himself for saying the name of the hotel. Three hundred quid a night for a room. This lad couldn't afford that. Bit out of their league. 'For the moment, there is no evidence that she has been in this area at all.'

'What about the picture on the laptop?'

'With respect, sir, it's a picture on a laptop. I've got the moon on mine. I'm sorry. She is not answering her mobile phone, as you know. It's up to the Met now to run a trace, which I am sure they will do. Here, this is who you should talk to.' He pushes a paper across the desk. 'Please, ring that number if you have any more information. If it relates to activity in this area they will tell us and we will act.'

'I'm not giving up. I'm not just walking away.'

'Sir, you have the freedom to do as you wish,' says the weary sergeant. Then, under his breath: 'So does she.'

'What are you saying?'

Sergeant Ravi answers carefully. 'We are taking this seriously. You have reported your wife missing. Sir. We are investigating. My colleagues will take you to the Gap, where I believe you have a car.'

'I won't go home.'

'I thought you might say that. There's a room going at the pub there. They told us to let you know, if you needed it. Ask for Magda. She's the woman who helped you there.'

Jack takes his things, turns to the officers who are waiting for him, follows them through the door, fingers drumming on a bag strap. He does not hear what the big sergeant says behind him.

'Good luck, yeah? To the both of you.'

Ten

Jack says he's fine, he'll take a cab later, he's got things to do in town first. So the officers let him walk away around the corner to a row of shops, where he pops in and asks directions. The Grand is a large white Victorian hotel on the seafront, easy to find.

'Good morning, sir,' says a commissionaire in a black coat hung with gold brocade, dropping a shoulder to pull open the heavy brass door so that Jack may pass into a dreamlike place, a haze of light, a constellation of bulbs and lamps and electric candles reflected in mirrors and gilt and leaf.

'Welcome to the Grand,' says a woman in a black suit whose hands are clasped in front of her. 'How may I help?'

'Yes. Thank you. Please. I'd like . . . coffee.'

She takes him briskly away from reception and down the hallway to a large, circular space with a massive ornamental fireplace on the far side. 'This is the Great Hall, where tea and coffee is served,' she says, already spinning away. 'Someone will see to you.'

Struck dumb by the quiet, he can hear the hiss of the gas feeding the fake flames, the rattle of a silver spoon in a coffee cup. The clock on the mantelpiece tut-tuts time.

'Would you like hot milk or cream?' The waitress is short, slight, pale. She speaks with a soft French accent, eyes averted. She's pretty.

'Milk. Thank you.'

She sets out a silver pot, a silver jug for the milk, a silver sugar bowl and a silver spoon. A white china cup on a white china saucer decorated with silver swirls. He taps the spoon against the cup and is startled at the clear ringing sound, which makes heads turn. Stop, he tells himself. Concentrate. It's hard when he wants to scream and shout out to them all, 'Where is she? Have you seen her?'

Cookies arrive on a side plate, wrapped in triangles of white tissue paper. They came here for afternoon tea just a few months ago, after walking on the Downs. It was a mistake. The staff kept looking at their walking shoes, which had traces of mud. It's coming back to him. Sarah was in a state, saying something about a woman in the bathroom just now and telling him to look across at an elderly couple, eating their tea: he with a large cotton napkin tucked into the collar of his shirt as he demolished a vanilla slice; she polishing gold-rimmed glasses on the same kind of cloth, with a tiny slice of fruit cake uneaten on the table before her. The woman had been in the bathroom earlier and had washed her hands, dried them on a fluffy white towel, looked at Sarah and said to her face, simply and flatly: 'Black bitch.'

Jack found that hard to imagine. His face must have said so.

'Why don't you believe me? This is a different country down here. My country ends at the M25 or, I don't know, maybe the bloody North Circular!'

'You brought me here,' he said.

'I want to leave. Now.'

She was agitated, tugging at her sleeves, crunching sugar crystals under her spoon. She stood up and spoke loudly to the whole room: to the pastry couple, the waitress, the under-manager in her suit, the mutton-whiskered lords and ladies of the past whose faces looked down from portraits on the wall, the ghosts of luxury and exclusion. Sarah almost ran down the long corridor then, out through the revolving door, past the commissionaire, who nodded as though people did this sort of thing all the time.

Jack did not follow. He knew she would walk for a bit and come to herself. This agitated, paranoid woman was not Sarah as he knew her, the Sarah he loved. The fertility drugs were strong, the mood swings brutal. He was willing to wait. He wasn't expecting the doorman with an outstretched hand.

'Excuse me, sir. Madam asked me to give you this.'

A sheet of thick, creamy paper with 'The Grand Hotel' embossed in gold at the top of the page, and Sarah's tight little letters forming black words on a slight diagonal. 'Jack,' she had written. 'Go home.'

He found her on the promenade by a squat Napoleonic structure called the Wish Tower. Three wishes. One, for this to end. Two, for Sarah to return to him, the way she was. Three, for a baby. Or no baby. He didn't care any more; he just wanted it over, one way or another. She was walking up and down the seafront, waiting for him to find her, sorry to have spoilt things. So as Jack searches for her again now, he wonders whether this is really the right place to look. It costs a fortune, but in her state of mind anything is possible.

'Excuse me,' he says to the under-manager. 'You've got a guest here, Sarah Jones. Could you let her know I am here to see her, please?'

'Of course. Who shall I say is asking for her?'

'Her husband.'

She frowns, just for the briefest moment, before professionalism wipes it away.

'Sir, are you sure?'

'Please, tell her.'

More guests arrive, with expensive luggage. They wear formal clothes, as if for a wedding. They need help with the revolving doors. An elegant elderly lady moves slowly across the reception area, immaculate in a navy suit, floral blouse and pearls. She must be ninety, at least. 'Yes?' She is speaking to him, in a thin, reedy voice. Her lipstick is bright red, her skin mottled, her hair a whisper. 'What is this? Young man? I am Sarah Jones . . .'

And so, a few moments later, a retired judge is left standing in the lobby of the Grand Hotel, sincere in her hope that the anxious young American gentleman finds his wife very soon. At the police station, the detective in FCUK glasses is trying to imagine what Sarah is like as she dials her mobile number one more time and gets the answering message again. In another room, the big duty sergeant is thinking of Sarah too, as he finds her profile on Facebook. Not much to go on, but a looker, certainly.

He clicks on 'send' and a report makes its way to his colleagues in the Metropolitan Police. Another sergeant, seventy-five miles to the north, reads the name of Sarah Bramer and a description of her circumstances, and begins to formulate a response plan that will involve knocking at the door of her flat, speaking to her neighbours to see if there is a key, going to her place of work and calling her next-of-kin, who is listed as her father. A reverend.

Meanwhile, Jack is in a taxi heading for the Downs. The officers who offered him a lift earlier are already there, taking one more slow drive out west along the coastal road to the Gap, where they will pull in to speak to Magda. They know her well. She is also thinking of Sarah, with little more than a name to go on, as she hoovers the bedroom at the pub, which has not had a guest for a while. In the bar, the coxswain of the local lifeboat is working his day job as a painter, stirring emulsion and wondering if his boat will be called out to recover another woman today, as it was yesterday and a few days before. Something weird is going on. There are more people jumping than ever before. He hears the thrum of a helicopter and knows the pilot will be looking along the rocks or in the water. There's an alert out, the police gave a name. All of these people are thinking of Sarah, wherever she may be.

Sarah Bramer, formerly Jones, reported missing 18 April at 10.13 p.m. Female, 30 years old, born in Birmingham, United Kingdom. Address: 263 Francis Road, Leyton, London E10. Married to Jack Bramer, 30, of the same address. Ethnicity: M1, Scottish and Jamaican. Occupation: teacher at St Joseph's Community School, Leyton. Height: 5ft 10ins. Hair: reddish brown curls. Distinguishing marks: birth mark on left breast, small tattoo of a soul bird on upper right buttock. Eyes: green like the sea on a hot day. Smile: intoxicating. Laugh: mesmerizing. Brightness: dazzling. Beauty: silencing. Mood swings: infuriating. Sadness: heartbreaking. Whereabouts: unknown.

Eleven

She hangs in the morning air, caught between the sea, the earth and the sky. He has nothing but a thought, a feeling that Rí is out there, outside the lantern room, looking in through the glass. Watching him. It's impossible. He is thirty feet above the ground at the top of the tower, more than four hundred feet above the sea. But he won't look up from his work, in case the feeling goes. 'I saw you on the hill today. I shouted out but it was someone I have never seen up here before.' He could have sworn it was her, walking like an adventurer, striding out, head wrapped in a bright scarf with a long coat trailing behind. 'Must have frightened the life out of her.' The window frame rattles somewhere. His yawn is long and hard. The coat was the right shape, but it wasn't made of patchwork, velvet and silk, fragments of colour and texture stitched together by a magpie mind like hers. It wasn't the first time. What they don't tell you, what the counsellor with her tissues doesn't say, is that it all gets so bloody routine. After the adrenaline wears off, after the challenge of survival has been met, the grinding grief remains. The yawns never end.

'I'm sick of it. This. Without you.'

The Keeper is on his knees, digging into the soft wood of a rotten window ledge, causing the paint to buckle against the blade of his chisel. Clearing the bad from the good, dislodging flakes of wet, black-brown wood, spraying tiny splinters over his knuckles. Working away to the song of the wind, and talking as the red light of the mini-recorder glows by his side. If he sits and tries to talk, he can't do what the counsellor asked; but if he works, he forgets himself. 'In the morning . . . when I wake up . . . sometimes in that moment, before my eyes are fully open, you could be there.' Beside him. Supple and close. Breathing lightly. She's here now. 'Your knees in my belly. Your hand over your eyes. Your pillow all scrunched up under your neck. I could reach out and stroke

41

your head and kiss your neck and smell you, sweet and dark. But the moment I think of it, you're gone.'

His hands have stopped working. His eyes are closed.

'Then I'm falling. It feels like I'm falling. My insides, my spirit, my person is still there, still up there with you, but my body is falling away, to the truth.'

Just the dust, and the whisper on the wind. His voice is barely there.

'I can't breathe then, or move. I want to stay as I am, between the sleep and the dream.'

He could sleep here and now. Why not? Who cares? He doesn't sleep in the night time, so why not sleep in the day? For the same reason that he still gets dressed properly, still washes, still shaves. Still works. Whatever that is. He has to get up in the morning. Make a coffee. Turn on the radio.

'Sometimes I turn it over because you like music in the morning and the DJ is blethering on about some old nonsense, then he puts on a song and it's one of your songs and I just can't do it, I can't do it . . .'

Eyes open, seeing nothing. This is not the absence of feeling but the overwhelming presence of it: sorrow, grief, loss, confusion, pain, frustration, fear, all fighting for the air inside him. If he could open a door in his chest, it would be like a medieval painting of hell in there. Bodies writhing. Open, screaming mouths. Wild animal panic. He does not dare open the door; that's why the counselling had to stop. The effort of keeping the door closed exhausts him as it is.

'I have to keep on. I don't know why. Sometimes I'm dressing for the memory, like this . . .' His fingers touch the piebald stone hanging from his neck. 'I wouldn't wear this. And then . . . and then . . . I have to start the day. Do the work. Make this place comfortable for people to come and stay, but I don't want that to happen. I don't want anyone to be here at all, except me and you. All I want is me and you, like it should be.'

Rí knew this place as a ruin in her childhood, but someone had worked on it and built rooms, made it just about habitable, before running out of money. This could be their place, she said. Their tower. He used his redundancy payment, along with what she had. Everything she had. When they got the keys it was cold and dark. They climbed the steps to the top and the lantern room, lit an old heater, spread a rug and lay down together in the glow of it, ignoring the heady stink of damp and paraffin. *El fuego que calienta mi corazon.* The fire that warms my heart. Maria had Spanish and Irish blood, the wildness was in her, she could speak both languages. The wild woman had shaved off all her raven hair and he was shocked by the pictures of her in the past, but she loved him to stroke that soft stubble, and her pale blue eyes would close in pleasure. They would flash open again quickly if he said the wrong thing, though.

'You argued with everything,' he says, softly.

No I didn't!

A shadow shivers through the room. Outside, there's a flash of bright colour, a half-moon of silk, a canopy gliding by the window. Beneath it a figure in black. A parascender riding the thermals like the spirit woman in an old Irish song she used to sing. 'I am come to you from among the waves, riding on the wind.' And gone. She's gone.

He is as high as he can get, at the top of their tower, between the earth and the sky. She comes to him here, but when she leaves again like this, he cannot follow. He feels as though he's falling, like the parascender, like Icarus with melted wings.

'I ought to leave this place, Rí. I ought to go. I don't know why I stay. Because I can't go . . .' The man they call the Keeper steadies himself with a hand on the window ledge and looks directly to the south, to the sea, to the light skittering off the water.

'Where on earth would I go?'

Twelve

The bell rings. A proper old ship's bell hung on a rope, echoing up the steps. But that's odd because it never rings, there's never anybody at the door. Those who come to the cliffs look in or rest by the wall but then walk right past on their way to the Head or the Sisters; and those who lurk on the edge at dawn and dusk with thoughts of going over seem to avoid the grey stone tower. That's the way he likes it. Until he's stronger. No vacancies, no visitors. Nobody he has to speak to. The lighthouse keeper goes slowly down the spiral of steps, wondering. Down another level, past the desk that is meant to serve as a reception. One day. Maybe. Through the toughened, frosted glass of the new front door he sees a figure in silhouette like a scarecrow: dark, skinny, long-limbed, with a shock of dark, messy hair.

'I'm looking for my wife.'

It's the boy from the pub. He doesn't look drowned any more, but he hasn't slept, that's obvious. He's looking in, trying to see through the darkness of the lighthouse. The boy hasn't shaved for a while, thinks the Keeper, touching his own stubble. Ah. Yes.

'You do bed and breakfast, don't you? Is she staying here?'

He must take the sign down. It went up far too early.

'Talk to me. What's the matter with you? Are you shitting me? She's in there, isn't she? Sarah! Sarah! I'm here!' Now he's shouting. This could get out of hand. On a better day, the lighthouse keeper might have taken the boy in, offered him a cup of tea; but right now, his head is full of his lost love. That wasn't the boy going past the window just now, was it, with a parachute? No, surely not.

'Let me see her. Where is she?'

This startling scarecrow tries to push into the lighthouse, and without thinking the Keeper steps across him, accidentally grinding his arm against the wall.

'Shit, what are you doing? Man! Jesus!'

The boy throws a sudden punch, fist whipping in from nowhere, catching him on the eyebrow, stinging. Bad move. The old instincts kick in. The old training. He grabs the boy's swinging arm and pulls him in close and tight, their faces almost touching. Hot breath, a fleck of saliva landing on his lip. There is no choice but to speak now. 'Listen. Understand. She is not here. This place is closed. We're not . . . I'm not . . .'

The confusion in his voice gives the boy his cue to wriggle free, and he jumps back, bouncing on the step, waving his arms. 'You hurt me! I'm getting the cops! Sarah? Sarah!'

The Keeper stands with his arms by his sides, waiting for the manic young man to shout himself hoarse. Deep breaths. Someone has to be calm. 'Please.' He speaks very quietly, very matter of fact, as he learned to do from policemen and soldiers at crime scenes and in war zones. 'Let's start again. What is it that you want here?'

'Jesus. I want my wife. Sarah. She's missing. Don't I know you? Is she in there? I've been walking, looking for her, I can't find her. These hills are so steep. I've been walking and walking, she's not here. I can't see her, she must be there, inside your place; that's the only place, there's nowhere else she can be. Is she there?'

'I'm on my own.'

'Sure?'

The lighthouse keeper does not answer but his eyes say yes, trust me.

'Jack. I'm Jack.'

'Yes.'

'You know that? How? Shit! Get her, will you? Just let me talk to her.'

The Keeper tries to fill the doorway. Of course he doesn't know this person's name, he was just responding. This is what always happens. Misunderstandings. He'd like to help this Jack, he'd like to help him look for this Sarah, he'd like her to be here . . . but his eyebrow smarts and his head is thumping and he just wants it over, to get this guy out of here, away. 'Please, go.'

Surprisingly, Jack does. 'Tell her. I'll be back,' he says, stumbling over the gravel, out of the gate, looking back over his shoulder, then disappearing behind a wall. Thank God. The glass is cool against the lighthouse keeper's forehead. So one man stands in the darkness of his hallway, another slumps in the sunshine, his back against a drystone wall.

Neither sees the other's eyes filling up with tears.

Thirteen

This is ridiculous. The boy has got to him. He's been threatened by far more dangerous people than this, but his hands are trembling. He can't stay here, he's got to do something, so he chooses to run. He puts on his shorts, an old T-shirt, a thin Lycra hoodie, then his trainers – silver Nikes with a rip in the right toe, a bit battered like himself – and he finds his phone and earphones and runs down the steps, through the gate, along the path, in the opposite direction to the way the boy went.

The air is heavy, the sun is still shining, but there's a breeze blowing up from the valley, across his body, from land to sea. He presses play with his thumb and on it comes, the track that gets him going, the one he always runs to first: 'Move On Up' by Curtis Mayfield. His left foot goes down on the one, right foot on the two. His hips jolt as his feet find rabbit holes, and dusty chalk patches to slide on, but otherwise the ground is soft, springy, a wide carpet of flattened grass along the back of the hill with the drop on one side and a line of gorse bushes on the other.

It's a long, downhill slope towards the Gap and gravity drags him along faster, his pace getting ahead of the song; but as his shoulders shake down and his hands loosen at the wrist he begins to relax and let his breathing come naturally, listening to the scratchy guitar, the stabbing horns, the swooping strings and the rattling congas. As always, the memory comes. They were in the car, on a hot, sunny day. The soft top was down, the wind ruffling his hair. He had one hand on the steering wheel, the other reaching out along the top of Rí's seat. Her bare feet were up on the dashboard, the summer dress riding up to the top of her legs where the last of her hidden stars were waiting. The tattooed stars that cascaded down one side of her body, spilling across her stomach, burning out on the soft, pale skin of her inner thigh.

'Hey, Jensen Button! Watch the road, will you?' she said, laughing, pinching the hem still further up, until he really did see stars.

The country roads were winding, the Triumph Spitfire was on song for a change, he was steering into the turns, going much too fast, hoping there was nothing coming the other way. Knowing there wouldn't be. The road stretched out ahead, appearing from behind trees and barns, towards their destination. The Gap. A birthday trip down South with a proper wicker picnic hamper and a coolbox of wine. That was the day she made him drive on to the lighthouse, marched him up the hill and said, 'What do you think?' As if it was a work of art, not an abandoned building. As if he should have been able to guess what she was thinking. How ridiculous.

Now he's running back down the hill with her in his mind, in his eyes, in the music. 'Move on up.' One-two, one-two, one-two, running, breathing, banging out the rhythm on his chest as his hands rise and fall, tripping and slipping over the grass, down towards the steps, down the steps, across the gravel of the car park, past the pub. Down more steps to the beach, the drum break echoing from ear to ear, the bass kicking in at the base of his neck, still in time as he hits the pebbles, losing it then, falling over, laughing. Getting up with a push, pulling out the earphones, losing the music and hearing it crackle as he wraps the phone in his T-shirt and leaves it on a flat white table of chalk and runs towards the water, still in his shorts and trainers. Still keeping up the rhythm of the song, bam-bam-bam, still banging his chest, running over the chalk bed, over the sand, into the sea, feet slowing, hands scooping up water for his face, feeling the salt-sting, going deeper and deeper then diving, straight and flat, into a tiny wave.

He stays under as long as he can, eyes open and hurting, then comes up gasping, into the light, flicking his head, seeing more stars and diamonds and dazzling beads of sun-caught water flying around him. God, it's cold, it's freezing, his body in shock, his breath gone; but how wonderful, how wonderful, how wonderful to be here, falling backwards, arms out, lying like a starfish under a cobalt sky. *Move on up.* She's singing to him, and he loves her, he loves her. He loves her. He loves this life. With her. He loves her. *You'll be okay.* He hears her. *Move on up. You can do it. Move on up!*

Zinging from the swim, he lies on the hill with his hands behind his head, thrilled by the glory of this place, the profound energy that shines in the grass, the chalk and the sky, that skitters over the sea. He wouldn't want to be anywhere else right now, other than here under the passing sun, wrapped in the warm breeze, loved and loving in the landscape that is his home. He puts in his earphones, pulls up his hood and lays back to listen to a piano, the music of Erik Satie. The sound of calm. The pianist plays slowly, so slowly it is almost awkward, leaving the notes to fall into stillness. Rí is beside him now, he can sense her in the warmth of the ground, the scent of the grass and the flowers, the kiss of the breeze. The flecks of jade in her eyes, the flashes of blonde at the tips of her lashes, the tiny, light brown mark on the skin of one cheek that nobody had ever seen before him. Tracing her cheek with his lips, down to her neck and throat and to the stars, the stars, falling and flying, far away.

Fourteen

'You okay, mate?' The Guardian approaches with caution, seeing a male of uncertain age and origin on the ground a little way back from the edge, lying on his side with his hood up. 'Everything all right there?'

Michael Bond, a big man with a cannonball belly and a black, piratical beard flecked with grey, stops for a moment to lean on his carbon graphite trekking poles, catch his breath and assess the situation. He knows exactly what the Guardian training manual tells you to do in a situation like this, because he wrote it: keep your distance but stand within earshot, stay calm, begin a conversation. 'Frontline Alpha to Frontline Zulu,' he says into his radio, contacting his colleague back in the lay-by, who is watching him through binoculars. 'Male, hooded jumper, running shorts and trainers. Lying down. Not responding. Will attempt contact again, over.'

'Roger, Frontline Alpha. I have you in sight. Advise if help required, over.'

'Roger. Will do. We're okay for now, maintain contact. Out.'

His eyes are on the man. His prayer is quiet. 'Lord, guide me.' This one could be drunk or high, he could be sick or desperate, he could get up suddenly and run. 'Can you hear me, mate? Are you okay? We're on patrol up here, really just trying to see if anyone needs help, if they are feeling down. Because, you know, this is a place of suicide . . .' Call it what it is. That's the word that makes people turn around, usually. Not this time, though. 'Look, mate, I'm sorry,' he says, keeping a good six or seven feet away, because you don't want them to grab you, definitely not. You don't want to be in a wrestling match. Talking is much better. 'If you were sitting on a bench in a park, I'd leave you alone, but you're not. I just felt a bit of rain and this is a fairly remote spot. Can you hear me? You are close to the edge of a cliff. This is not a normal situation. Do. You. Understand. What. I. Am. Saying?' He can't see the face but this man might be an illegal with no English. That will be tricky, there are no translators up here, they'll need to get the police involved. Hope not then. 'We have a duty of care to the people we see here. If there is something bothering you, can I help? Come on, son . . .'

The lighthouse keeper whose love has gone hears none of this. He is lost in the memory of her skin, the softness of her lips, until a shadow across his face calls him back. Somebody is watching, from behind a disguise. No, a beard. It's a big man with a black beard and shades. A white shirt open at the chest, under a red fleece. Oh great, that's all he needs to spoil his mood. The Guardians do a lot of good, there's no arguing with that, but they will keep coming up and asking if he's okay. He's seen this guy before but they've never spoken and right now he really doesn't want to have to explain his presence here yet again. But here we go anyway. This one has bushy black eyebrows and eyes that are expectant, so he pulls out his earphones to get this over with.

'—for disturbing you. It is what we have to do. You understand that. Better to be safe than sorry.'

He doesn't want to reply, or talk at all. Not to this guy. He wants her.

'Mate, speak to me. Where are you from?'

'Here,' says the lighthouse keeper, despite himself.

'No, really.'

'Go away.'

'I'm not going to do that.'

Fine, he thinks, rolling the rubber tips of the earphones between a finger and thumb of each hand, then pushing them back into his ears, feeling heavy bass notes drop.

'Hey, would you mind turning that off so I can speak to you?'

The music stops and he nods but keeps the buds in. The Guardian breathes hard, nearer now and struggling to get down on the ground, belly shifting as he goes. 'Sorry, I'm sorry. It has been a hard day. Let's try again. I'm a Guardian. We're here to help.'

'I know. I don't need any.'

Hair whips into the lighthouse keeper's eyes as he lowers his hood, then the Guardian's face changes. 'Hang on, I've seen you before. You're a runner, aren't you?'

Very observant. His legs are bare and threatening to cramp. But he might as well answer, this guy won't go away otherwise. 'I live in the lighthouse.'

'You're the one they call the Keeper. Magda says. From the pub.'

'If you say so.'

'Funny. They call me the Chief. Taking the mick, mostly, but I don't mind. Used to be a chief constable in the Met, now I'm sort of the leader of the team up here. Player manager, if you like. Got a name though: Michael.'

He offers a hand and the Keeper shakes it, but doesn't give his own first name, or say anything else in response.

'You're doing it up then? Big job.'

'Yep.'

They sit together in silence, except for the fussing of the wind and the gulls turning circles close overhead. A lobster boat is making its way through the bumpy sea far below. The Guardian takes off his sunglasses, squints and smiles. 'Not suicidal then?'

'I wasn't.' The Keeper pulls a zipper up to his throat and tucks his legs in under himself, rubbing the tops of his thighs. The wind is gathering, he should go.

'Okay, fair enough. Sorry to disturb. We have to ask. I know you're not one of the main ones we're after today anyway, you don't fit the descriptions from the police: Asian man, late fifties, in a parka; white lady in her twenties, white puffa jacket, pushing an empty buggy. Had to give the baby up. Let me know if you see them.'

'How?'

'Here's my card. Hard to get a signal up here, sometimes text is better. Or just call the police, you know? We work with them. People don't usually come up to this bit by the lighthouse, I grant you. They mostly go to Beachy Head itself, because they've heard of it and the bus stops there, by the pub. Early in the morning or in the evening, often. No crowds. Your place puts them off, like a watchtower.'

'Should you be telling me all this?'

'It's okay. There's a lot of sadness in this world, but I've seen hope too, believe me. We are hope. The Lord is hope . . .'

'Are you allowed to try and convert people?'

'No, sorry, never do that,' says the Chief quickly. 'I was just talking about why we do this . . . Never mind, what did you say your name was?'

No answer. Something has caught the lighthouse keeper's eye, in the distance.

The Chief doesn't notice as he wipes sweat from his face with a hankie. 'Listen, please, don't let me give you ideas. Not today, I couldn't take it. Stupid of me to talk this way, but I've had enough. There've been more than usual lately. You must have seen the choppers and the cars. I don't know why. Lads in the force are giving me grief, saying we should all keep our eyes open more, but I tell them, we have a good team, they are all well trained, we would know, we spot things. If we can just talk to people, let them know someone cares, it breaks the spell. They know that. They appreciate that. Everyone's on edge right now. No pun intended. Listen, you haven't seen anything unusual, have you? Anyone hanging about? Up here, on your own?' A dark thought gathers in his mind like a cloud over the Channel. 'Hang on, have they talked to you about this? Hey, mate, wait! Where are you going?'

The Keeper is up on his feet, slipping past the Guardian and away.

'Come back! Oi! Get back here!'

The Chief's hand goes to the radio in a holster at his hip. 'Frontline Zulu, come in! Frontline Zulu! Alert our friends. Suspect running.'

'Roger, Alpha, repeat please. Mike, did you say "suspect"?'

'Roger that. Blue lights go. White male, hoodie, shorts.'

'Suspect for what?'

'What do you think? Why would he run? Quick! Am in pursuit!'

But it's not a fair race. By the time the Chief has hauled himself to a standing position with his Elite Alpine walking poles, the man in the hoodie is yards away and moving fast. Running up the slope, pumping hard, past a young couple eating a picnic on a rug a safe distance from the edge. The man and the woman are waving their arms and pointing fingers at each other and having a great big row, although the words are taken on the wind and they have not noticed that the one thing they agree on – the one thing that is good about this bloody relationship, the one precious person who has made life bearable these last three years, even when he's being a lazy bastard or she's a moody cow – is no longer sitting in the buggy having a snooze. Their little daughter Poppy is going for a stroll. She's tottering like a drunkard towards a rabbit, which is sitting in the sun, twitching its nose, nibbling the grass, looking up again, near the brim of the cliff. The toddler in her pink padded playsuit and pink woollen hat laughs and stretches out her hands to this bewitching creature, who stares back, blinks and bolts for it, leaving Poppy just a few baby steps from a very long fall.

'Oh my God! Oh my God! Oh my God!' shrieks her father, rooted to the spot, flapping his arms while his wife is already on her way. But she will never get there, she is too late. 'Poppy!' Alarmed by the speed of the rabbit, confused by the sudden sight of the drop, the little girl stumbles and falls.

Fifteen

Sometimes, death is ordinary. Sometimes death comes in the middle of the day, without warning and just like that, between the boiled eggs and Müller rice pots of a picnic on a rug in a beauty spot. Sometimes you take your eye off what matters most to you and indulge in yet another argument – because everything else in the world is okay in an ordinary sort of way and you've got to fight to keep interested – and while you're naming names and telling lies and making claims, the person you really love just drops out of the world. Gone. Without a whimper or a cry, that you could hear anyway. Vanished.

But sometimes life wins. Sometimes, a man you have never met – and whose name you will never know – comes running out of nowhere with all his strength, flies past you like an Olympian and gets there – he gets there – just in time. He is just in time. He scoops her up as she is falling over her feet – your daughter, your precious little girl – and with one arm he scoops her up and holds her close and stumbles on the uneven ground but regains his balance and still has her as he slows, and stops. He has her, safe.

Poppy screams, red and furious and magnificently alive, letting the world know that she is not done yet and she will be heard. Who is this man and what is he doing? Where did the rabbit go? I liked the rabbit! Mummy! The Keeper kisses the child on her woollen hat, ignoring the screams, catching her scent. For him, this is suddenly a good day. A great day. He feels like Superman, Batman and Wonder Woman all at once. Nothing can stop him now. Nothing.

'What the hell do you think you're doing? Put her down!' The father, flushed by panic, lashes out. 'What's your game? Stop! What's your name? Stay there. Don't you move.'

The Keeper does set Poppy down gently, close to her mother, who grabs her hood immediately and pulls her close. Dad glances at a mobile phone, which has no signal even for an emergency call. Top of the range, of course, but useless here. He's a Bodenista, one of the tribe of affluent Londoners who descend at weekends to cottages in the picture-book villages of Alfriston and Jevington, places that have been in the family for generations, since Virginia Woolf was renting, or else have been bought lately for extraordinary amounts of money. They come in their Range Rovers and their Hunter boots, their red trousers, their green Barbour jackets, like this man with his weekend beard, his tweed cap and his swagger, barking an order: 'Don't you run!'

The mother's shouting too, inventing a threat like him to hide their shame at having lost sight of their daughter for one terrible moment. 'I saw you!' She's holding Poppy tight, the girl's face buried in her chest. At least they're working together on this, their differences forgotten. 'You're in a lot of trouble, buddy,' says the father, lunging for the alleged child snatcher. But he's out of shape, out of breath and dizzy with anxiety and embarrassment, and misses completely, stumbling dangerously towards the edge.

'*Okay! That's enough! Both of you.*' The Chief has caught up at last. 'I saw everything that happened, sir. This man was trying to help. Your daughter was in danger.'

'Who the hell are you?'

'I'm in charge here. Look.'

The red sweater, the badge that says Guardian-in-Chief, the impressive radio and the commanding voice are persuasive: this man represents authority. The father deflates, with one last gasp: 'He tried to snatch her!'

'Then why did he give her back?' The Chief turns and winks secretly at the accused, who suppresses a laugh – adrenaline still sweet in his blood – and starts to walk away, until the big voice sounds again. 'Come with me. I need to talk to you.'

The Chief catches up and walks with him. 'You can't do that. You can't just go around interfering up here like some kind of self-appointed policeman.'

'That's a bit rich.'

'All right, listen, I can't have you acting like this. People might get hurt, you might get arrested. Leave it to the professionals!'

'For God's sake. You're amateurs.'

'I'm paid to do this. Respected for it, I might add. We work with the police. The others are highly trained. I lead them. You get my point?'

'Not really.' The adrenaline has given way to a sadness. The lighthouse keeper just wants to be back in his tower. 'If you're not going to leave me alone, can we sit down?'

He plonks himself on the grass.

The Chief does the same, more slowly. 'It is, by the way,' he says. 'For God's sake. Otherwise I wouldn't be up here, let me tell you. Scares the living daylights out of me sometimes. You've got to have faith. Guts, too. Determination. Patrolling this place in all weathers, day and night. I'm full-time but the others are all volunteers. Thirty or so we've got. A teacher, solicitor, brickie, retired, whatever, they come up here for a shift – once a week, usually – in pairs, on foot or in one of the Land Rovers. We've got the lot: heat-seeking cameras and really powerful lamps that cut right through the dark – they're amazing.'

'I've seen them. What good can you do really? If they want to jump . . .'

'They will. Yeah. Hard to stop someone who really wants to. So many are not sure, though: they're trying to get up the nerve or they want to be stopped or they're lost to themselves through grief or anxiety or medication, whatever it is. So we try to have a word. You know: "You don't have to do this, mate. Somebody cares." If they say anything in response – even if it's just to tell us to get lost – there's a chance they'll come away. Have a cup of tea back at our hut. Then maybe make a call, get someone who loves them to come and collect them. Or the police.' It's been a tough day. The Chief feels like talking. Something about this guy makes him think it's okay. 'Some poor souls come here again and again because they've got nobody else to talk to. It's so sad. Nothing gets funded. Nobody wants to know. So they end up here, with us. That's okay. We're called Guardians because we're here for everyone, as long as we can meet the need.'

He leaves a silence, hoping for the question. It comes.

'How many?'

'Hundreds come here, every year. The number is going up all the time, but until now the number of people actually going over has stayed the same, at about thirty or so a year. We must have been doing something right. There's a line I use to churches and so on: we stand in between life and death and insist that life is better, however much it hurts. And it does, let me tell you. For them, of course, and their families. For us, too. But the last couple of months, there have been more than anyone expected getting through; it's heart-breaking. And baffling. We lost one this morning . . .'

The Chief is glad to get this off his chest, but he isn't just rambling, he's also got a plan: share a bit, watch for a flicker in the eyes to suggest he might know about the death already, or is excited by the thought. Anything that might implicate him.

'My colleague Magda was on patrol. She was in pieces. It's harder on the ladies, but she is remarkable. I told her, "It's not your fault. You were doing what is right." She went home after that, but I couldn't keep away. I'm in charge, you see? This is my place. There is nowhere else I can go. I mean, nowhere else I should be. The Lord sent me here, He will keep me safe.'

The Keeper's silence is taken for approval. It encourages the Chief to go on, still watching for a reaction. 'I miss the force, I've got to be honest with you. Camaraderie. Mates. The kids have all grown up too and gone away, they're doing well for themselves. I tried retirement but it wasn't really for me. Shirley, my better half, said I didn't know what to do with myself all day. She was busy with the church and the golf, so I offered my services to the Lord in prayer. He saw fit to answer in this way. Long hours, low pay but good work. I have been running the show for a year now; it's going okay.'

The Keeper's calm, unfazed gaze invites him again to carry on. He's not to know that this is instinct kicking in, a legacy from the Keeper's past: the habit of keeping quiet and looking sympathetic, nodding to show he's interested, letting the story unfold.

'I reorganized the whole thing, of course. The two pastors who started the patrols were sincere, willing men of prayer, but we needed organization. Proper training. It's not for everybody. We have

58

torches, but when the moon goes behind the clouds and you stumble, then you think you're a goner.'

'I know. I live here.'

'Yeah. Course. Okay. Well, discipline and training help and the Lord gives me courage. There are times when I have to break the rules. Grab 'em and pull 'em back. It's dangerous but the Lord protects me. As long as I am doing his work he will protect me and no harm will come to me.'

The Keeper looks away, disturbed now. Not going along with it any more. He runs a hand through his hair, glances back at the Chief and mutters irritably: 'No.'

'Excuse me?'

'Sorry. I'm not having it. God, I really don't want to do this.' The Keeper stands up, stretching his legs and arms, looking the Chief right in the eyes. Staring, almost. 'That's not how it works, is it? Do you really believe what you're saying?'

'Yes, I—'

'And it's not just you – the same protection goes for everyone?'

'If they love the Lord and they're doing his work, then yes . . .'

'You're sure?'

'With all my heart.'

'Then you're a bloody fool.'

'It's easy to hurl abuse—'

'I lost someone. She had a faith. So strong. Put yours to shame. It didn't save her.' The Keeper is aware of his legs juddering; he could lose it now, not having talked to anybody about this in a long time. 'Right. So. This is bullshit.' Keep it all in, he tells himself. Keep it all in. 'Will he save you now, if I push you over?'

'You threatening me?' The Guardian struggles to his feet, but when he gets there meets only a smile.

'No need. You're a danger to yourself. God help you. I'm going home.'

'I can't let you walk away. I am in charge here!'

The Keeper puts his earphones back in, pulls up his hood and turns on the music, not Satie now but Curtis Mayfield again. Move on up. He slips easily past the Chief and runs up the hill towards the tower, his lighthouse, his sanctuary. Running for home.

For half a mile he runs, fast. The tower appears over the hill and grows larger in his sight, but when he is almost there, almost home, his eyes are drawn to a white shape, away to the right. It's a man, a little man, sitting right on the edge where the lighthouse wall ends, where the ground is dusty with loose scraps of chalk and flint, and he is afraid to go. Very afraid. There's a white number six on the red England shirt hanging from the little man's bony shoulders. The back of his neck is glistening below the buzz cut. Long white pedal-pusher shorts flap around the knees. His feet are actually over the edge. Bloody hell. He's kicking off a sandal by the heel, flipping it from his stubby feet with their blackened toes. Watching the sandal turn and fall. His lips move. He is trying to count the seconds until the splash. It's too far to hear that and there are too many ledges that might snag it on the way down. Now the other sandal is going the same way. Why stop to talk to him? Why care? There is a faint shush from the waves below. The little man twists around.

'What's your problem, mate?'

Bloody good question.

'Come on, what is it? "Why are you sitting there? What are you gonna do, kill yourself?" Ha!' The laughter is hollow. '"Why would you want to do that, eh? You've got so much to live for, aintcha?" Listen, pal, you think I wanna top myself, just 'cos I'm having a nice sit down?'

That's weird, he's turned it all round. I'm supposed to say that to you, thinks the Keeper. What can he say in response? 'Er . . . the sandals?'

'I like bare feet. They was broken anyway. Bugger off, will ya?' The little man laughs, wheezily, until a cough comes up. 'I'm bird watching.'

Without binoculars or a camera? Sure. No problem. Really. But if he does go over, right here, outside the lighthouse, there will be trouble. Better to say something. What did the Guardian say? 'If we can just talk to people, let them know someone cares, it breaks the spell.' Okay, so say anything. Hang on. Classic England shirt. Number six. Who is that? Bobby Moore. West Ham United. 'You a Hammer?'

'Very good, Columbo. I know what you are. Chelsea. You'll like my name then. Frank. Fat Frank.'

'Right.'

'After the player, Frank Lampard? You know? They called him Fat Frank when he was a lad, when he had puppy fat. It was a joke, really. He was never fat. I was enormous, me. Ma-hoosive. Ha ha ha! Then I lost it all. Misery diet, best diet there is. Ha-ha ha ha!'

'Not my team.'

'Let me guess then. Three guesses. How much?'

'What?'

'Let's have a bet. How much? My life?'

Is he serious?

'You win, I won't do it,' says skinny little Fat Frank. 'I win, you watch.'

This is getting out of hand. The lighthouse keeper sits down on the wall. He has no choice, his legs have gone. This is bizarre, surreal, dangerous. Still, Frank is talking; that must be good.

'United?'

The wind has dropped, it is very still, or they could not hear each other.

'No, hang on. Too obvious. You sound like London, that's all. That would make you a Man U fan, wouldn't it? Ha-ha-ha! Not Spurs, you're not one of them. A Gooner wouldn't live up here. QPR?'

Rí grew up not far from that ground in Notting Hill, the hungry child of artists, caught between suburbia and bohemia – she was Maria then. But that was her, not him. 'East . . .'

'Ah. Gotcha. Orient. Leyton Orient. Poor sod. So, deal's a deal, you watch me.' Frank shifts his bony hips and pulls up his legs as if to start a roll. He's going to do it . . .

'Mervyn Day. Billy Jennings. Tommy Taylor,' says the lighthouse keeper quickly for something to say, reciting the names of men who wore the white and red of the Orient when he was a boy. Former West Ham players, all of them. 'My grandad's fault. He played for them, so he said. I don't know. Never seen the evidence. He took me to my first game.'

'Bleedin' curse. Still, you gotta stick with it,' says Frank lightly, as if they are in the pub together after a heavy defeat. 'I like the Orient.'

'Come and talk about it. Over here.'

Astonishingly, Frank stands up. He steps away from the edge, to a slightly safer place. This is going well. It's going to be all right.

'Tell you what,' says Frank, 'it don't half make you feel alive, thinking you're gonna die.'

'We're all going to do that. Not today though, eh?'

'I'm wrong in me head,' says Frank without prompting, looking up at the sky. 'I get things wrong. I know, I sound all right now. It comes and goes, but it's getting worse. My daughter, Sophie, she ain't told her boy. Billy. I love that little monster. Love him. He's a bit tiny, poor bastard, but he can play. I wanted to tell him what was wrong with me, but she says he'll be scared. Won't let me do it. We had a row, now she won't let me see him at all. I'm scared shitless, mate.' He taps his head and rubs it, as if trying to fix something in there. 'I don't wanna forget his name. Don't wanna see him and not know him.'

'I'm sorry—'

'So I thought, you know what? Go quietly. Just do it. Spare them both seeing that. Spare myself. Get out the way. Somewhere nice. It's nice here, ain't it? Beautiful.'

'Yes,' says the Keeper with some effort, reaching for the other man's small, cold arm. 'Billy needs you, Frank. Keep trying. Go home.'

'Yeah.'

And so it ought to end, with Frank walking away from the edge, but it doesn't.

'*Come away!*' It's the bloody Guardian again, shouting out, doing his best to run. 'You're putting yourself in danger. Back off!'

'He means you,' says Frank, and he's right.

'I told you, I can't let you do this. Get away from that man.'

Frank looks across like a child who has just got his best mate into trouble in the playground. 'Listen, cheers, yeah?'

'Yeah.'

'You need to leave,' says the Chief, breathless.

'I told you. I live here.'

'Please, for your own sake, just back off. Leave it to us.' He's annoyed now. The Chief's dark glasses have slipped down his nose. 'This is stressful enough. I told you that. We know what we're doing. Let us do it.'

'Whatever you say, sir,' says the Keeper, letting the last word trail with irony. He wants to get away anyway, get inside his tower and lock the door. Be alone. 'Take care, Frank. Go home, yeah? Go home.'

'I will, yeah. Cheers.'

The Keeper turns and jogs away, then runs up the hill, but at the door of the lighthouse a great sadness comes over him. He turns back to see Frank and notices a second Guardian arriving down below. A woman. That's good, she will understand. Okay, maybe all will be well. Frank will go home. Maybe for once there will be a happy ending.

Sixteen

'Fudge?'

Frank looks into the white paper bag. 'Ta.'

'Shall we sit?' They both do, riding side-saddle to the slope of the land. The edge is still close. Frank watches the runner at the top of the hill, near the lighthouse.

'I'm going,' he says. 'Better be off.'

'Of course,' says the Guardian, a woman whose name Frank didn't catch. 'My colleague will go on foot. I have the car, I can take you. Sit, first. Rest. How did you get here?'

'Taxi.' Frank rubs a hand on his shorts and arranges himself, cross-legged.

'Who knows you are here?'

Nobody, says his eyes, searching the horizon. It's warm enough, the wind has dropped. The fudge is good.

'More?'

'Yeah. Why not?' The dry, dusty, nervous laugh doesn't feel like his. He's so tired. 'Mind if I lie down a bit? While we're 'ere . . .'

'Be comfortable.'

So Frank lies on his back, hands out and palms down, like Billy doing a snow angel. Scraps of rain-dark cloud move fast above him, threatening change.

'You can talk, I am listening.'

So he starts to talk about Billy, the clever little sod, and Sophie, and all that, but his heart ain't in it. He's had enough today. 'My mind wanders.' The wind picks up and blows sweet nothings in his ear. This place is noisy, for somewhere quiet. The kerfuffle, a couple of birds, the flap of a corner of the fluorescent yellow coat his listener has spread for them to sit upon. The waxy white paper of the empty fudge bag crackles as it is rolled up.

'Are you afraid? That's okay. It is a scary world.'

'Yeah. You got a fag? No, course not. I forget things . . .'

This little world they share is interrupted by the rip of a sports car, going far too fast. Silver convertible, bottom waggling over the bumps on the long road. What are they called, those? He can't remember.

'My name is Frank. I know that. I am not fat.' He can't be bothered to explain. The words swell in his mouth, crowding out his tongue. 'I . . . they tell me . . .'

Another long silence.

'You forget things?'

'Bit by bit. Getting worse, I know what's coming. I've seen 'em, sitting there dribbling. In the home. Don't even know their kids' names. Don't even recognize 'em. My old man was like it . . . you know?'

The clouds are bunching up. Plotting in the sky over to the east, above Beachy Head. He should have gone straight there, instead of walking, but it was so beautiful. Such a lovely place. Find a quiet place, he thought. Get it over with.

'You are a strong man,' says the Guardian. Frank won't return the gaze at first, then he has no choice. 'Protecting Billy, and Sophie. Yes. I see. You are strong, Frank, you were stronger before. Young, fit. A handsome man.'

His mousy face pinches in pleasure. Yeah. He was a player.

'You are clever, quick. Billy loves you, he looks up to you. Sophie is your daughter, you are her father. Daughters admire strong fathers. You have been a good father and grandfather. Billy will remember you, playing football in the park?'

Frank's eyes glisten.

'Yes,' says the Guardian, slowly. 'Football. Good times. Not this other person you will become. Sometimes it is the brave thing.'

'You telling me to do this?'

'No. I can't do that. God sent me because he wants the best for you. God is good. God does not want us to suffer. My mother suffered, Frank. I prayed and prayed and one day her suffering stopped. I will pray for you. I can take you home if you like, Frank. They will be worried. Scared. Angry, maybe.'

'You're not bloody joking,' says Frank, face flushing suddenly at the thought. 'Sophie will do one. Lock me in or something. Make my life a misery. She'll say it has started. They're gonna put me away like him. I can't take it! I'm not some child. Sitting there, gone. Screw that!'

He contracts suddenly and curls up like an embryo, arms over his head, covering his face. The Guardian leans over and touches his shoulder, making soothing sounds.

'Hey, Frank. Come on. Okay. You are in control. Your life, you choose. There is no need to suffer. No need to make Billy suffer, seeing you that way.'

Frank goes limp at that. The Guardian gives him space. Frank uncurls, unfolds his body and rises, putting his hand out on the grass, then on the Guardian's shoulder, until this skinny, trembling man with the pedal-pusher shorts flapping about his bare legs and the England football shirt hanging off his bony frame and the tears drying fast in the wind on his sharp face is standing up, breathing deeply, arms by his side, looking out to sea.

'This is why I came. It's for the best,' he says and takes a step, then another. One more. Filling his lungs with the fresh sea air. 'Thank you.'

The Guardian's eyes close. There's a shuffling sound, a sigh lost in the wind; and when they open again there is a boat with a red sail out in the Channel, nosing through the waves. The hill is a peaceful, glorious place in a wash of sunshine.

The Guardian walks away from the edge, as if Frank was never there.

Seventeen

Now here's Jack. Standing by the door of the lighthouse, twisting yellow flowers in his hands. 'Are these yours? They were blowing away.' The flowers have been shredded, by the wind or by him. Most of the heads have gone. 'Were they for a friend? I'm sorry.'

'Go away,' says the Keeper, exhausted and irritated and desperate to get indoors, but Jack is not going. Sorry for what, exactly? He looks as if he's been mauled by a beast. This boy – he's ten years younger, maybe – will keep coming back; the only thing to do is to let him in, let him look around, then get rid of him as quickly as possible.

'I hear they call you the Keeper. That's weird.'

'It's a lighthouse.'

The guest rooms are mostly in the outhouse, the square block that was built on to the side of the tower as accommodation for the old keepers. It leans into the hill, rising up through three storeys. The first guest room is just inside the door and he opens that first, for Jack to see. A table, a chair, a bed with the mattress on, still wrapped in clear, thick plastic for protection against the damp.

'There are six of those. They are all like that. She's not in there.'

Jack must believe it because he doesn't ask to see the others. They go no further. The Keeper offers Jack the chair, and sits himself on the edge of the bed, feeling the chill of the plastic beneath him. He breathes deeply, pausing in the moment to reflect that he doesn't have to do this, he need not ask, he could just leave it and tell Jack to go, and return to his world of silence, but today is not working that way. Today, people keep putting themselves in his face. He doesn't want to care, but here we go.

'Why are you so sure she's here?'

'I'm not.'

'Right. Wasn't expecting that, to be honest. From your behaviour.'

'A feeling? I don't know where else to look. What am I supposed to do? She's not at the pub. I checked the hotels in the town, most of them, but there are so many. The police don't care, they think she's left me. I can't raise her father, he's away. Our friends . . . her friends haven't heard from her. They want to come down, but that's humiliating. I don't want them here. I have to find her, talk to her. Magda – you know her, don't you? I stayed there last night, she has rung some people.'

'Did Magda say your wife . . .'

'Sarah.'

'Did she say Sarah might be here?'

'There was something. When she talked about this place. About you.'

'I see,' he says, but he doesn't.

'They don't know your name.'

Jack's fingers are drumming on the table, tapping like a tele-graph, while his eyes skitter over the walls, the door, out into the space beyond the windows.

'Call for her. Go on, if you don't believe me, call out. She's not here.'

'Sarah?'

That's really loud. The sound of her name makes the Keeper flinch. He wants to shout for Rí too, get the balance back. He should throw this boy out, but the restlessness, the panic, the fear is familiar. They've both been shredded, like the flowers.

'Sorry about your eye,' says Jack, noticing a cut and a yellow bruise. 'I didn't mean to. Well, I did, I meant to, sure, Jesus. I got you, didn't I? Didn't want to. Reflex action. You got my arm . . . yeah, well, anyway. We came here before, she loves it. She could do anything out here. I don't know her any more. The drugs do things. She's a danger to herself. We're trying to have a baby.'

Of course you are, thinks the Keeper.

'That's all she ever talks about. We've had our last go. I've got to find her because I know it won't work, I know what that will do to her. She's on her own. I don't even know if I want a baby with her any more. It screws you up, this thing.'

68

'I know,' says the Keeper, softly.

'You do?'

The floor needs a damn good sweep in here.

'Yes. You didn't hurt me. Not much. I've had worse.'

'Damn. I thought I had a good punch.'

The Keeper looks up quickly enough to see the spark of a smile on Jack's tired face, before it vanishes. Their eyes meet. 'You should go home.' He seems to be saying that a lot today. 'She might turn up back there.'

'She's here. I can feel it.'

'Not here,' says the Keeper.

'I mean, out there. Somewhere. Not far.'

'I hope . . .'

'Thank you.'

But all the while he is listening to Jack, a question turns over in his mind. He tries to ignore it but the question won't go away; it just keeps repeating as Jack goes on about his life in that nasal, fidgety way, like a comedian without any jokes. The story Jack tells is all about Jack, and why would it not be? He's here, it's him. Still, it is intensely irritating. What about Sarah?

Slowly, the man they call the Keeper feels himself becoming what he was before he came here: the special correspondent, the man in the blue flak jacket seeking tears in the dust. A mildly famous face on the television news. The sympathetic one, the empathetic one who sat for hours with weeping, frightened people who had it far, far worse than Jack, in faraway places first – in bombed-out houses, in refugee camps, in boats smashing against the rocks – with a cameraman and kindness, nothing more. Then back in this country with the mothers and fathers of the disappeared. Milly. Shannon. Young girls, gone. Abducted. Murdered. Crime stories. He doesn't want to remember. There are too many stories, locked away inside his chest. Too many to bear, as it turned out. They're calling. He doesn't want to hear them, doesn't want to feel it all coming back, hates to find himself listening like this again, biding his time, noting the ticks, the drumming, the tone of all Jack is saying. Waiting for the narrative to be spent, for the moment to arrive – as it always does – when he can put the question that matters, the one that might unlock the story. Whatever that is this time.

Then Jack stops talking. He has nothing more to say, and looks embarrassed, as if he has just woken up from a dream. There is nothing for it now, no choice but for the solitary lighthouse keeper who was once a coaxer of stories from the hurt and the angry, to remember how to do this.

He leans forward a little on the bed, takes a deep breath, looks at Jack until their eyes meet and asks: 'Tell me about her, will you? What about Sarah?'

Eighteen

She was a miracle child. That is one of the many things Jack does not say. 'You will not conceive,' a doctor said regretfully, but Jasmine Jones smiled and told him she was already pregnant, thank you very much. 'You will not survive,' said a second doctor, but Jasmine gave birth, noisily, at the height of summer and lived to hear her baby cry. A third doctor warned her, 'The child will not live long.' But the child was a month old and unexpectedly healthy when the Reverend Robert Jones paused on the threshold of their tiny house in a suburb of Birmingham, beaming like the sunbeam Jesus had always wanted him for. In his arms was a Moses basket and in the basket was a baby girl.

'You do know you'll have to give in, don't you?' said his wife, her hand on the small of his back, as much to help her stand as to urge him forward.

'I don't think so.'

'I really do think so.'

'Both names then? But mine first.'

Jasmine Jones snorted a laugh, shaking her head in mock dismay, spraying raindrops on the hallway's old orange wallpaper. 'You lovely, stubborn man.'

Jasmine had been raised to know her own mind and to get her own way. Papa had spent a lot of money making sure that was the case, sending her down from the mountain to the finest school in Kingston, probably the whole of Jamaica, where she had learned far more than he knew. When Jasmine and her friends walked out through the town in their starched white uniforms on sunlit evenings in the seventies they were well aware of being watched by men in cars and sidewalk bars. They kicked their heels, showed their legs, threw back their heads and laughed because they felt a hunger too, but theirs was different. Their lust, nurtured by their folks, was to Do Better. They were never meant to stay.

So Jasmine left the island and went away to Oxford, where she met a man. 'His face told me to trust him,' she wrote to her mother long after meeting Robert in a coffee shop on a corner near her college. The letter was written a good six months after they met, but it was all news to her mother. By then they had studied together for their finals, the serious young ordinand and herself, a different kind of believer, working as hard as him but always trying to make it look easy. Sharing the same library table in silence, divinity and law books spread out side by side. 'Tell Papa not to worry,' she wrote, but she knew that was in vain. With the letter, she sent a wedding invitation. It was fast, too fast maybe, but it was also too late for Papa to stop her then, if he wanted to. So of course, both men were nervous when they met for the first time at the college chapel, on the night of the wedding rehearsal.

'Look after her,' said Papa, pulling back his shoulders and pumping the hand of the groom. It was what he had to say. He had prepared the words. His face was stern and his stare was fierce. For a moment, he was every disapproving father in history. Then a twitch on his lips became a smile, as his worried daughter watched. 'Don't worry!'

Papa knew all about Robert Jones, she found out later. Papa had been to Oxford too, he still had friends from those days, only now those friends had influence and access. Questions had been asked, files checked, bishops consulted on the sly. This young priest was well thought of. He might not make a fortune, but he was a man of God.

'I know you will look after my daughter, I can see that . . . my son.'

'Done,' said Jasmine to her husband, closing the door against the traffic that was swooshing its way through another miserable day. The child was home. Back in the sun, her aunts and uncles would be muttering over their tea cups about what a shame it all was, how bright little Jasmine would probably never return to the law now, after all that money had been spent on her education. But Papa would be coming soon, to see his grand-daughter.

Jasmine would tell him this was her home now and he was welcome. She would not say how little time there was left for her to live in it. She had neither the strength nor the will for a fight on the day her daughter came home, but she was sure this child, this miracle, should have a name as big as the wonder she inspired.

'Both names,' said Robert Jones as he bent to kiss the forehead of the sleeping child, who wriggled in her snug of pale pink terry cotton. 'Your mother is crazy, but she is almost as lovely as you.'

Jasmine, who was about to draw the curtains, paused at the sight of her porridge-pale man and his lovely daughter. Her lovely daughter too, caught in a bar of swirling sunshine. One precious column of light had found a way through the rain clouds and smog, through the smudged window pane and thick house nets and was spending itself on them both. Let them be like this, she thought. Remember this, Jasmine. Remember.

'I love you,' she said, moving close to him, but he did not take his eyes off the baby. They both looked down and surprised themselves by saying the first of her two given names together, softly. 'Sarah . . .'

She knew none of that, of course. Her eyes had yet to open. She was not told the story for a very long time, because for years she did not want to hear anything about it or about her mother. But there was one thing Sarah could never easily put out of her mind: her earliest memory, the blinding white light. She saw it when she was three years old and holding the hand of her grandmother, as they turned from a hospital corridor into the room where her mother lay. There, surrounded by a dazzling haze of light, was Mummy on the bed, strangely yellow between the sweetie pink of her nightie and the bone white of the linen sheet.

'What is in your nose, Mummy?'

Sarah pulled herself up onto the bed by the green blanket, nearly kicking over a vase of daffodils on the bedside cabinet with her shiny patent shoe. She felt the hands of the nurse, a grip strong enough to lift her off.

'Oh darling.' The nurse's uniform was dark blue, she was in charge. 'Mummy is a little poorly just now, best not climb on her.'

But Mummy spoke. She whispered. 'Please. Let her.'

The voice did not seem to come from her body but from the air, floating down like a feather, startling Sarah and making her want to cry. 'Come here, my angel.' Mummy reached out, trailing the tube attached to the bruised back of her hand. Sarah knelt on the bed and cool palms cupped her face; she was pulled in tight towards her mother's lips, mouth to mouth, feeling and tasting tears. The tickle of eyelashes. She was too young to see the wildness in her mother's eyes: the look of a woman trying to inhale her daughter's energy, her love, her life, trying to suck up something of Sarah to stay there with her, in that room, a little light to burn when the darkness came. Sarah just felt herself squeezed so tight she could hardly breathe, and heard her granny's voice.

'Come on, love. Let Mummy rest.'

Not fair, thought Sarah, you are hurting me, Mummy. She wanted to say that, but she could not speak. Then the arms around her relaxed and fell away, back down to the bed, like the arms of a puppet whose strings had been cut. The arms of her mother, bare and motionless on the bed. The skin was pale, powdery, dry.

'Goodbye, my precious.'

Mummy hissed it, swallowing with great effort as if there was something dusty, spiky in her throat. She pursed her cracked lips in a dry kiss. 'Be a good girl.'

Why was Mummy angry? Sarah saw light blaze from her eyes and the room was crowded with whirling angels flapping fiery wings, and she was scared. She did not know that Jasmine Jones was raging, raging hard, but not with her tiny, precious daughter. Not at all. Jasmine did her best to smile, to fight it. To reassure. 'See. You.' She said it so quietly that Sarah could only just hear her. 'Later. Angel. When. I get. Home. Yeah?'

No.

No.

No.

She never did come home.

Nineteen

This will pass, they said. Trust us. But Sarah called out for her mummy in her sleep and in her waking, and she ran downstairs still befuddled from the tossing, turning night, shouting: 'Mummy? Mummy? Where are you?' There was only her father, a shadow in the doorway, bending down to pick her up. Sarah never cried, not even when he held her hard and pressed his face into her shoulder and her *Little Princess* jim-jams grew wet there, where his eyes were. 'Don't cry, Daddy,' she whispered. 'I'm sorry.'

She learned fast. She learned that some things hurt more than others; that the photographs of her mother, and her mother's clothes, and the books that had once been read aloud – 'all the better to eat you with' – and the mug Mummy liked to drink from were like bits of broken glass scattered around the house that cut her when she was not looking. She learned to find other things to do when Daddy had pictures and papers spread all over the kitchen table and he was sorting them, flicking them, working through them fast as though he had lost something among them, or when the music in his bedroom was loud. She kept away.

'Do you remember the monkeys at the zoo?' he asked her one bedtime. 'They were gibbons, I think – a yellow one and a black one and they had a little baby. They were swinging around and bouncing off the branches and Mummy said they were us – the two of us swinging, with you in her arms – do you remember that?' He was talking and talking, sitting on the edge of the mattress. He had stopped stroking her hair as he thought of it, but his hand was on her forehead, just there. Warm. 'You used to say the same thing all the time after that. "Mummy, Daddy, Baby!" Do you remember?'

She said nothing. She felt a bounce in her chest.

'You're tired. I've gone on too long. Mummy loved you, Sarah, she still does. Never forget.'

He left a warm space in the bedclothes, and she thrust her legs into it.

'Goodnight, my angel.'

'Night, Daddy.'

That was all. It took her ages and ages to get to sleep.

She loved Saturdays when his sermon had been written, her homework done and there were no weddings, so they could go for long walks in the forest with the curate's dog, that smelly, disobedient hound called Tutu. Then to the pictures. Her father grinned stupidly and squeezed her hand and ate popcorn (and let his eyelids close sometimes, she saw him) through *Toy Story* and others that blurred into primary colours over time, until she became a teenager and toons were no longer really her thing at all.

'Do you like this?' he asked once in the dark, their faces reflecting the action as some prince or other flashed his sword at a dragon.

'Not really.'

'Well, thank goodness for that.'

They got up, laughing, shuffled past a lot of grumbly people with awkward knees, and went for pizza. 'Next time,' said Sarah firmly, 'I will choose the film.'

She chose badly. A tale of pirates and romance, with not much blood, no swearing and only a bit of kissing, so that was okay, but all she could think of in the lovey-dovey bits was a boy from her class called Stevo, who flicked pellets of chewed paper into her hair with his ruler and would look dead cool with a cutlass in his hand. She burned up in the dark like a Ready-Brek kid, glowing with embarrassment at sitting there thinking and feeling those things while her dad was there, shoulder to shoulder.

Luckily, he had fallen asleep in his seat.

He will want to talk later, she thought, but she did not mind. They talked a lot, more than other girls and dads. They liked a natter, when there was time between the church and meetings, swimming and drama group, piano lessons, tennis and laying on the floor listening to soppy songs. Oh, and reading, she did tons of that: increasingly grown-up things like the Edna O'Brien novel a woman in the congregation called Suzy put her way. The words in the books were like a code – they had structure and meaning deep within them but Sarah could not quite grasp the whole, only catch fragments. Vivid, intense, adult fragments that thrilled and frightened her. She could not ask her father about it; that would be embarrassing. And he would try to make it lead on to talking about her mother, which she would not do. Under no circumstances. That was a given. There were things Sarah and her father did not talk about, for fear of spoiling what they had. Boys, for one. And two and three. But also, mainly, Mum.

Twenty

'Do you love me?'

His hair against her face made her want to sneeze.

'Tutu! Stop it!' The dog was tugging her away to play among the forest leaves with no idea what his monochromatic eyes had just missed: her first ever real kiss. With tongues.

'Of course I do,' she said, rubbing her nose with a mitten. Sarah had known this boy James in junior Sunday school, when they were very young, then waved him off at the airport when he left with his family for India. They had spent a fortnight together every year since. Strong, bright and funny, James told stories about the missionary life and teachers who thought they were still living in the Raj. He was smart and sensitive, the things she thought she wanted. And he made fun of the Lord with jokes, which was way cool.

'The nun says to Mary, "Why do you always look so solemn in your statues?" So Mary says to the nun, "Between you and me, I wanted a girl . . ."'

Back at the rectory, her father was saying to James's parents, 'They're good for each other. As friends, I mean. Obviously. They're good friends. Oh, I don't know, doesn't it scare you how fast they are growing up?'

The parents sat over cold tea and uneaten crumpets confessing that yes, it was alarming and it did make them feel old. They were all praying together, Robert and Tom and Judy, holding hands and asking the Lord for strength and wisdom, when Sarah and James were under the forest canopy kissing, trying to work out where to put their noses.

'I am in love.'

The first time James wrote those words to her was on tissue-thin blue airmail paper, sent from India seven days after the kiss. She wrote back, 'Thank you for what you said, but I am afraid to say that I think a proper relationship requires more than a fortnight a year of proper contact in which to flourish.' She felt very grown up, writing that, and it was only half serious, but it was also true. Sarah wanted a boyfriend whose hand she could actually hold. Lovely as he was, James would not do. They traded letters once a month, but by the time he returned to England a year later they were like brother and sister again, mooching around dusty museums and playing long games of chess.

'I am in love.'

The second time James wrote those words, he did not mean with her. They came after a complicated, lingering description of an unnamed school friend, which was confusing to her for reasons she could not immediately identify.

'This is it, Sarah. His name is Parv.'

Ah. Then she knew what her father would want her to think, but she was not going to think that, thank you. This was great: James was a secret friend, far away, who knew her like nobody else and had found a love really worth writing about. What a great secret. She was just a little bit jealous, though. Not of Parv, but of the passion.

'I love you too,' she wrote. 'I always will.' She meant it. 'I will be as loyal and faithful a friend as you have been to me, James.' Very Jane Austen. She was pleased with that. 'I do not suppose there is much I can do to help you tell your parents. You *are* going to tell them, right?'

Right. Her father called out as she passed the half-open door of his study later that day. 'Honey . . . I guess you know about James then?'

She was disappointed to lose her secret, and also very worried. She had heard her father preach. Love the sinner, hate the sin, he said. It was against God's will. 'It is different when you know somebody,' he said gently, as though stumbling on a thought for the first time. 'I suppose that is true. When you love them.'

He pushed his glasses back up his nose and shuffled his papers in the wordless way he had of saying that he needed to be alone to work now, thank you. His sermons changed after that. He began to quote Tutu – the archbishop, not the dog – so often that the phrase became his catchphrase in the church. 'Love is stronger than hate. Light is stronger than the darkness. Life is stronger than death. Love changes everything.' Sarah didn't know whether to tell him the last bit came from *The Phantom of the Opera*.

The Reverend Robert Jones said those things so often to his daughter because she would not let him say what he really wanted to say, never ever. He wanted to talk about his wife Jasmine, her mother, but Sarah would not have it. He very much wanted to give her a letter that Jasmine had written for her before she died, but Sarah would not take it. He tried on her eighteenth birthday, then her nineteenth and her twentieth. He tried again on the morning of her twenty-first birthday, holding out a blank white envelope. Inside, he knew, was a much older letter with her name on it, written in her mother's flowing hand.

'Please?'

'No. You can't make me.'

The eggs were burning in the pan. There was smoke in the kitchen. He pleaded, cajoled, paced the room, circling her, shouting, even cursing . . . and finally, when his eyes were blind with tears and his face flushed with exertion and he seemed about to lose his temper in a way that frightened Sarah, he went quiet. 'Fine. It is your choice.' He kissed her on the forehead, wetting her hair and thinking, you are so much like your mum.

Twenty-one

Sarah stood by the window in the tatty, untidy schoolroom and felt the heat of a radiator on her legs and the warmth of the sunlight on her face, or as much as could get through a pane of glass cloudy with handprints.

'Shall I compare thee to a summer's day?'

They were supposed to be doing Shakespeare but the teacher was off with the flu, suddenly. Sarah was shadowing Mr Alvin for a fortnight, getting her first taste of what school was really like for the people up the front. Or at the side. You should be the guide at the side, her college tutor said, not the sage on a stage. Let the children speak. But Mr Alvin said that wasn't easy when what they had to say was so often challenging, or just so bloody rude. She had been thinking about that earlier, when the Head found her.

'You can fill in this morning, Miss Jones, can't you?'

That was an order, Sarah realized as she watched Mrs Khan stride away down the corridor, ploughing through the crowd with her silent presence, scattering kids to either side. Genghis, they called her in the staffroom; but it was only a joke, born of admiration, because everybody knew what a tough job she had, holding the school together. The place was in trouble: they were five staff down already and the term was only a fortnight old. Summer term, the year almost done. Teachers were just dropping out, giving up, calling in sick. Too much pressure, not enough time, all the lost weekends and mountains of paperwork, politics and safeguarding pressure and abuse from kids who didn't want to learn. They bitched about it in the pub, then some just went missing. They just stopped turning up. Sarah still loved the idea of teaching, with the innocence of a beginner. It was nearly time for her first-ever solo lesson and she heard her chest whistle, felt a tightening. Closing her eyes, she concentrated on the warmth entering her body and on her own breathing. In through the nose, out through the mouth.

'Y'all right, Miss? Where's Calvin?'

Danny George swept past, all swagger and poise, and took a seat at the back, legs spread. Sarah knew where the nickname came from, she had been there. Mr Alvin bent over in class to retrieve a book from the floor and revealed the underpants at the top of his trousers. Just a peek, but enough for the class to see they were somewhat grey, somewhat the underwear of a man who lived alone.

'Them Calvins, sir?'

Danny's disciples had laughed at that. His status was already sealed. Star striker in the football team, he was going to be a pro, no problem. He'd wear Calvin Kleins all the time then. Real ones, not knock-offs from the market that went grey in the wash.

'You've got me today,' said Sarah without thinking and she immediately felt Danny staring at her. His confidence was unsettling. His eyes seemed to say yeah right, that would be your lucky day. What had she got herself into? But he looked away, sucking air in through his teeth, and Sarah felt relieved as the rest of the class came in like a crowd storming a palace. Now the babble was at its loudest, with shrieks and calls and the clatter of stuff and scraping of chairs, and it went on and on echoing back off the high classroom ceiling and Sarah thought about calling them to order but she knew this class, she had watched Mr Alvin struggle at times. They'd wind her up if she took them on. So she handed out the worksheets for Sonnet 18 instead and discovered a universal truth of teaching English: that nobody wants to read Shakespeare aloud in class except the show-offs. Danny volunteered to go first, stood up, threw a pose and read the first line with controlled aggression, like an actor in an action movie.

'"Shall I. Compare *thee*. To a summer's *day*?"' His eyes were on her the whole time. Then he shrugged and said, 'Nah.'

His people jeered, Sarah smiled. 'Thank you for that, Danny.' She'd got her bearings now and wasn't going to let him rattle her. This is going to be okay, she thought, although the volunteers dried up quickly and she had to pick readers from around the class. A girl called Kiké – Sarah checked – stood up, but nothing came out of her mouth; tears looked likely, she was trembling, so Sarah invited her to sit down. Another girl was asleep, oblivious to it all.

'That's okay,' said Sarah. 'Let her be.'

She knew the reason but couldn't say. Anastasia was the carer for a mother who was very ill, in constant pain and in need of help or company many times through the night, every night. She was struggling – anyone could see that from the poor girl's ghostly face – and the social workers knew it but nothing was ever done, apparently. Mr Alvin had warned that Nasti – as they all called her – might doze off. There were others like that too in this school. Every school. What could you do but feel for them? So Sarah moved things on and the class quietened after that, as if to let Anastasia rest.

'Kiké, come here, will you?'

The shy girl in braids stood up, unsure what to do.

'Come and sit with me.'

So she did and Sarah sat beside her, both of them perched on the front of the desk, facing the class. 'Do you feel lovely today, Kiké?'

Some of Danny's boys made highly inappropriate noises but Sarah waved them down, and Kiké said, under her breath, 'No, Miss.'

Sarah smiled, holding her attention but speaking loudly enough for everyone to hear. 'You are, though. You're lovely, Kiké. Are you as lovely as that summer day out there?' A few heads turned towards the windows, where the sunlight held up ghostly palms. 'No, you're much lovelier than that. You don't blow hot or cold, you're just right. Some days are so windy they shake the blossoms off the tree, you've seen that, right? Some days are way too hot. And summer's over way too soon, isn't it?'

Kiké looked at her blankly.

'Lovelier than a summer's day. How does that make you feel, Kiké?'

'Special, Miss. I guess.'

The low, teasing wolf-whistles came again.

'Well, you are. And that's what Shakespeare is saying to some-one in this poem. You're lovely, in a way that lasts for ever. Class, who do you think he's writing to?'

'His girl!'

'His batty boy!'

At least they got that this was love. Unfortunately, Sarah then lost them completely. The answers became cat-calls and shrieks and jokes, it all got out of hand and there was a near riot that caused a passing PE teacher to rush into the room and bellow at everyone so Sarah felt as though she had failed, which was true. But she learned lessons of her own that day and didn't give up. And when Danny and his disciples had gone away and there were only a few stragglers left in the classroom, Kiké came over and said softly, 'Thanks, Miss.' She looked happy in a way Sarah had never seen before. That's it, thought Sarah. That's why I'm here. But Anastasia was still asleep, face down on the desk, cheek on her pencil case, the last one left. So Sarah went over, squatted down beside her and put a hand on the poor, exhausted girl's shoulder until she came round, startled and afraid.

'It's okay. You're okay,' Sarah said. And when the pale, skinny girl was more awake, thrusting her stuff back into a bag, mut-tering apologies and rushing to get out of there, Sarah said as kindly as she could, still learning and feeling her way: 'It's all right. Anastasia, isn't it? Don't worry. Listen, is there anything at all we can do to help?'

Twenty-two

The second miracle of Sarah's life had an edge as sharp as the first. Granny was lying in a bed in the nursing home under a thin, pale blue blanket. Her hands were all red and gnarled, laid out flat as though she had been smoothing things down, making her bed in the morning. Someone had brushed her hair so silver-yellow strands swirled on the pillow around her head. A mermaid, underwater. Her eyes were closed, her mouth open. This is it, thought Sarah, taking her turn at the end of the bed. Just a matter of time. She was a trainee teacher now, in her early twenties, but this was a study day. Granny shivered and Sarah realized she was waking up. Why did she shiver? The central heating was turned up too high – there was a thick odour, the smell of bladders not attended to, bodies wasting away. Through the window, behind Granny's head, she saw a chestnut tree, branches jostling like the heads and shoulders of a waiting crowd. The memory of the blinding light returned. Sarah felt exhausted.

'Hello, Granny,' she said softly, not expecting an answer. Granny had not spoken since her fall, months before. She bent and kissed her grandmother on the forehead. 'Rest, eh?'

Granny breathed. A little sigh, every time. One more hill to climb, then down the other side. Rolling home. There was a hymn-book on her bedside table. The words stamped on the black leather cover had lost their gilt. Sarah opened the book, releasing the scent of childhood Sunday mornings. 'Amazing Grace, how sweet the sound, that saved a wretch like me,' Sarah sang softly in that hospital room, surprising herself. Almost not singing, then singing a little louder, then singing to her grandmother. 'I once was lost but now am found. Was blind, but now I see . . .' She sang with gathering strength, songs she had not sung for years. Sarah slipped her fingers between the cool, bony fingers of her grandmother and imagined that she began to sing too. She imagined a groan becoming a wheezy, wordless harmony, and she found to her astonishment that this was not just imagination. She felt those fingers squeeze her own and heard a sound.

'O Lord my God, when I in awesome wonder . . .'

Softly, Granny was singing with her. When Sarah faltered, Granny caught the melody. Sarah sang now with purpose and vigour, as if she could drag her grandmother up and out of the bed with the power of the song. But her throat tightened and she stopped. There was quiet. Birdsong. The radiator gurgling. A buzz of applause from a television in a distant room.

Then Granny, so quietly, began a song on her own. 'O Love, that wilt not let me go . . .' First line. Page three hundred and fifty-two. Sarah joined her, tentatively. 'I trace the rainbow through the rain.'

They sang together for ten minutes, an hour, she didn't know. Granny sat up a little, she smiled a lot, and when they ran out of tunes she fell back on the pillows again and hummed notes that tripped and slurred and sounded like hymns even though they were only the faintest of breezes passing through the Aeolian harp of her chest. She got fainter and fainter, until she seemed to have sung herself to sleep.

'Thank you, love.'

She had spoken, for the first time in months. Sarah couldn't believe it, but Granny smiled as though it was perfectly natural. There were even more remarkable things to come.

'I could drink a little soup.'

Granny got stronger in the following hours and days and weeks. She swung her legs out of bed and was wheeled into the garden and walked a few steps herself, out in the sun. The nurses said she laughed a lot but was difficult. 'Do come forward,' she told them, as though back in the Scottish Presbyterian revival meetings of her youth, throwing her arms wide. 'There's plenty of room at the front here!' She didn't know where she was sometimes; but she was happy.

In lucid moments, she gave orders about her forthcoming ninetieth birthday to Sarah's father. This was important, there were things she had wanted to say but not been able. 'I want you to sing, dear. In the park. Sing with the birds. Have a drink, too. To your health, not mine. That would be a little pointless, wouldn't it? Ha! I'll probably be stuck in here; don't look at me like that, I'm not an old fool.' She reached out and held her son then. It was that way round, for the first time in years. 'You must have champagne. There is so much to celebrate, it has been such a lovely life.'

Twenty-three

They were to gather at the Lido Café beside the Serpentine for Granny's birthday breakfast, with Bucks Fizz but no Granny. They would ring her and sing down the phone. The morning was fresh, with the hope of serious heat later. Sarah got there early, to walk for a while by the water, which was still. Three swans: a mother and her daughters, one of them white and one of them brown.

'Excuse me, Ma'am, is this the way to the palace?'

Ma'am? Sarah Jones looked at Jack for the first time then, in the park, with the swans on the lake and footballs flying through the air and airliners overhead and the breeze blowing up and the shouts of children and a woman in bright blue lycra cycling past, and she saw a weird, spindly creature, wearing too much black. Skinny jeans. Bird's nest hair. Ugh.

'Hello?'

He was swaying. Standing there with his mouth open. Spaced out. Sarah turned back quickly and walked off. That brought him to life, like a jolt of electricity: 'Hey, I'm sorry to bother you, Ma'am, please forgive this intrusion, I only ask for a moment of your time; you see I am a little lost, lacking in direction, I need someone to help me get my bearings. Show me the way, so to speak. Would you be so kind? Ma'am?'

He was following her, two steps behind, leaning in, bending round to look into her face. A torrent of words suddenly, hands hacking the air, his eyes wild, his fingers clicking a rhythm to match the rat-a-tat rattle of his language.

'I am looking for the palace, that is the truth, the palace, yes, but I see I have found a princess . . . would that be an imposition to say?'

'Yes,' she said, stopping and looking at him. 'Yes, it would. And very, very cheesy.'

'Then forgive me again. Yes. Forgive me. I am a poor boy washed up upon your shores, a stranger in a land far from my own.'

'You're American.'

'This I am. Ma'am. At your service.'

She smiled, but shook her head. 'Which palace?'

'Your city is charming. You yourself are charming—'

'You said. We have many.'

'I had no idea.'

Already, there was something that both of them knew, but it kept slipping away from him as his eyes lost focus, before they snapped back on her again. He stopped walking, and she stopped to match him without thinking about it, and they stood there on the path by a litter bin and a patch of grass, at a crossroads.

'Could you tell me, would you mind . . .'

'Probably.' Her arms were crossed, her head tilted to one side, a turquoise teardrop set in silver hung from the ear he stared at as if he wanted to kiss her just there.

'Can you tell me, what . . . I mean . . . what are we talking about?'

'Palaces,' she said.

'Ah. I knew that.'

'Then why ask?'

'About palaces. There are many. Locating them, you see, this is the issue. My issue. I am meeting friends later. At the palace.'

'You need to tell me which one.'

'Soccer. Not soccer,' he said as if to himself.

'What?'

'I am not a fan of that sport, although of course I do see why others are, please don't be offended if you are one of them, but I am not in a particular hurry to see Crystal Palace. The main attraction there burned down a long time ago, I believe. I don't have a passion for the Duchess of Cambridge either, unlike some of my fellow countrymen, so Kensington Palace does not particularly interest me. I'm looking for an upgrade on that.'

'You know your palaces.'

He laughed. 'So it would seem.'

'You were having me on.'

'Pardon me?'

'Pulling my leg.'

'Yes. In a way. So, Bucking-ham Palace. But which way?'

'That way,' she said quickly, pointing to the right-hand path, the one that would lead to Hyde Park Corner, Constitution Hill and ultimately the palace. 'It's quite far.'

'I'm obliged,' he said.

'No problem.'

'I'm delighted.'

'Okay.'

'I'm enthralled,' he said.

'Are you now?'

'Utterly. Entranced. Beguiled. Enchanted.'

'Right.'

'Bowled over. Knocked for six. Gobsmacked. Is that right?'

'I don't know. What are you saying?'

'You're . . . let me get this right . . . a bit dishy.'

Sarah laughed and turned away, stepping on to the forbidden grass.

'I'm sorry,' said Jack. 'Is that wrong?'

'No,' she said. 'Well, yes. Where did you get it from?'

'A gentleman I met in the pub. A senior. What I mean to say, Ma'am, and I hope you will forgive again the intrusion here, is that I am transfixed at your beauty, mesmerized by your grace, seduced by your presence, even though we have just met I feel—'

'Does this usually work?'

He looked hurt. 'What?'

'This . . . crap.'

'Nicely put.'

'Thank you. Does it?'

'No,' said Jack quietly, sounding confused. 'No, I mean I don't know. I don't usually . . . look, forget it, okay? Forget it. I'm outta here. Mistake. My mistake.'

'Don't be angry,' she said, as he strode away, and she found herself calling after him. 'What's your name?' He kept walking, but she put a hand on his shoulder and the boy stopped suddenly as if arrested. Or electrified. 'My name is Sarah.'

They kissed for the first time a few hours later, in the half-light under the branches of a tree near the Italian Gardens. He had walked beside her and talked too much at her and tried to make her laugh, then he had made her laugh – at his accent, just like in the movies – and then he had waited while she went into the café to see her family. Two hours he had waited on that bench. More. He thought she would never come, but he could think of nothing better to do than to wait for her, just in case. She was startled to see him still there, this startling boy with the motormouth and the daring eyes, but she also saw that he was calmer now. If he had been on something earlier, the effects of it had gone. And then they were alone again and walking, for such a long time, who knew where, to the palace first, because he was a tourist after all – and she wanted to be sure that he actually was calm, not dangerous but as cute as he seemed and that the glimmer of something was real – then they went back through the darkened park, around in circles and she was stopping and kissing him, to both their astonishment.

'Sarah!'

Jack said her name like a man seeing a marvel for the first time. For a second they were in symmetry: each touching the other's face with their right hands, then the left hands joined. Their bodies moved closer. They kissed again. Sarah closed her eyes and the spirit moved across the face of the waters. Let there be light. From then on, as if it had always been meant, Jack and Sarah were together.

'I thought you looked a bit of an idiot,' she said as they walked hand in hand on the way to the station that night.

'Thank you, Ma'am.'

'No. Well. I thought you must have something to hide. Nobody wears that much black except a priest. Do you? Tell me.'

'Do I what?'

'Have something to hide.'

He stopped and bent low like an Elizabethan courtier, sweeping away all objections with the back of his hand. 'Nothing. Not from you.'

And at that moment – for that moment – it was true.

'What do you dream of doing?' His voice was close, quiet; she felt his breath on the back of her neck. Sarah was lying on her side on the dog Tutu's old tartan rug, a month after they met. They were under another tree: this time a solitary, wind-bent cedar on Haven Brow, the first of the Seven Sisters. Seven hills in a row by the sea but cut in half all the way, making for a rollercoaster ride of a walk across the tops, with a sheer drop always to one side. From the beach at the Gap they had looked ahead and seen them there like seven women shoulder to shoulder, shawled in green with veils of white, looking out for a lost ship. Jack lay behind Sarah on the grass at the summit with his groin close to her backside and she was trying to ignore what she could feel going on back there.

'Who says I dream of anything?'

'Come on. We all do. What is that thing of which you dream?' he declaimed like a ham Shakespearean. 'What manner of dream is this?'

'What are you on?' She felt a tingle of warmth on her neck again and regretted the question quickly. He was clean now, as far as she knew. Not using anything. Promises had been made. Jack shifted his weight up on to his elbow, and she wondered if he was offended. It was so hard to tell. What did he expect of her? Relax, she told herself; but he never seemed to do that and the knot in her stomach would not loosen when he was around. 'What about you? What do you dream of?'

'Oh, that's easy,' he said, and he eased back down, his arm still under her head. 'Peace, justice, freedom and equality! Don't think I'm shallow or anything – although of course you know by now that I am – but I do believe there are things wrong – really wrong – and I want to change them.'

When he spoke like this, there seemed to be a much bigger audience in his head. She already knew better than to say so.

'So this dream I have, it's like Live Aid, you know? There's this vast crowd and they're all singing along to my song. Hands in the air, living it, loving it. It's about love and hope and pride and dignity, and anything seems possible because we all have those things in us. We're all human, we all have such enormous potential.' She let him talk. 'You think it's corny, don't you? Cheesy, you'd say.

My dad says music can change the world, because it can change people.'

Jack had not mentioned his father before. She was intrigued.

'Is he a musician?'

'They changed the world that day.'

'Live Aid? Seriously? What band? Why have you not told me about him before?'

'Things are different when I tell people.'

'What is the matter?'

'They were there, in Philadelphia. Low on the bill. They really believed all this stuff and lived it too: no big deals, they shared their money, shared a house, singing about things that mattered. Then Live Aid happened. He rocked. I mean, really rocked. All those people in the stadium. Like in my dream. Only I don't screw it up like he did. I use that energy to make things better. He let it get to his heart, thought they were loving him. Not themselves. He went solo after that. Got blasted. The usual. Can we change the subject?'

The clouds shifted. She felt herself closing up. He would tell her more, in time. She was afraid of something, but what? It would not come to the surface. Jack leaned forward and nuzzled her face, lifting her chin with his cheek, and he kissed her. Then he said: '"It is easier to love and be loved by lots of people badly than by one person properly." That's what he says. I hope to do better.'

The wind picked up and the air was gritty. Something got in her eye and she said, without thinking: 'Do you want children?'

'Now? Oh yeah. Definitely. Let's get started.' But he saw that she was serious. 'I don't think about it. I suppose I just assume I will, yeah. You?'

'I always thought so. I have this feeling, though . . .'

'What?'

'It's okay,' she said, rubbing her eye as the wind faded. She wanted to go home. 'Another time.'

Twenty-four

The sun was shining and Jack was smiling, but he wouldn't say why. They walked across the wobbly bridge under a wide blue sky and all the way along the South Bank from the Tate Modern to Gabriel's Wharf and beyond, chatting about this and that and nothing and everything, laughing and teasing each other as they had done for many months now; and becoming aware, as they walked, of the warmth on their skin, the slow rhythm of the water beside them and the promise there was in everything. Jack was smiling because he knew that he had done the right thing. They paused for a while to look at the books under the bridge by the National Film Theatre, trying to pick out the most inappropriate purchase they could find for each other. She chose a book called *The Art of Silence* for a man who would never stop tapping his fingers, which irritated her, but she tossed it aside because she was in love and it did not matter – the relentless tapping, never stopping – because he did not realize he was doing it, until she told him to please just give it a rest for a moment and let her think while she was marking school books or watching *The West Wing*. It was easier to understand the accents now she and Jack lived together and she heard an American talking all the time. He said the same thing in reverse about *Doctor Who*: 'Why do all the aliens in the universe sound like they come from London or Cardiff?'

'Captain Kirk killed all the ones who sounded like you.'

'Funny.'

Then they browsed the books for sale under the bridge, each to their own but always aware of the other, looking up from time to time, at the same time, and smiling; and he actually found a *Star Trek* annual from 1979 and showed her because they could not afford to actually spend a pound – a quid, he was learning to say – on such a thing, there was a cat to feed.

'Ugh,' she said and held it up between finger and thumb as if it were a disgusting item that one of the boys in one of her classes had brought into school in his bag by accident or design. A week-old banana or perhaps a dead hamster.

'You touch, you buy,' growled a grumpy-looking geezer prowling along the line of books. Sarah had seen him before. He was one of those men you find on the South Bank: sixty something, wearing a dark blue cotton Chinese worker's coat with epaulettes and Mao cap like he used to when he was leading sit-ins and dreaming of revolution, and a soul patch on his chin and a flinty, mean look on his face that ought to disqualify him from conversation with the young women she had seen him haunting in the National Film Theatre café. He sat too close to her once but said nothing and she wondered what he was up to, then realized he was sniffing her, sucking her up into his nostrils like a drug. Sarah moved away then and he didn't recognize her now. She replaced the book carefully and gave a smile that was meant to dismiss but was accidentally kindly. His delight made her shudder.

Sarah slid her arm inside Jack's arm and they began to walk, falling back into step with each other, feeling light and easy and alive. Then there was a guy walking beside them with knitted Rasta hat and a wispy ginger beard and a funny little drum, a hand drum he held under his arm and patted with the flat of his hand. *Pat-pat pause, pat-a-pat pause. Pat-pat pause, pat-a-pat pause.* He was smiling too but looking ahead. Sarah wondered when he was going to ask for money. Jack didn't seem to notice. But there was a woman in an open Afghan coat with fur on the cuffs and collar, walking in stride with Jack on his other side, clapping and swaying her body to the same rhythm. *Pat-pat pause, pat-a-pat pause.* They passed a busker playing an electric guitar, a skinny guy with a tweed jacket and a cocked hat who nodded a greeting and started playing chords in time with the rhythm, which was now being joined by a group of half a dozen friends, who turned and walked in time and clapped their hands too, and snapped their fingers and made a little humming noise. *Pat-pat hum, pat-a-pat hum. Pat-pat hum, pat-a-pat hum crash!* The drummer playing a full jazz kit on the far side of the promenade caught the rhythm in a splashy, thunderous, boozy, drawling kind of way and Sarah was bewildered, she thought she was in a dream; what was going on? Jack didn't look round, he kept walking, slower though, with his arm tight against hers.

'Are you doing this?' she asked.

'No,' he laughed. 'You are!'

By now there was a crowd of people walking with them: a young mum with a buggy and a toddler girl waving her arms, shaking a yellow rattle; a couple of hipster lads arm in arm, with matching beards and dreamy eyes; a guy in a suit with a briefcase, banging on his back as he showed off some serious hip swivels; an elderly lady with her gentleman friend, rubbing her hands between claps; and a choir. Wait, seriously? A gospel choir?

Yes. They had it written on their black T-shirts: 'Gospel Train Leyton, all ages, men and women welcome.' Big guys, skinny girls, bigger girls, muscle boys, skipping in time and swaying and singing – and now she knew the tune, even though she could not believe it was being sung to her by a crowd and a choir that was suddenly beside her and around her and filling the pavement, and the people who were not in on this were laughing and clapping and filming and looking astonished – except the ones who thought this kind of thing happened in London every day. She so wanted to tell them that it did not, but what was happening, exactly? Jack was looking so pleased with himself, high-fiving a guy with a razor-cut who did an extravagant bow, held a microphone to his mouth and sang to the whole assembly – with a battery-powered amplifier on his back – the melody and words of a song she absolutely loved about how his girl was amazing. He was nailing it and the guy was singing to her, as if in wonder, with the sound of the whole South Bank banging out the rhythm and she was caught up in it, feeling as if she would burst, feeling like an idiot in front of all these people, thinking she would give Jack what for when they got home, but loving it, loving him, the daft boy. 'You're amazing . . .' They were all singing now, a sound like being lifted on the shoulders of the crowd; it was all for her. They were dancing and swaying and stopping. Then everything stopped.

The words, the music, the rhythm, gone.

The silence broke like a wave upon her.

She heard a bird cry and a boat blow its horn and saw them all pointing upwards and away towards the Hungerford bridge where there were other people, she did not know them, standing on the footbridge waving back, unrolling white sheets. 'I,' said the first one in a big bold blue letter. 'Think,' said the next, in red, hand painted with flowers at the corners. 'You're Amazing,' said the third in yellow. And these sheets were massive, they were filling up the line of the bridge, getting to halfway. 'Will,' was the next in green. 'You,' in purple was followed by red again. 'Marry Me?'

'Read it,' he said but she had and she put her fingers up to her face without thinking, as if to hide but there was nowhere to hide. He spoke into her ear, close and personal, just for her. 'Will you?'

Shivering, she threw her arms around him and buried her face in his shoulder and heard the applause that began around her like firecrackers at her back and spread out through the crowd, up the steps of the bridge and across the bridge, and the drums rolled and the guitar kerranged and the song began again and she was crying, crying, for what? For happiness. For goodness' sake. What a daft thing to do. What a daft and great and bloody lovely and wonderful thing to do.

He could have ruined it. He could have forced her to say something to all these people. Instead he kissed her on the lips, held it there, then stepped away and put his hands together over his head. It was like magic. Jack clapped twice and they melted away, becoming smiles, strangers again, dispersing, each playing their own tunes now, except there was a hum in the air like happiness and Sarah had never been more sure in her life that this man here, this Jack, this daft skinny American boy, was the boy she loved and would always love, for ever and a day.

She could not have said no, of course. There was no way to decline in front of all those people, even if she had wanted to. Which she did not, she told herself quickly when the thought occurred to her, as he was leading her towards a wine bar. So she never really gave any further consideration to the way he set her up that day. Or the way he controlled the crowd. Or where he got the idea from. She did find something similar on YouTube later and realized that he had copied someone else's proposal, but it was still a great gesture. So romantic. There was no way to refuse. Anyway, what did it matter? She was in love.

Twenty-five

The church was full, Sarah could feel it before she saw them all. Their expectations spilled out through the open doors to summon her in from the blustery day.

'Ready then?' asked her father.

Her arm was linked through his. She was weak, fizzy, unsure of herself. Ready though? Yes. Ready for this man. Coming, ready or not. She and Jack, the poor, imperfect dreamer, the wanderer, lover-boy, generous, considerate. Wilful. Stubborn. Gentle. Scatty. Strong. She was ready for anything with him. Side by side. But there were hundreds of people in that church – her father had insisted on inviting the whole congregation – and they had come to see this. To say how lovely, what a lovely dress and how much she looked like her mother.

She was trying to deal with that thought when her father urged her forward. Sarah took her stride from him. Under the arch they passed, walking slowly, and she began to see them in full, the faces turned towards her, the startled looks. One of the women in the choir put a hand up to her heart as if shot, or as if Sarah had turned up eight months pregnant with a space-hopper stomach. Halfway there now, her father was still keeping the pace, nodding to people. Smile, girl, smile. James was there with Parv; she saw them both laugh and give her the thumbs up. She saw Jack turn; he hadn't guessed her secret but he could see her coming to him. He could see it now. His eyes widened and he laughed too, his shoulders shaking, his whole face alight. Through the bells and the music she could hear the happy, fantastic sound of him and she knew it was all right. His laughter was the cue for applause that began at the front and rushed to the back. They were applauding her, the bride, the beauty, the woman of the day, beaming and daring in her gown of gorgeous, glorious red.

*

Her father held the Bible open with the rings in the crook of its pages and asked his daughter to repeat after him a name he had not used for her since she was born. The name his tearful, grateful, stroppy wife had ordered him to write on the birth certificate to mark the arrival of a child she had been told she could never have. Sarah saw him glance down over her shoulder to the front pew, where the mother of the bride should be. She sensed his balance shift, but not the ripple of longing that ran through him. She could not read his thought that he must smile whatever now, because his wife Jasmine – the great fortune of his life, the mother of this astonishing bride – would have wanted him to do that. Sarah saw him look at her with a love that could have stopped the devil. He winked. She winked back and repeated after him, in full, the name she never, ever used:

'Sarah . . . Hallelujah . . . Jones . . .'

The mother of the groom was there, immaculate in a vintage cream Chanel skirt suit that certainly made the most of her legs, as was remarked upon more than once or twice in the pews around her. She caused the men to prickle with sweat at the collars of their badly fitting wedding shirts. The women wondered at her poise, her elegance, her confidence and apparent youthfulness. Calculations were quietly made as to how old she must be now and how old she must have been back then, in the days when it all happened, you know? Surely you've heard? She was friendly enough when spoken to, but mostly kept her silence and an enigmatic smile, under a broad-brimmed black hat that a few people recognized as having been made by Philip Treacy. She was classy, but they were also looking around for the father of the groom. This was a big congregation. Robert thought it was because the church had turned out to support him, but actually the Girl Guiders and the plumber who fixed the vicarage pipes and many of the rest were there because they wanted to see a man in the flesh who was known to them all by a single name. An elder statesman of rock. Snake-hipped, rake-thin, with a wolfish smile and a sexuality that swept ahead of him like a tsunami. And a heart. A conscience. Presidents and prime ministers fell for his charms; Bono was an ally of his. He was said to be a recluse now, prowling through Manhattan in his pension years with his hood up. His voice was gone, his mind too, some said, but those were just rumours. Surely he would come to his son's wedding?

Jack had the same vulpine look and restlessness, his eyes always seeking the next thing, his fingers always drumming (even at the altar), although his company made people edgy, rather than beside themselves with excitement. Sometimes he tried just a little too hard to be like the old man. He was very fond of quoting things his father had said, as if they were rules for life: 'I have two instincts, as a rock star. I want to have fun, and I want to change the world.' The difference being, of course, that Jack was not a rock star.

The apology for his father's absence came by motorcycle courier just before the service, with a gift in a little red box. Two Cartier rings, side by side in velvet. Eighteen carat white gold, with diamonds of course. Far too expensive. Sarah looked at them and tried not to think of all the things she could have bought with the money. A washing machine, for example. And a car. It was going to take her a long time to feel able to wear that ring on the street without fearing muggers, but she would wear it in church today, that would be okay. There was no way to refuse. Jack was happy. His father had blessed them from afar; his mother was pleased to be there, drawing the eye but certainly not competing with the bride. Chana was her name, meaning 'grace' in Hebrew, and she embodied that virtue in the way she walked, the way she sat. She was flirting again with the faith she had rejected as a child, which appalled her son. She had a sense of humour about it, though: when the father of the bride asked if she would like to choose any readings as part of the ceremony, she offered him Woody Allen: 'If you want to make God laugh, tell him your plans.' But that was just an opening shot. They were able to agree on another text from the same source, which she read beautifully. First she waited at the lectern for the congregation to settle and become quiet, so that there was a great sense of expectation. They were all wondering about her anyway, more so in the absence of her former lover. Then she spoke the one line slowly and with great care, as if it were Scripture.

'Maybe the poets are right. Maybe love is the only answer.'

And that was it. That was all. There was silence as she took off her glasses, picked up the slip of paper and stepped down – then a quick bubbling up of ahs and murmurs of approval. They liked her style. She was flying home to America after this, back to her interior design company. Back to a tiny apartment in Forest Hills that none of her clients would ever see. She had chosen Chana as a new name for herself and then later for her company, after hearing a song that said 'grace finds beauty in everything'. It was not one of those written by Jack's father. She had not listened to his music willingly for a very long time. Not since the day Jack was made.

Twenty-six

'Where are you, love?'

The voice calling her suggested the streets of London, a city she had never seen. She was too young to hear the way America had bled into his voice, his vowels had changed and his drawl had lengthened to be more familiar to the kids who bought his records, to seduce boys and girls just like her. But those others were not there, in the room. Only she had been chosen. She was the one in the Frank Sinatra Suite of a grand hotel in Las Vegas on that enchanted early morning, the dawn of his fortieth birthday, holding a glass of Jack Daniels and Coke and looking out of the tall, wide panoramic window on to the Strip. Five o'clock. The sun was already up behind the Nevada mountains, soaking the sky with a rosy glow. The lights of the Strip were softening, getting gentler on her brain, which she knew must be fried but did not feel it. She felt sharp, alive, quick. Bright, funny. Clever, sexy.

'Darling?'

She went to his call, naked under the kimono he had given her the first time, a fortnight ago, in another city far away. He had seen her in the crowd of young women waiting after the show and sent his bodyguard to find her, to bring her to him in the long black limousine, for oysters and champagne. It was so romantic. They would be together for ever now. Somehow he had known she was there for him. He was her first lover and she was now all his. He did not ask her name. There was no need, he said. Their spirits had met. He was so spiritual. She was glad to be somebody else now, someone grown up and exciting. He wore a red cotton thread on his wrist. He was deep. Love had won, against the odds.

'Ah, there you are, you look divine, I could eat you . . .'

She was fourteen years old.

Twenty-seven

Fourteen years and nine months later, almost to the day, a skinny kid in black jeans, a black T-shirt and a black jacket, with his dyed black hair all-a-mess in the wind coming off the Hudson, made his way down a street in Greenwich Village. Jack the spider-boy saw gargoyles high on the apartment blocks, leering across the rooftops. There were palm trees on the terraces way up there, waving like fans at a concert. His father had the penthouse in a magnificent building from the thirties, like something from *The Great Gatsby*.

'Hey, watch it, son,' said the doorman as they collided. Jack stepped back from him and was questioned: 'Can I help you?'

'Oh, yeah. Okay, sure. Thanks.' A new boarding school was teaching him to be polite. 'Excuse me, sir. I would like to see my father.'

The doorman was wide and solid, in his fifties, with a purple bulb of a nose and rheumy eyes from the street wind. He looked kind, in a gruff sort of way. Probably had kids, even grand-children. He would understand, Jack knew it.

'Your father?'

'Yes, sir. He lives here.'

'Got a name, or what?'

The doorman stood between Jack and the door, an old mahog-any affair with plate glass and impressively shiny brass fittings. Inside, he could see a polished panel of buttons, one for each apartment, a grille for the intercom. What should Jack say?

'Paterson. Colin Paterson.'

The doorman frowned at a name he had not been expecting to hear. The real name of the famous man who lived in the pent-house. Everyone else called him by his stage name, unless they knew him well. The doorman took out a burgundy handkerchief that matched his uniform and wiped saliva from his mouth. He ought to tell this young buck to get out of the way, stop making a nuisance of himself, but there was a chance he might be telling the truth, in which case the client would make trouble. Big trouble. On the other hand, the kid was clearly desperate. He was tapping his leg in time, rolling his fingers in a rhythm, like he was up to something bad.

'You got proof?'

No, Jack hadn't thought of that and it made him panic. When he panicked, he came over as cocky. 'What do you want, a DNA test?' Damn his smart mouth.

The doorman threw up a hand. 'Funny, kid. On your way.'

'Oh, come on! I am sorry, sir. Really. I mean no offence, believe me. Will you please just buzz him and tell him I am here?'

'Yeah. You kidding me? Because some kid on the street says he wants a present from Daddy? Get outa here.'

'I'm telling you the truth. Please!'

Just then a lady in a long white coat stepped out of a long white Lincoln, letting her little white poodle dog run under the awning first, on one of those leads that extend like a wire. The doorman gave Jack a hard stare before standing to attention and opening the door to the dog. 'Thank you, George,' said the lady almost imperceptibly.

If this had been a movie, now would have been the moment for Jack to dart around her, through the open door and buzz his father on the intercom. He did indeed try that, then tripped over the dog. The poodle howled, the lead snagged Jack's foot and he fell hard at the feet of the doorman, who kicked his legs. 'Get up!'

The fine lady disappeared, cooing in alarm, with her pet skittering after her into the darkness. The door clicked shut. The doorman was gone now too, having hurried inside to placate her ladyship. The sidewalk was empty, but Jack felt as if he was being watched. Not from within, so from where? From above? He took a step beyond the awning and looked up to where he guessed his elusive father was at home, but it was impossible to see from this angle. There was nobody in the cars along the kerb, unless they were behind the blacked-out windows of a luxury SUV. Maybe. Then he saw the man on the other side of the street. Jack saw him over the tops of yellow cabs and limousines, between trucks and buses, standing on the sidewalk over there, hands in his jeans pockets, hood up, wearing wraparound shades. He was slender like a shadow and on his toes, ready to dance. Jack knew him at once.

'Dad!' Jack shouted and ran, ducking past parked cars, twisting over the tarmac, risking the wrath of cops and drivers, defying death.

'Dad!'

Breathless and desperate, he made it to the other side. The slender shadow man took off the sunglasses and pulled down the hood. Dark hair spilled out. It was not a man at all. Pity and apology were in her smile, then she shouted over the noise of the traffic.

'I really am *not* your father!'

Twenty-eight

Every Easter after they were married Jack and Sarah went down to the coast, to stay in an old farmhouse on the Downs, within walking distance of the Seven Sisters. It was cosy when the fire was on, but this was a tight, dark house built for a farmer long ago. It was cheap. They couldn't afford much. After a few days, it always started to get to both of them.

'I am going mad,' she called out, after hearing the door. She had been reading, legs stretched out to catch the last heat from the morning's log.

'Going?'

'This place is driving me crazy.'

Jack flicked on the kettle in the kitchen and picked up a leaflet from the worktop.

'The Long Man? Like the guy in the West Country but with no balls. You read this?' The leaflet showed the outline of a person on a hillside, holding two long sticks. A figure drawn in chalk on the green and brown land, like a huge prehistoric crime scene. 'Says here he may be a symbol of—'

'I know.'

'The f-word,' he said, wandering through to her.

'I have read it, actually. I wonder how he manages, without the necessary.'

'Science. Or magic. We should go.'

Sarah let her book drop into her lap. 'Why?'

'He's a symbol. And we're trying for a baby.'

'For God's sake.'

Jack was smiling as he pressed on, half teasing, but she couldn't see it. 'A change of scenery. You brought the leaflet home. You must be interested.'

'Whatever,' snapped Sarah. 'I have got to get out of here.'

So they drove, eight miles inland. Fifteen minutes that felt to Sarah like returning from the edge of the world. As the car plunged and turned, the hills acquired trees, the buildings became less rare. They passed sheep on the road, a tractor with orange lights flashing from every angle and men in goggles trimming trees, cottages covered in rambling ivy and high flint walls protecting old manor houses. They had to pull over to give the right of way through one-street villages, and slow down to miss Range Rovers coming out blind from late-afternoon sessions or red-faced pedestrians stumbling out of the gloom of the half-slumber ploughmans-and-pint pub into the blue light and the damp air. Over a hill then, high up with the Weald spread out under the mist, then he was at their shoulder. On his back in a field, although from here it looked as if he was standing up. Cut from the earth, in chalk, as odd as anything that shouldn't be there, as unearthly as a spaceship on the hillside. No facial features, no clothes, no massive genitalia, just the white outline of a figure, arms bent and fingers pointing away from himself as though dancing to Bollywood music, with a pair of straight white lines, one on either side, that might have been staves or shepherd's crooks or spears.

The Long Man was a giant who fell here and was buried at the top of Windover Hill. Or he was a dodman, an ancient surveyor laying out the ley line running through this swooping landscape. Or he was Beowulf with a spear in each hand. He was Woden or Thor, Solomon or Samson, a Roman or Mohammed, a Green Man or a Lone Man, a Lanky Man, holding open the gates of dawn, or heaven, or hell. Everybody had a story, nobody knew the truth. He was best seen from a distance, said the sign at the car park on the edge of the village. They took no notice and walked over the lane, through a gate, along the side of a hedge, then climbed a wider path cut from the tracks of a tractor. The slopes closed in on them as they walked, huffing and puffing as city folk do, until they reached another gate and felt themselves somehow on the inside of a huge green bowl. They could hear the sound of the traffic on the A27 nearly two miles away, and their own laboured breathing, and something else. Strange. The pluck and munch of grass in the mouths of cows, amplified by the curve of the hill. Black and white ones, brown ones, golden ones with shaggy white heads, munching away on a field higher up the slope, staring down at them.

'What do you think? What's the best way?' Sarah pushed away the snout of a sudden dog, a greyhound perhaps, a sharp black face pushing into her lap. The owner was approaching them in a long overcoat, stern and mythical, his crown of white hair glowing in the growing dark.

'You wanna walk up there a bit, to the left,' he said, pointing a stick that had a cleft at the top, like an extra knuckle. 'See, the fence stops. Go round it, otherwise you've got a nasty climb the other way.'

'Thanks,' said Sarah, because his words had been addressed entirely to her. His eyes were taking her in, frankly.

'It's bricks. You'll see. Used to be chalk. Lots of bricks now, concrete painted white. In the last war, there, they painted all the bricks green, so the Germans couldn't see him.'

'Why would they do that?' She surprised both of them with her question, but had to follow through. 'Why would the Germans want to bomb a chalk giant?'

'Well, lovely, they wouldn't,' he said slowly, as though to a beautiful idiot. 'But they might like to use him to see where they was.'

Jack had already gone on, making his way up the rutted, muddy field like a crab on the shingle, taking care not to step in the fat pats of cow dung. One had a hollow in the middle filled up with rain or cow urine and there was a rainbow swirling on the surface. 'Stay Off The Long Man. Soil Erosion.' The words had been carved or burned into wood and painted red. 'Go No Further Than This Sign.' He did, of course, but kept close to the fence. Away from the feet of the giant. He told himself this was because he wanted to preserve the ancient treasure. It was really because somebody might shout.

'Hey! Wait for me.'

Jack put out a hand to steady himself, realized he was about to touch barbed wire and placed a finger between the twists, which left him standing there awkwardly, balanced on one leg.

'This is a woman,' said Sarah, chasing her own breath.

'Sure.'

'No, look at her.' The change of perspective had made the giant's arms go wavy and squashed the head, but that was not what she meant. 'Chunky thighs. I thought that when we were back down on the ground, but the hips are the thing. Look at that pelvis.'

'Big calves, like a football player.'

'Women's rugby player. You men are all so self-obsessed, bet none of you has seen it. How many years has she been here?'

'He. I don't think anyone knows.'

'She. These cows are sinister. Are they bulls?'

'Definitely. Female bulls,' he said and put his spare hand – the one not balancing his weight on one finger on the wire – out towards hers as he had done many times that week. Usually, she let it fall. Things were not going so well. They were trying for a baby, yes, but they had been trying for longer than either wanted to think about.

'I love you,' he said gratefully when she took his hand.

She ignored him. 'Looks like the hill is on fire.' Up ahead, on the curved crest of the bowl, the clouds were racing past so close and so quick they could have been smoke.

'So . . .' he said.

'So what?'

'Here we are.'

'And?' The hand that had been cool in his own went back into a pocket of her fleece.

'You know. What about it?'

'Are you saying what I think you are saying?'

'Dunno, it's—'

'Look at the ground. It is soaking wet, and covered in cow excrement, and there is spiky grass sticking up everywhere, and it is nearly night time and it is cold and wet and you really are a moron.'

'Sorry, I wasn't—'

'No. You didn't think, did you? You just dragged me here to a hillside in the rain and made me look at the second biggest fertility symbol in the world and I went along with it. And you thought you would get a shag.'

'You wanted to come, that's not—'

'Shut up. Leave me alone. Just leave me alone.'

'What the fuck is your problem, Sarah?'

He knew exactly what the problem was, they'd been over it a hundred times, he'd seen the diagrams, had the patronizing talk from the doctor, been for the tests himself. This wasn't about that. It was more than that. 'I was joking, actually. But I just want to make this work – is that really so bad? That I bloody care about you? That I fancy you? I want to make love with my wife!'

'Not here, you idiot.'

'Not bloody anywhere unless you say so, right?' He was shouting properly now, to hell with whoever could hear him across the fields, in the mist. He'd got his balance back but was ankle deep in mud. 'I get it, this is a pretty lousy place, I was only fooling. If you weren't so wrapped up in yourself you'd see that, but come on! You just give the orders, don't you?'

Come now, she wrote in texts. *It's time*. Sometimes they were funny: *Your Assistance Is Urgently Required*. Mostly, they were not. The time was right, the temperature was right, she had called in sick, she was waiting. Get home. Get here. Get off your drums or your computer. Get your trousers off. Get inside me, quick. Do the business. Deliver your load. Then she was, like, roll off and make a cup of tea or something, let me put my legs up against the bedroom wall and shake it all down to the right spot. Go on! Sometimes he just couldn't, there was a deadline or he was knackered from a gig and he just couldn't face it, and she was, like: 'Do you not want a baby? Is it just me then, going through all this shit while you mess about with your mates?' He'd say, 'You're interested now, when your little thermometer says so. Time for the production line. I'm not some factory, you know.' And she would say, 'That is bloody obvious. If you were a bit more productive we would not be having this problem.' And he'd have to say: 'No! It's you! It's not me! How dare you?'

But he knew she didn't really fancy him any more. His hair was grown out, it got greasy real quick. He was putting on weight, but they both ate for comfort and there were a lot of takeaways coming in to the house. She was getting fat and greasy because of the drugs, he was all Super Supreme and misery. The worst thing was, he had no control over any of this. He was powerless. Without saying anything, she had started avoiding films with any whiff of a child in them, and books, and songs. 'Baby, now that I've found you.' 'Don't you want me, baby?' They set her off crying. Life was a minefield. 'Hey babe,' he would say and she would shout at him. 'Let's go and see our friends,' he would say and she would shout again. 'How can I spend a day with their brats running round and that woman cooing over them? She is so bloody protective, and she never wanted a kid in the first place – never mind twins. What a shitty idea!'

Sarah was so angry and so disappointed and everything seemed to hurt her. She ran away once when she saw a granny give an ice cream to a toddler, just got on a bus that happened to be at the stop and left Jack calling after her like an idiot. Like a kid without his mummy. She was in control, always.

As for sex, there was none. Nada. Not unless she said so. Not outside the appointed times. Before they got married, their sex life was great. Really great. When she was relaxed and happy in the holidays, in the old days, it was great then too. When she thought he was hoping to get off with someone he worked for, she was mad for it then. At times of celebration, desperation and potential conception. Now? No. Sex on demand, but only when it was required for the purposes of making a baby. No build-up, no hugs, no foreplay, no joy; just do it and get off. Some guys would be happy with that, sure, but he was hurting. He was burning, he was angry, getting angrier all the time, with every time she turned away. Even here on the hill in the cold in the coming dark, when he hadn't really meant it but she just assumed he did and pushed him away again, like she was always pushing him away. Well, screw her! Jack didn't know where to go with this, what to say that would get through to her, where to put his flailing hands as the rage surged through him. Grabbing her by the shoulders, he yelled in her face and let it all go, fuck the consequences; she was going to see his truth, all of it, right here and now: 'You're not going to do this any more!'

He pushed her too far that day. He was sorry afterwards. Really sorry. It is not easy to stomp down a hillside when there are ruts and cowpats and the matted grass is slippery, when you're hurting and crying and cold with rage and numb with shock, but Sarah managed to do so and somehow retain her dignity.

She was a class act, he had to give her that.

Twenty-nine

These are the stories Jack does not tell, because he doesn't know them or he doesn't want to know. Instead he paces the room in the outhouse of the lighthouse, six or seven steps to the wall, turn and back again, turn and back, a tiger testing the cage, sniffing the wind, working out strategies to escape these close, dark circumstances and pursue his own desires. 'Tell you about Sarah. What do you want to know? I can smoke here, right?'

Without waiting for yes, Jack produces a battered brass Zippo and flips it in a single movement, letting the little flame burn blue at his thumb while he finds a cigarette with the other hand. The tip glows and after a moment he exhales, clouding his face.

'I'm the victim in all this. I didn't do anything wrong. I could walk away, you know? Walk away. Right now. But here I am, up here with you, trying to find her. Why would she run? Tell me. I care. I do. I love her. More than I can say. So strong, it hurts. She's beautiful. Hair like fire, face like . . . like . . . I don't know. How do you describe one face to another? Yours is drawn, man; you need some sleep. You been crying? Looks like it. What's the story? She's beautiful. Everyone says so. People turn around in the street. Guys. I could kill them. I can't kill them – I couldn't kill anyone. I'm not a fighter. I love her. Love. She rescued me. Then she threw knives at me – has she told you that? Big kitchen knives, could have killed me. It's the drugs, they make her dangerous. To herself, to me, to you. Have you got her? Is she here? I don't think so, or you would have given the game away, my friend. I can tell. I know people. Where else do I go? What am I supposed to do? I've been to the farms, they won't talk or they don't know and anyway I don't believe in that: Sarah hiding in some lousy bed and breakfast with cows and chickens in the yard; too much, what's the word? Fecundity. This thing you got here, unmissable, sticks out like a cock on the hill. What do you want to know about Sarah? It doesn't matter. I just need to find her and take her home.

Make everything all right. Back to what it was. Before. Just us. She has to love me, just me. Why am I not enough? If I can get over this, why can't she? I would be happy, just her and me, for ever. No kids. I mean, I want them, but not like she does. It's . . . pathological. Obsessive. Too much, man. Way too much.'

'How did you meet?' asks the Keeper, because the only way he can think of to stop him coming back again is to let Jack talk it all out.

'I was high when I met her – did you know that? How could you know that? Spinning round in the park and she was like a vision, couldn't believe it, thought she was in my head, kept talking and talking, I don't know, but she talked me down. Talked. Me. Down. Like a guy on a bridge. Or up here, I guess. Walked me round, talked me down, sucked my face off! Ha! I was like a little puppy – her puppy, her boy, her project. A wild one. For a long time. But you know what? Puppies grow up. They get a bark. And a bite. I'll bite you, buddy, if she's here. It's not my fault. I don't have the problem. I'm good. The target's screwed, man. I could just walk away. Who do you think I am?'

'Who do you think you are?'

There's a sudden almost-silence; Jack standing in the corner, in the shadow, looking at the wall. Drumming on the wall, hand at head height, as if looking for dry rot in the woodwork. *Tap-a-tap-tap.* Jack smiles, a distracted, disappointed smile. 'I'm nobody. Come from nowhere. Here, there, everywhere. I'm sorry, I am a guest in your lovely home. Maybe do something about the damp? Please make allowances for my distressed condition. I've had a drink. Jeez. I'm lost without her. Where is she? Have you seen her? No, you say no. Of course. I'll bite you, man. I'm a stingray!'

'You can try,' says the Keeper, but Jack does not hear. He shakes his head as if to clear it, tapping on a temple with his fingers.

'She rescued me. I want to rescue her. It's hard, you know? When they fight back, when you're trying to put the lifebelt over their head and get them out of there, out of the sea, save them from drowning. And they fight you. Hard. We went to the hospital dozens of times, I was there to be the husband: stand by her, see her through. To whatever conclusion. Then it all hit home.

115

Hospitals make me anxious. When I'm anxious my stomach gets all tied up, like cramps. I needed the john badly. You feel the blast of heat and the smell clamps itself on your face. It was such a hot day, but I think I was wearing my heavy coat. I don't know. You don't dress up for the doctor. We were going to have it out with him. Sarah was going to do that, I was there to hold her hand while she let rip. That's what I thought. So here's how it goes, right? The waiting area was not the one we had been in before, that was being decorated or something. And here's the thing. This is the thing: all the women who couldn't have babies and their men – and the frightened ones who hadn't found out what was wrong yet, and the ones who couldn't believe it was happening to them, and the ones like Sarah who were recovering from operations, with battle scars to show how much they really want a baby; more than anything else in the world, more than life, more than their husbands. And all the husbands struggling to understand, who can't help feeling crushed – they're deeply, deeply worried, you know? Deeply. We were all put in a waiting room for kids. Paediatrics. Can you believe that? Thomas the Tank Engine pull-a-longs. Fisher Price garages. Rupert the Bloody Bear and Winnie the Pooh and Tigger too, on the walls, all looking at us through their big mad cartoon eyes, thinking, "What the hell are you doing here?" The chairs, brightly coloured plastic, red and yellow, green, like in a kids' library and our butts were way too big for them. Like Goldilocks on Little Bear's chair. I know the stories, I'd be great at telling them, I'd jump about and do the voices and roll on the floor and make the kid laugh. I wanted to pick up the soft octopus with the bells in his tentacles and hold it in my arms like a baby and walk back down the corridor, go to the desk and ask for the person responsible, the jerk who thought this would be a good place for us to sit and wait for hours, and I wanted to shove that soft toy down her throat.'

He glances at his audience, to check he still has one. Or that he is believed.

'I didn't do anything. I just sat. Like Sarah, like all the rest. The fight gone out of us. And I got this pain ripping through my stomach. I didn't want to say anything, she had pains of her own, this was nothing. I had to find the john. I just managed to sit down in time. Then I fainted. Hmm.'

The cigarette has burned down in his cupped hands; he looks around for a way to get rid of it and sees the window open just a crack, so pushes it wider and flips it out through there. It lies on the windowsill for a moment, lifts a little in the wind, a worm with its head raised, then disappears.

'Sarah got worried. Of course she did. Her calling out brought me round. I made myself decent, got dressed, but my legs were shaky. I fell into a chair. I was thinking, "This ain't right, I'm letting her down." The nurses let me out the back, at the end of the ward where there was a little grass area, and made me sit in the sun with a breeze on my face, sipping water, until I was ready. The nurses both smoked. They took that chance. They couldn't believe someone had decided to put us all there, make us wait in the kids' room. They didn't know who was responsible. It was an hour before somebody called us in to see the doctor. And you know what he said? "Forget it. This hospital won't give you a baby, the system's broken. It ain't happening. Unless you go private . . ." And he slid his card across, cool as you like. Private clinic.'

'That's terrible.'

'I thought it was just her problem, I guess. She talked about nothing else. I thought she was exaggerating, she couldn't really be hurting that much, she was getting obsessed and it was making things worse. I had to hold in my feelings, keep whatever it was I felt (and I really didn't know what that was) inside, and be strong, look after her. I thought everything would be all right in the end, if I could just do that. Stay in control. For both of us. Nice to have the chance. Felt good. Strong. But that day . . . I knew, deep down, that everything would not be all right. A bit late, I know. If I was going to spend the rest of my life with her, then it would be just us. No kids. I had thought that didn't bother me, it was all her problem. I was wrong. The truth gave me a great big poke. Red hot poker. Joke. We were walking past the ambulances. I sat down on the sidewalk just like that, one step and sit, on the concrete, up against the wall, with her shouting at me, 'What are you doing?' This little girl stepped over me as her mom pulled her away from the crazy guy, and I sat there, just crying my bloody eyes out.'

Yeah, thinks the lighthouse keeper. That's how it goes. But he's had enough of this, so he says what he's thinking for a change: 'What do you want, a bloody medal?'

Thirty

The helicopter clatters overhead as Jack goes storming out, cursing the lighthouse keeper, who is glad to see him go. The Keeper longs to be wrapped up in silence again in the weary light of afternoon, when the chopper has gone. He watches Jack stride away, out of the gate, down the slope. He's heading down past the bench and into the dip where the coaches stop.

Oh no.

The black and yellow helicopter is like a huge wasp hanging just beyond the edge of the cliff. People are standing on the grass and in the lay-by looking at it, some daring to step forward and try to see down over. Careful now. Christ have mercy. Lord have mercy. They must have found another body. Three this week. What's happening? Not Frank, surely? He was going home.

The Keeper begins to jog down the hill. He sees a police car, and recognizes the two officers from the pub, standing with the Chief. Jack is there too, shouting at them: 'Is it her? Is it Sarah? I told you, why didn't you believe me? You could have saved her!'

'Sir, *please!*' The male officer steps in front of Jack, both palms up, trying to calm him down. His female colleague intercepts the Keeper and diverts him by a few paces, turning so they both have their backs to the others. 'Sir, could I have a word? The gentleman says you were talking to someone on the cliff here earlier. Is that right?'

'A lot of people come here.'

'This person, in particular, was distressed.'

'What did he look like?'

'I only have a description at the moment, sir. A smallish gentleman, shorter than average. Slim. He was wearing a white football shirt, I believe.'

Frank. The helicopter is still hovering over the edge, the downdraught whipping into faces. A few people push against it and dare to lean forward and look over. It's a long, long way down. If the chopper goes, the wind will drop and they'll fall.

'He was fine. I don't understand.'

'Sir, the Guardian says—'

'He was really angry.'

'People sometimes are, sir, when the time comes.'

'Not Frank. The Guardian was angry. He said I should keep my nose out of it. I just talked to him. Frank, that is. He seemed fine. Better.'

'Look, sir, can I be honest with you? These Guardians, they're not police officers. But they are trained, sir.'

'Meaning what?'

'They know what they're doing. It's best we let them get on with it.'

The man they call the Keeper sees the Chief throwing a glance his way.

'Are you arresting me?'

'Should I be, sir? At this stage, I'm making enquiries. Now . . .'

The clatter of the helicopter makes it hard to think, but the Keeper tries to recall the things that were said, tries to make sense of what happened with Frank. He can't believe it. What about Billy? *Go home.* That's what he said. *Go home.* 'I didn't mean jump—'

'What, sir?'

'Nothing.'

'So as I was saying, if you wouldn't mind, sir, just let us know if you see anything out of the ordinary, living where you do. Another pair of eyes. Living up here. Here is my mobile number, just in case. I wouldn't want you to be overly concerned; it's just there has been this increase of late, and we would like to know . . .'

Where's Jack? He's not by the police car. Not with the walkers and students trying to peer over the edge. It's not Sarah they have found, thank God for that anyway, but poor Billy, poor Sophie. Poor Frank.

'Your phone won't work up here,' he says to the policeman. 'You know that, though. Will you talk to Jack? Please?'

'Ours do. Sorry, sir, I'm not with you.'

Jack is nowhere to be seen.

Thirty-one

The wind comes up in the early evening. The shush of the sea comes with it, rushing up to the balcony around the lantern room at the top of the tower. Relieved to be alone again, he's out here now after his shower because he can't keep his eyes off the edge. Not since Frank, who was the seventh or eighth in the last month. That's not normal. It's a story; he should ring someone from the old days, but he's not going to. Better to think of the beauty up here. Such beauty. The white horses on a gunmetal sea, the powder blue sky, the clouds racing each other for fun, so low overhead he can almost touch them. The gulls turning, calling. High above them the trace of a jet gives itself away. Heading west towards the sun. The wind steals his breath, wraps itself around his body like a lover in the dark, then runs off around the tower, coming back at him from behind. There's a chill in it, an echo of what has been. The hard winter. Then a warmth in the buffeting, tumbling that says summer will come.

Now the sky is full of light as the sun breaks through again, the air itself is dazzling. Hand up to shield his eyes, he sees through the haze the figure of a woman coming towards him up the hill. Magda, in the red fleece of a Guardian, her bleached white hair trailing. She stands out against the furrowed green and brown, but that is the point. You're supposed to notice the Guardians, if you're desperate. Red means danger in the animal kingdom but here it means rescue, although that didn't help Frank. Was it really his fault? They think they own this place, walking past with torches in the night like prison guards. But if they take care of the lost and the lonely, then the lost and the lonely won't bother him.

Magda waves. She's closer now, she's seen him at the top of the tower. She's smiling and waving and making some sign with her hands, trying to tell him something. Come down. No. He doesn't want to do that. He's safe up here in the golden sky, in the haze,

in the sunshine dream world. I'm okay. Go away. Leave me alone.
Let me be.

'Look at the light, the sky is so full of light,' said Rí the first time
she brought him here. 'The air itself shines.' You could see the
sun rise in the morning and set in the evening. They watched it
all once, more or less. She was reading a book about the place,
the old green book he still has on a shelf somewhere downstairs.
They lit a brazier in the courtyard in the afternoon and as the
wood of an old pallet fizzed and crackled she told him what she
had read about the men and women who once danced through
the smoke and ashes of a great bonfire here on the hill, seeking the
blessings of Belen, the old sun god who rode across the sky in a
chariot of fire.

'How do you know they did that?'

'Well, I don't. It's in the book. But there was a sun god. There
was a Roman too, who threw himself off here in a bid to become
immortal; and a saint called Wilfred who saw a long line of men
from the settlement that was here all jump together, hand in
hand, to save the last of the food for their women and children,
after three years of drought and famine. Isn't that a sad tale,
now?'

'Saint Wilf?'

'Sure.'

'A drought? In Sussex?'

'It was a very long time ago.'

'There's a reason everything's so green. Where's your evidence
for all this?'

'Feel it, loverboy.'

'Feel it?'

'Yes. Feel. It. Do you know about Parson Darby's Hole?'

He laughed, but she was serious. This wasn't a dodgy movie.
A priest in the village a couple of miles inland got sick of burying
sailors, long ago. He spent too many hours searching in the rocks
for survivors while the people from his parish filled their baskets
with beach booty from wrecked ships. Those were smuggling
times. So he carved a staircase into the chalk and dug out a cave

123

in the cliff face, high above the water line. And he sat there in the dark on stormy nights, holding up a lantern as a warning.

'Maybe he was working for the wreckers, luring the ships? There was enough room in that cave for a load of brandy. We should go and see it.'

'Gone. The cliff has fallen way back since then.'

'When?'

'Seventeen something. I read he was just trying to get away from his wife, sitting in his cave all night. A proper man cave. Halfway up a cliff.'

'Wouldn't work for me. No stereo.'

'A table, a bit of carpet and a Bible. And a lot of brandy, maybe. She had a vinegar tongue, they said. Annie. His wife. Poor woman, I bet she bloody didn't. There's a reason it's called his-story. She lost a son and then a little baby, then she died too. The parson caught a fever. The Sailor's Friend, they call him, on his gravestone.'

'Hello sailor!'

'I like him. He cared. The first light keeper. At least he had a light. Grand. I love the stories about this place. Someone called Mr Thunder built a cage that he slung over the cliff and lowered to the beach to save lives.'

'Did he really?'

'Yes. Probably. I don't know.' She caught him smiling at her. 'Definitely. Hundreds. Thousands of lives. He'd get a Queen's Medal now.'

'Or he'd be locked up. Good way to get barrels of brandy off the beach.'

She began to read the book aloud to him at nights, and his favourite character by far was Mad Jack Fuller: Georgian plantation owner, slave owner, rich man, MP, enthusiast, constructor of obelisks, pyramids and other follies in otherwise empty fields. Mad Jack, whose other nickname was Hippo, whose proposal of marriage was turned down by the only woman he really loved. The sight of a shipwreck moved him to pay for a wooden platform on Belle Tout, sending out a warning light. This worked well, so a proper lighthouse was called for. Blocks of granite were brought down from Aberdeen by boat and hauled across the Downs by teams of oxen. Steaming with the effort, caked in clay, they heaved up the hill in the early 1830s. The stonemasons created a tower fit for Rapunzel, and the representatives of the landowners of the area – the men of the grand houses of Cavendish and Gilbert – rode out to see the opening of the lighthouse. The band played 'God Save the King' and all was well in the world, all was safe and well. The lantern burned bright in the room at the top of the tower, a clockwork frame of thirty lamps that burned two gallons of oil a day. The light shone in the darkness and the ships were saved.

Until the mists came down. Then the ships could not see the light. Then the lighthouse on the hill was lost in the night by the men looking out for it on the black sea. Then the rocks had their way again. The ships were lost. The *Dalhousie*, bound for Sydney. The *Rubens* from Buenos Aires. The *Coonatto*, almost home to London after a long journey from Adelaide. All too close to the cliffs, all caught on the razor rocks beneath the surface of the sea, all battered and smashed and sailors drowned, for the lack of a warning. The lighthouse was useless. 'Another folly,' she said. 'Hey ho, there you go. Mad Jack was dead by then anyway. Long gone.'

The light was put out and a replacement was built down on the rocks a mile along the coast in 1902. It was hard to get to except in certain tides and living in a new lighthouse was enough to befuddle any mind. 'The grey Channel on one side, absorbing thoughts and swallowing sanity, and the sheer face of the cliffs on the other, looming like a jealous giant,' wrote one visitor. A first lighthouse keeper went crazy, living all on his own, so they put two lighthouse keepers in there together, to keep each other company. They fell out during the winter months – an oil lamp was left unfilled, the porridge was lumpy, or some small thing. They stopped speaking. Trinity House in London received a wire, requesting help. One of the men had died of natural causes, a boat should be sent for his body. The crew arrived on a boiling sea to find the corpse strung up on the outside of the lighthouse, tied by his hands and feet to the curve of the lantern room so that when the light shone, his shadow cast a cross on the sea. The survivor said he did it to keep out the smell, but nobody was sure whether to believe him. 'From that time on, there were three light keepers,' said her book. 'Two for the light, one to stop them killing each other.'

The original lighthouse tower – their tower – was handed to the local landowners and sold on to a surgeon, who had seen it as he was motoring along the coast. This was meant to be his refuge from the pressures of treating the nerves of wealthy London folk, but the sickly King George sought out his adviser even in this sanctuary, in 1935. Queen Mary climbed the breathless steps to the lantern room and called down to the monarch, 'George, don't come up here, it's too steep for you.' His Majesty's lungs were riddled and his body failing, but he called back, 'Damn it, Mary, I'm coming.'

Within a year, he was dead.

Then came the war. German bombers used the tower as a guide to help them find their way home, and dropped the last of their load here to speed their way. Spitfires chased them, dancing in the summer blue, their pilots using the tower to make sense of the whirl of land, sea and sky. The Army built a little railway on the edge of the cliff and ran a tin tank along it for target practice. They missed the tank and hit the tower – by accident, they said. They blasted away with their big guns, the shells exploding here and here, chalk and rock spiralling into the air; then closer; then the fire fell on the house and finally the tower itself, taking great bites from the side.

And when the war was over, the tower was broken and empty. Except for the birds that crept in to nest. Except for the rabbits. Except for the walkers whose dogs came for a sniff around and the hikers who slept in its ruins. For a decade, the shattered tower offered shelter to anyone who wanted it, until its broken body was redeemed by love. Boys and girls came running through the grounds and inside the tower in the late fifties, chasing each other up the narrow staircase to the top. A doctor with a family had a dream to restore the tower, picking up the pieces, clearing the yard, paying men to come and build again and helping them with his soft doctor's hands. They hardened. There were happy summers and secure winters for the family that lived in the tower then, before the children grew up and it was sold. Somebody tried to make a go of bed and breakfast here; they built the rooms but they ran out of money and the lighthouse was left empty again.

The sea mist fingered the latches, rusted the hinges and split the frames, so the place was in a poor state when Maria came to paint, as she had done as a child, only now she was Rí. Despite the dripping ceilings and the rags at the windows to keep out the draughts, she was enchanted again. She brought him to the tower and he loved her. He wanted a life that was new. To step out of his own and into another. With her. This fairytale tower on the edge of the world felt like a good place to start.

There was even a good omen. They were up on the balcony around the lantern room, trying not to fall through the holes in the wooden floor, when they heard a noise that was something like a song and a growl. It grew louder and louder and seemed to be coming out of the sun at them on this dazzling day. A pair of great elliptical wings shadowed their faces for a moment and he knew it was a Spitfire, the most elegant flying machine ever created, more like a bird of prey. The Spitfire climbed steeply above the Downs, showing its back, then slipped sideways through the sky, levelled up and came in low towards the lighthouse at an impossible speed, so fast and so low that they both ducked for fear of losing their heads; but the wings tilted again and it was gone, the throaty song trailing behind. Rí stayed on her knees, pulled out her sketchbook and was marking the swoops and curves of flight when the Spitfire came back along and below the line of the cliffs, flying from right to left, lower than the tower. He could even look down on the cockpit and saw the pilot wave, as if from the past. *Over to you, then. Over and out.* This was their place. They would have all the time they needed to begin again. That was how it felt then.

But here and now, the cold wins.

The golden light vanishes as the sun drops. Shadows spread over the downland like a bruise. A murder of crows shifts shape overhead and passes out of sight, heading for the trees in the Horseshoe Plantation at the foot of the hill. The last fragment of sun disappears into the horizon and green flashes on the faces of the Seven Sisters. The chill is sudden. He watches the great dome of the sky light up one last time, then darken into moody blue. His cheeks are numb. His bones are damp.

Enough. The day is done.

Thirty-two

His shoulders bump either side of the narrow space, a hand running over the guide rope, but his feet know the way. The wind whines and comes slipping down behind him as he reaches the base of the staircase where the circle is wider and a room is tucked behind the steps. The Keeper's Cabin. That was the name she painted in bright, bubbling yellow on a piece of driftwood and nailed to the door, not knowing it was a prophecy. The room in which he sleeps, on a high bunk above a wardrobe. It's a tight space, up there. You lie in bed with the grey stone ceiling right in your face. More than once he has cracked his head. There is a security in this confinement, though. A sense of being hugged by the tower. The thick, stone walls, strong against the night. Safe. He shrugs off his shirt and jeans, feels the cold tighten his chest and finds old jogging bottoms and a T-shirt, the memory of a festival long ago now. They lay in their tent and listened to the rise of a hundred thousand voices as Primal Scream began their set. The thump of the drums and the jagged chords of 'Get Your Rocks Off'. Get your rocks off, honey! They turned their faces to each other in the shadows and he can taste her now. The soft lip. The soft bite. He stands with his hands on the wall like a usual suspect, until the surge of feeling passes. Sweet, sharp, dark like wine warming the stomach. He gulps in air, then sighs to let it go.

Let it bleed.

The cabin bed is only just big enough. Happier in his tight space, he waits. His eyes become accustomed, he can see the arch of the window set against deeper black. Out there are the shifting shadows of the sea.

Goodnight, my love.

Goodnight.

*

There are always sounds in the night. The rattle of this, the tap of that; sometimes the crash of another as the big bad wolf of the wind tries to blow the tower down. Tonight, a storm is rising. 'South-westerly severe gale force nine, increasing storm force eleven imminent, perhaps hurricane force twelve for a time.' The voice of the shipping forecaster is eerily calm as she predicts mayhem for those at sea, out in the Channel, on the ships that have not put into port, but pitch and roll in the churning waters, tankers tossed like tugs.

This tower will not fall to the storm, but the outhouse is more vulnerable. All the beds wrapped in plastic, waiting for him to . . . what? Get over it? Rí was going to sleep in each room for a night, and name it the next morning. Now they are just empty spaces locked up in the dark, and he can't sleep. Of course not. Every night, he lays here. Every night, he hopes. Breathing deep. Breathing out. Trying to relax his body. Wide awake. His back aches, his throat is dry and his eyes are open. Again. Every night, he flicks the torch on and reads a few lines before they blur. Every night, he tries something different. Shakespeare offered no way to sleep, perchance to dream. *The Selfish Gene* was a jealous god. There was no balm in Gilead. What is it tonight? *The Tommy Cooper Joke Book*. 'Side-splitting one-liners from the hapless genius of magic-based comedy,' says the cover.

'I painted my wife in oils. She looks like a sardine.'

Maybe not. Side-splitting is what the sea-soaked, salt-worn timber window frames in the outhouse are probably doing right now, prised apart by the blade of a gale. The Keeper rolls from the bunk and drops to the floor without finding the ladder, the stone cold against his bare feet. He scoops up a sweater, pulls on leather mules and pads down to the wide space where the base of the tower meets the top storey of the outhouse. Shapes loom in the dark, but they are familiar to him. Boxes, cases, piles of books. The horn of a gramophone; a modern sound system; an easel. Her easel.

The wind grows louder, then fades, then comes back louder still. He listens for the whistle that will tell him a crack has appeared somewhere, but there is nothing like that, just the fussy gale. Downstairs there is damp in the air and a sense of expectation, like a dog awake in the night. Is this the master come to wake me? Is it now the fun begins? No. He closes and locks each door and pushes on it to be sure. The ground floor rooms are the same. Open, look, nothing. Open, look, nothing. Open, look . . . wait. There is something wrong here. The door is not locked, a draught is coming through the window. The table and chair are as they should be, but there on the mattress is the something. Someone has been here. They've ripped open one of the boxes and unfolded a blanket, and left it curled on the bed like a question-mark. No, hang on. He can't see properly, he can't be sure, but isn't that a body? There's no rising or falling, no sign of movement, but yes, it's true. Here in the night, in the storm, in a blanket on the bed, is a body. The body of a woman.

Thirty-three

He sees her now in his sleepless confusion, as the light changes and silver ghosts her face. There is a body in his house. He lives in a tower on a hill. He lives alone in the tower and there is a body in his house. There is a husband out there looking for a wife, a furious husband shouting for his wife. There is a body in his house. In his knackered state, in his up-late, day–night delirious state of mind, body, spirit, he feels panic. He should call the police. The rain sounds angry, like it wants to come in, like it knows she is here. Like Jack. He should ring Magda – she will know what to do. There is no signal on his phone. It is like that up here, particularly on stormy nights. The last place in the country to be so inaccessible. Magda would know what to do. She will be back from patrol, alone in her bed in the back room while Tony sleeps and snores elsewhere. She would know what to do, but he can't call Magda. Or anyone. There is a body in his house and nobody to call. Stepping closer, he peels back the edge of the blanket and reaches out with the softest movement to touch the marble flesh. To be sure. And as he does so, stressed and breathless, leaning over the woman, she moves.

Her breath is on his fingers. She shifts and sighs in her sleep. What to do? The lock is useless. That would be imprisonment. She's not a burglar. He is not afraid, having seen her. He has looked into the eyes of women who would have killed him without flinching – women to be scared of – and she is not one of those. She is sleeping and therefore not dead in his tower, and for that he is very, very grateful. Okay, so. If she needs shelter for the night, let her shelter. Let her sleep. What choice does he have? In the morning she will be gone, hopefully. So he turns back up the stairs to the kitchen, to make tea and sit in the dark, waiting for sleep or for her to wake, or the morning, whichever comes first. Soon there is music from the speaker. A solo piano. The notes dropping softly among the sounds of the storm.

He wakes in his armchair, shuddering with the cold, into the sickly light of dawn. Hot water from the kitchen tap eases the stiffness in his hands and brings his face back to life. Then he remembers. He takes the stairs carefully, barefoot for stealth, toes frozen. Listening, as he reaches the ground floor. Nothing. The bedroom door is open. The blanket has been folded up and put back in the box; there is no sign at all of a visitor except for a slip of paper half hidden under the bed, an envelope with no name on it that he tosses on the bed. There's nothing wrong in the room. He must have left the door open when Jack came, when he was rattled. The front door, too, unless she came in through the window. Jack left it open a crack when he threw out his fag.

'Hello?' His voice cracks at the first attempt, brittle in the early morning. 'Hello? Are you here?'

The wind sighs, a long, sceptical sound as if to say, *Really? You're asking that question? You want to know? You want me to tell you? Well . . . no. She's gone.*

There's a fire in his blood, a sickness from so little sleep, a shot of relief that she has gone and a burst of energy like a high, so he feels the need to run again. To get out there into the simplicity of morning and run through the lilac light. In shorts, a T-shirt and running shoes he slugs juice from the carton and crunches a cereal bar, looking down through the window to the new lighthouse, winking in the dawn. Let's go. 'Move on up.' The drums and bass kick in as he closes the front door and the rhythm pushes him forward, over the paving stones, over the gravel, vaulting the wall. Slipping on the dew, reclaiming the beat, running down the whale's back.

Far away beyond the Gap, the waves advance in long, sweeping lines towards the Seven Sisters. He might go for a swim, he's thinking – elated again by the raw pleasure of this place: the wide sky, the storm-cleared air, the rush of oxygen – when he sees her. Standing on an outcrop, close to the edge. Very close. Arms wide. Face up towards the sky. Good for her, he thinks. Quite right, enjoy the place. He's running on, running on, when a thought makes him turn and look back, and he stumbles and his foot catches in a rabbit hole, and he curses and he sees the wind jerk her back suddenly, like a push. She twists forward, tries to adjust and goes down hard on her side. Get up, get back, he thinks, get away – and she's trying to do that but there's something else: the lip of the cliff is coming away. Underneath her. He can see it from here, the crack in the creamy white, the landslip and the fall. She's going to fall. He can see that and he's running, lungs burning. Running, stumbling, running. Reaching out, fingers stretched, too far. Grabbing air. Come on! Flailing, finding, feeling her coat in his hand, pulling hard. Yanking her away. Wrenching his shoulder, going down with her, hip to the ground, breath gone, dizzy but fighting, reaching, pulling. Saving.

In the moment that follows, as his head thunders and his bones burn, he looks at her. She looks at him. A moment of recognition. Nothing to do with the wind, the racing clouds, the ambitious sky, the shimmering, snakeskin sea. Nothing to do with the crumbling chalk, the breaking cliff, the clattering stones, the fleeing birds. Two people, each looking into the other's eyes and seeing something they recognize. Something they understand, for a moment. Then it's over.

This time he isn't interfering. This time he has actually done some good. But what to do now? He's panting like a dog, she's lying here beside him. Get up, come on. Get up. His legs are shaky, they give way as he tries to stand, then the blood seems to surge back down through the knees and he's okay. Breathless, dizzy, but okay. 'Let me . . .'

She won't take his hand.

'All right, all right.' He backs off, palms up. Here we go again. Leave her, he thinks. Walk away. Let it be.

She looks up at him, quickly, then back at the edge. She's not getting up, but staying down on her back. Closing her eyes and seeming to sink into the grass. A tangle of curls. A face he sees upside down, the chin where the forehead should be, the hair like a beard. Then a black top zipped up to the throat, a bright scarf and a long, almost ankle-length, black greatcoat twisted underneath her. Black boots up to her knees and rusty red jeans. She's lovely. The thought flares and dies like a match flame in the wind. Her fear is more powerful, he can sense her distress.

'Are you okay?' Stupid bloody question. Stupid, stupid.

She doesn't answer.

What's he going to do? Get down on the ground. Kneel down, lie down beside her. Not touching, he makes sure of that. Above them a wisp of high cloud is unravelling. Coming undone.

'What's your name?' he asks, although he's sure he knows, and waits. And waits. A bird passes over them, a predator. 'You were in my house.'

She glances at him sharply, then rolls away, on to her side.

'It's okay,' he says as softly as he can manage and still be heard. Now what, though? There is nobody up here, it is still too early for walkers. The Guardians will be along, but after yesterday he doesn't trust them. If they see him lying here, with a young woman who is obviously in some kind of trouble, they'll call the police. Or she might end up like Frank, God help him. She must be the one the ragged boy is looking for. He scans the broad back of the hill all the way down to the Gap, looking for Jack. How long has she been sleeping in the bedroom? Surely he would have noticed before now? It was closed up, he thought it was locked, he hadn't looked into the rooms for months, and when he opened that one for Jack there was no sign of her, no sign of anything. Jack. That boy really worries him.

'Will you come back inside and get warm?'

She doesn't respond.

Okay, so. 'I'm going to put the kettle on. The door is unlocked. But you know that, don't you? Come up the stairs. There's a fire.' He keeps going, without encouragement. 'Right then. That's me. In the lighthouse. Come and get warm. Have some breakfast. When you're ready.' And as he walks away, not looking back, he is thinking, I will turn around when I get to the lighthouse and she will be gone over. Christ have mercy.

The walk is no more than a hundred yards but it takes a while. When he reaches the wall and turns, she is still there, lying on the grass. Facing the tower. Facing him.

Thirty-four

'Are you there? I have to do this. Don't know why,' he says to nobody but the wind and the memory, not expecting a response. He needs strong tea, and something to eat. There is honey somewhere here. He scoops it up with his little finger and sucks, loving the sweet hit. She's not out there now. He hears the door opening down below and the sound of her boots on the stairs. Right then. Right.

'Up here.'

This slender, angular woman stands slightly stooped, coat wrapped tight around her, her posture an apology for existence. I am sorry that I am here. And yet he also feels obliged to apologize, looking at the chaos of the lounge-to-be and the only slightly less chaotic kitchen space. 'It's a mess. Look, here, this is comfortable.'

The old red leather armchair in which he listens to the piano at night is saggy, but the best he has. She lowers herself into it like a gymnast coming down off the bars, and tucks her knees up to her chest, arms around them. Defensive, he thinks. Fair enough. He feels more secure here, in his home. His tower. More able to talk to her. 'The kettle's boiled. Tea? I've got builder's or Lapsang. Coffee maybe?'

The woman says nothing, so he settles for an ordinary teabag to match his own. She is remarkably still in the armchair, tucked up, eyes on the view.

'Milk? No sugar, sorry. I do have honey, though.'

He gives her milk and puts the honey jar on the floor beside the chair, with a teaspoon sticking out. He clears a pile of unsorted books from a kitchen chair, turns it round and sits down astride it, mug in hand.

'Well.'

Well, indeed.

'So then. Music?'

He finds a remote, and the small black stereo blinks back into life, the first notes of a *Gymnopédie* beginning to fall among the boxes and chairs. His knee is jumping. What is he doing? Trying to help. First, find out who she is.

'You didn't say your name.'

She's not going to now, either. Cupping the tea in both hands, with the steam twisting up into her face – a sharp face with high arched eyebrows, a long nose, a rosebud mouth with the corners dragged down by sorrow or fear, a gap in her front teeth, a dimple on the left cheek but not the right, her eyes almost closed – she seems oblivious. Could she even be deaf?

'Sarah?'

She looks startled by the sound of her name, clumps the mug down on the stone floor, spilling tea, and starts to get up, to leave.

'Wait. It's okay. Really. Sit down.'

Sarah stares, alarmed and puzzled, trying to work something out. Her eyes are wide, bright. Frightened.

'Lucky guess. I heard someone of that name was missing. That's all. Honest.'

After a moment, she does let herself sit. Best not mention Jack, or the police.

'Don't let the tea go cold. I'm . . .' Is he going to say his name? Self-protection says he shouldn't. If he doesn't tell anyone, he can't be called back to that life. He can stay here, in the tower, with Rí. 'The Keeper' will do. But he can't say that out loud; it's weird, isn't it? He can't say that to this woman, when he needs to know her secrets in order to help her, so maybe he should give her his. Okay then.

'My name is Gabe.'

That's it. A relief. Big moment; not that she has even noticed. 'Gabriel, really, obviously, but Gabe is better. If you like. You're safe. There's nothing in the tea,' he says, but the thought had obviously not occurred to her until now, because she looks down, frowning. Oh God, he sounds creepy. 'You can get up and walk out, it's fine. Go, if you like. I won't tell anyone – you obviously don't want them to know where you are. It's okay. I understand.

Why do you think I live in a place like this? Everybody's got to get away sometimes.'

'Why do you think I live in a place like this?' What are you talking about?

Rí's voice, suddenly close, causes a shudder.

I'm sorry.

You should be. Who is this anyway? She's pretty.

'I found her . . .'

Did he say that out loud? Sarah seems not to have heard as she ponders her tea. He needs to get out of here, go upstairs, get his head right. 'Excuse me . . .'

The lantern room is a rainforest shower of light. It's a bright, sharp morning, the storm blown away. Out on the balcony, on his own, he grips the red iron railing, knuckles whitening. 'She was out there, she fell—'

I know.

'She needs help.'

So you only help the pretty ones?

'No, listen, I'm not . . .' He tries to speak quietly, for fear of being heard below, but he knows he's getting agitated, getting louder. 'She's not . . . for God's sake, Rí. For God's sake.'

Nobody else has been here.

'Please. Rí. Don't do this.'

Nobody.

'Give me a break.'

Why her?

'Why can't you just bloody leave me alone?'

It's hard to know how long he is on the floor of the lantern room, or which of the anguished, animal noises he makes can be heard below. The grief exhausts itself, eventually. He lies there in the bright morning light, coming back to his senses, suddenly craving a shower and some proper clothes, but not wanting to face Sarah again. When he does descend the stairs at last, she has gone.

Thirty-five

So, okay then, I have been reported missing; that is a shame, thinks Sarah. She does not mean to cause such trouble. Still, it's not time to go back yet. She isn't done. She walks out through the heavy black iron gate, arms crossed, getting away from the tower, knowing that she needs to be alone for what is coming. The moments and the seconds and the hours are slow for her, slower than ever, as she waits for the test. Then she will know what to do. Tomorrow. In the morning. First thing. Not before that date, the clinic said. When is that, though, to be sure? When the light comes up? After the first coffee? First wee. And where can she go now? Not back into the lighthouse. The strange, handsome, raggedy man who is trying to be kind makes her wary. What kind of person lives in a tower anyway? A knight. A battered one. There is no shining armour here. His clothes are loose and crumpled. His stubble is patchy, his hair explosive. That stone he wears around his neck on a piece of stretched leather obviously means something. Those are the colours of a lady, who is no longer here. There is a tone in his voice, a shadow on his face, some expression in those soulful, startled eyes that says he knows something of how Sarah feels. Somehow. Perhaps. But he cannot really. Nobody can. He means no harm, she believes that. So maybe she will stay. Until dark at least. Then she can walk down the hill unseen, follow the road back to the Gap, get a bus to the path to the farmhouse again. Even as she thinks it, she does not believe it. The wind is strong.

Sarah walks once around the outer wall of the lighthouse plot to the corner where it crumbles, then once the other way, before going back in.

She finds herself alone and starving, looking at a soup can on the table. Tomato. She fishes in the drawers, finds an opener, pours the thick, lipstick-red liquid into a saucepan. The scent rising from the pan makes her feel faint.

'Is there a reason you're not talking? There must be.' He is behind her, in the doorway, hair wet from the shower. 'That's funny. It's my thing. I like the silence here. I don't talk much, to other people. Or I didn't. It's okay, I get it. Just give me something, though, will you?'

'Good soup,' she says, very quietly.

'Right. Yes. Thank you. Have it all. You look famished. How have you been eating?'

She pours the remainder into her bowl and looks up.

'Right,' he says, getting the message. 'No questions.'

'I was okay. On the cliff edge. I wasn't going to fall.'

'No, okay.'

They sit and eat to music. Satie again, quiet and calm. The intimacy of the pair of them in this room disturbs him. She is lovely but young, too young. And anyway. Anyway. His head grows heavy, his eyes close and he rests on the table, the cool wood on his forehead, just for a moment. He doesn't notice Sarah, leaning back in the armchair, watching him. Waiting. When he starts to snore, she breathes deeply and allows herself to sink back into the same oblivion. So the strangers sleep, side by side in the same room, as the afternoon tires and the shadows deepen.

Gabe wakes with a sore neck and a flat face, to find anger pulsing in his temples and the woman talking to him urgently, saying things he can't quite hear.

'Why are you here?'

'Oh. Ugh. I live here.'

'Why?' She's kneeling up on the armchair, using the back as a shield. Staring. Studying him. 'What is this place?'

'A lighthouse. With no light. A darkhouse, Rí said . . .'

'Who is she?'

No, he's not talking about that. 'No questions. Okay?'

Sarah shrugs. They sit in silence again, at the table and in the armchair. She sits lightly, all elbows and knees, as if to spring up at any moment. The music has stopped, the wind has gone. The silence is awkward.

'I would like to know about this place. Please.'

Why won't she just go? He doesn't want her to go. She's in his head now. No, that's not happening either. So what now? In the other life before he was called the Keeper, when he was still the special correspondent Gabriel Keane, people told him things and he learned to hear them, even when they said nothing with their mouths. Silence could be eloquent. So, what is Sarah saying? He forces himself to think.

First, she doesn't want to talk about whatever it is that brought her here, not yet. That's okay. But the way she stretches her legs out now says she is starting to feel just a little more safe, starting to trust him a bit. Enough to risk pushing back at him with those questions. What else then? She has no bag. She hasn't been here the whole time; she must have been sleeping somewhere else before last night, and left her bag there, expecting to return. One of the farms, maybe. There are a couple of those within walking distance, two or three miles. It won't have been too hard to stay out of the way, under a different name, before the police were notified that she was missing and started looking. So she must have come to Belle Tout yesterday, probably on foot, without her bags. After Jack. Maybe she was caught out in the storm and needed shelter. If she rang the bell he did not hear it. The door was probably unlocked, because he's an idiot who should know better. She came in only as far as she needed to. That first room, by the door. You can't see into the tower from there. Still, she's brave. Tough. She looks slight, but moves with such composure. Her face makes you smile . . .

Does it now?

Rí, Jesus. Don't be mad. I'm yours.

I know.

Help me then. What am I supposed to do?

No answer.

Sarah is clearly not about to talk either. The other thing he was good at, back in the day, when he found himself sitting with someone, hoping for their stories to flow so that he could write them down, was knowing when to spin a tale, to share something of himself and show the way for the other person to follow.

'Okay,' he says to her. 'Okay, Sarah. I'll talk. Let me do that. They say we need to move it. The whole thing, back from the edge. You can see why: there's just that lip of land out there before the edge. Bits of the cliff are always falling away. The tower was fifty feet further back when it was built. They say we can build rails under the tower and pull it back. It will cost a fortune.' This is unfamiliar, talking this much – he has to clear his throat to keep going. 'I haven't got a fortune. Nobody has, for something like that. We got the place because of it.'

Sarah says nothing, head on her knees, not looking at him.

'We've got ten years – maybe a bit more if we're lucky. Maybe less.'

That's it. That's the story. She's supposed to respond. Sarah unfolds herself with quick grace, gets up and moves around, looks at a book or two, just by the window. Her face in shadow, the light on the long sweep of her neck. The silence is deafening.

Thirty-six

Tell her about the bird.

What?

The wheatear. That's a good one.

'The bird?' He says it out loud, too loudly, and Sarah turns to look at him. 'Er, you know the bird there, that went by the window? The little one there, just for a moment? You were lucky. It's called a wheatear, and there's a story. Do you want to hear it?'

She looks away as if it doesn't matter to her either way.

'I'll take that as a yes. There used to be a lot of them. Listen.' He picks the old green book from a pile and thumbs the pages. The cracked skin on his thumb is sore. 'Here. "In one season, shepherds on the Downs caught one thousand eight hundred and forty dozen birds. They sold them for a penny a piece." They hide away in rabbit holes now. You were really lucky to see one.'

Please respond, he thinks. Come on, work with me.

'Okay, so that's the bird. The wheatear. It used to be called something else, but the Victorians didn't like that. White arse.'

Is that a smile? Maybe a hint of one.

'So, the story. There was a guy called Wilson, who lived in a big house out there. This was during the Civil War. A secret royalist in a landscape full of Roundheads.' He feels his voice warming up, and takes pleasure in the physical sensation of talking like this. 'He didn't get out much. Gout. Leg like an elephant. All that claret, probably. So he was in bed when the soldiers came to get him. A whole platoon, a dozen maybe, I don't know, on horseback and armed, coming to search the house. The servants saw them coming, the Wilsons were warned.'

Is he getting this right? It doesn't really matter. There are brown marks on the edges of the page, literary liver spots. Sarah has sat down now, on the window ledge, and she's studying the hill. 'Mary Wilson was there when they arrived. The lady of the house. She was all smiles . . .'

Will he do the voice? No. Not today.

'She said, "Good afternoon, gentlemen." Something like that. She was scared. They could take him away and leave her ruined.'

He finds himself walking up and down the room, talking more easily. 'They would have rushed upstairs, but she had a plan. Well, a pie.'

Is Sarah listening or just sitting this out?

'She ordered the cook to bring out food and invited the lieutenant to sit down to eat something, it says in here. He was hungry. The barracks were half a day away. I don't know if he was surprised by her hospitality, maybe it was just expected. But he sat down and out came the most enormous pie he'd ever seen in his life. The size of a wheel. The depth of a bucket. It smelt gorgeous.' The word feels good in his mouth. '"What's in it?" said the soldier. She said, "White arse." Now he got excited. He thought she was flirting with him. They always do, don't they?'

Do they?

Is that what he's doing? His eyes are on the back of Sarah's head, the tight twists of copper on her crown . . . No, keep going.

'This was the most expensive pie he had ever seen. He wanted a taste, badly, but he also had a chance to show off to his men. No officer ever turned down one of those. So he commanded them: "Come here and feast." They made a right old mess of the table. Flakes of pastry and smears of pie all over the place, on the floor, on their uniforms. They were loving it.'

Gabe stops, suddenly too close to Sarah. Within touching distance, looking down on her head. She still won't turn around. He hears his own breathing and stops it, for as long as he can bear. But then he bursts, of course, and feels like a stalker. He steps back and folds himself down to sit on the floor. Closer to her level. But he doesn't reach out, doesn't encroach. He begins to speak again, more at ease with the telling now.

'While they were filling their faces, Mary slipped out of the room and upstairs to her husband, who was half out of bed, trying to hear what was going on. He said nothing, but pointed to the bottom drawer of his chest. Before he could make any kind of gesture to tell her there was a secret compartment, she had released the catch and pulled it out. That shocked him. What other secrets of his did she know? She took out a leather folder, emptied it of papers and pushed them into the fire that was heating his room.'

Now Gabe glances down at the book – he wants to get the next line right. 'Listen to this. "The flames rose once for his love for the king, once for his love of money and once for his love of another. Mary watched them burn." Lovely stuff.' He reaches a palm towards the wood stove warming this room, glowing orange, as if to push the papers inside. He knows she's listening now. 'So, that's it. They found nothing. William got away with it because of Mary's pie. He was made a baronet when the king returned. On his coat of arms he put a wheatear. Least he could do.'

There is silence in the room again, for a long while. Aware of his heavy breathing, Gabe gets up and moves away, puts the book down. The wind rattles a window frame.

'What happened to her?'

'I don't know. It's just a story.'

'You must,' says Sarah.

Oh God. Why did he start this?

Because I said so, Gabe.

He hands Sarah the book, his thumb on a paragraph. She reads out loud, which distresses him. '"After the death of his wife at a young age, Sir William asked a clergyman in Kent to take on the education of their six children."' The next sentence is underlined in pencil. '"It hath pleased God for my" . . . er . . . "sinnes to take from mee . . . my dear wife, one of the best of women, as being too good for me . . ."'

Oh Lord. He wants to be sick.

Sarah looks up from the page and sees his face changed. The desolation makes her go quickly back to the words, smoothing the page, running her thumb along the edge.

'It is a good story,' she says, wondering what else to say. Or do. She had not thought about that until now. He's skinny but tough, there is nowhere to run. Is that the cost of staying here? The surge of panic is a surprise, a jangling new sound in the white noise of her non-emotions. She is everything and nothing now, too far gone to care. She will see out her time, see the dawn and take her steps; there is no way to stop it now, nothing can get in her way, but here is this man. In her face. So sad. So hurt. Whatever he is, whatever he wants, he is not dangerous. Time is passing. The day is coming. She has nothing to say, nothing. But perhaps words are what he wants in return for letting her stay. Hopefully they are, anyway. We'll see. 'I have a question, actually.'

'Sure.'

'Was there a bird? Outside?'

'Yes. Of course.'

'A wheatear?'

'Ah. Maybe not,' he says, rubbing his cheeks, feeling warmth return to them. Feeling grateful to her for the jolt, for moving him on. The room is cold now, away from the stove. 'No, I have to confess there wasn't.'

'Pity. I like a pie. One other thing . . .' Such cool, clear eyes she has.

'Go on?'

'What happened to her? Ree, is it?'

'Yes, Rí. Maria.'

'Where did she go?'

Thirty-seven

Can I show her?
  Why do you want to?
I have to. I don't know.
  Why?
She wants to know.
  I don't care.
I want to show her.
  That's more like it. Why?
I don't know.
  She won't shag you.
I don't care.
  You want it then.
I . . . don't care.
  You're showing off.
Showing off what? Myself? No. You. I'm showing off you, Maria.
I'm proud of you. Who you are, what you did, what you made.
How you saw. How you taught me to see.
  Showing off the woman you made?
No. You made me. You saved me.
  I never understood how you could say that.
I never understood how you could not see it.
  Show her. I don't care.
I want you to care. I need you to care.
  You're asking for the moon, my star.
Yes.
  Yes, Gabe.
Yes?
  Yes.

And so he asks Sarah to follow him up the tight, narrow staircase,
conscious of his breathing again. 'Climb with me.' One turn and
another, almost to the top but not quite. And there he stops, with

148

the sky falling down from the lantern room, a cloud of light on the stairs. It is ignored, this time, for the sake of a heavy wooden door opening into a tight room with a high bunk, a curved room with a deep-set window. He lets her go through first. It takes a moment for his eyes to adjust and he knows when it is happening for Sarah because she breathes a little faster and she makes a noise, the slightest sound, like a sigh and a gasp together, at the sight of it, the wonder of it.

The room full of glory. The glorious room.

What does she see? First, feathers turning in the air by the door, close to her face. White and grey, silver and black, gossamer creatures trembling at her breath. The shadows of birds, the echo of wings, the rumour of angels. Then the faces coming into focus on the walls. Fine line drawings. A haunted old man, an elegant old woman, a young girl with sunshine in her hair, a boy with pride and terror in his eyes, his youth subsiding. There are more. Strong faces and weak faces, handsome ones and ugly chops, corpulent or arrow-sharp, each rendered with the same sure marks, the same fine detail.

'These are . . .'

Yes, wonderful. He waits. Outside, a cloud gives way. Fingers of light tickle the window frame and flick at the colours on the floor, ringing them like bells. Flashes of green and gold, stabs of yellow, fracturing blues, all somehow becoming music, a rising, shimmering, jangling, tinkling collision of colour and sound, and Sarah sees that it is a mosaic of sorts. A magpie mosaic made with scraps of this and twists of that: buttons and brass, fabric and foil, spirals of wire and tiny bells, set out as a picture wider than deep, organized in ways she cannot quite understand.

'Step back,' he says.

So she steps back and sees at last. The sea, the chalk face, the cliff tops. The hills, the valleys, the farms. The lighthouse with the lantern shining. 'That is amazing. It is just . . .'

'Rí,' he says, bending down to touch the materials. Caressing them, as if touching a beloved face. 'This is who she is.'

Sarah leaves him be and takes refuge up in the lantern room. There are ships in the Channel and clouds drifting back one by one from a moody gathering over France. Just inland, above the slope of the hill, a bird of prey is in her eyeline, hovering over the gorse and heather, letting the wind flow through its wings, looking down, watching and waiting. An angel with claws.

Gabe comes up at last, a lost look still on his face. 'I didn't . . . I haven't shown that to anyone.'

'No. Thank you.'

'She is more than that. More even than that. The one I cried out for, before I even knew her.'

Sarah looks at his hands turning over themselves in front of him, as Gabe sits down on the bench and leans forward. Tanned hands, trembling slightly. Strong wrists, covered by shirt sleeves. Is he strong? She cannot tell. He is burning energy all the time. His hair is like a Big Bang in slow motion, all grown out and left to stick up where it wants, but that's okay, there's a messy charm to it. His sideburns are ginger and silver, and his stubble sparkles. There's a stupid little burst of hair under his lip, a soul patch that makes her smile, how silly, but the scar next to it says no, take me seriously. And his eyes say something else. Look what I have seen.

'Tell me,' she says, a teacher again. 'If you want to.'

'There was a bomb. A mine. I was in the desert, in a truck with some lads. Embedded. We flipped over. Then it was dark and really quiet. The lad next to me was crying for his mum.' He looks at her, for reassurance that he should go on. 'My mum's gone, Sarah. Long ago. I was crying for . . . this sounds funny. Someone I didn't know. I'd been looking, all my life. The one who would understand, who would look at me and know me, everything about me and just get it. Accept it. I knew she must be out there somewhere. I wanted to live long enough to meet her. Sounds foolish.'

'Not to me. Were you hurt?'

'The lad lost his legs. They flew us home.'

Gabe turns back the cuff of his shirt, then pushes it up to his elbow. The skin underneath becomes hairless, pink and shiny like plastic, like the arm of an Action Man melted in a fire and reformed. 'It's not much . . .'

People flinch, he's ready for that, but Sarah wants to touch.

'After that, I didn't want to be the fearless war reporter any more. Turned out I wasn't fearless. So I stayed at home and made a new career out of talking to the wounded. Helping them to tell their stories. After a while, it was natural to start doing the same for other people: not soldiers any more, but mums and dads, brothers and sisters of the disappeared, mostly. Missing children. Names you might know from the news. When a little boy or girl – it was mostly girls – went missing, I'd go and see their parents, talk to the family, the neighbours, the teachers, whoever.

'The first time, your heart breaks. The second time, not so much. Third, fourth, fifth, whatever, it becomes routine. "Where was she last seen? Where might she have gone? Who might she be with?" The police are appealing for information, they are all over the reporters, we're their best friends, everyone in the village loves us because we're trying to help. Then a body is found, and the missing persons inquiry becomes a murder investigation. Suddenly they all feel like suspects, and we're prying. We're vampires. We should be ashamed, apparently. The circle closes, just like it does in the Army after a colleague gets hit or a soldier fires on a boy, by accident. I saw that. The back of his head blooming like a rose on the wall behind. Almost beautiful. Isn't that a terrible thing to say?

'I saw terrible things, wrote about terrible things, but writing about it does not remove the guilt you feel, as if you as the observer were somehow making it happen. And it got to me, Sarah. That's not how it's supposed to go. But listen . . .' He rolls down the sleeve of his shirt carefully over the pink, wrinkled skin and stands, moving to the window. 'I didn't come here to get away from anything; quite honestly, it was not to escape. It was to live. The Romantics came here to get their kicks, in search of the sublime. They felt more alive when they looked over the edge of the cliffs, or even climbed up them, because it was so scary. It doesn't do that for me, I stay away. But I do feel different here. Better. I did.

'I came with her to begin again, in simplicity. We both wanted to be in a place where it was simple – which is funny, because here there is simplicity on a grand scale, strange as that sounds. You know what I mean. Spectacular simplicity. Breathtaking. Look

151

out there. It does take my breath away, still. Huge skies, miles and miles of rolling Downs, immense cliffs, the wide sea. Something about the scale makes it restful. There's a peace to be had in sitting here, whatever the weather. There was, anyway.'

There was. Before.

'I have seen some beautiful places. The glaciers of Iceland. A pink lake in Senegal. The Bay at the Back of the Ocean on the island of Iona – there you go. But they are not mine and this place is mine, it felt like that as soon as I came here. Our place. We came together, but I was not just being nice or trying to get on her good side, although it was always worth being there. I meant it. I felt it. My place. There is a symmetry that appeals. The sea and the sky. The white and the green, the chalk and the down. The drop and the rise. Falling and rising. Falling again and rising again. The orderliness of the fields, the ordinariness of that deep, dark English greenery, that thousand-year-old landscape, farmed and tended and walled and sown and ploughed now as it was then. You can remember, here. Things you don't even know you have forgotten.'

'How can that be?'

'The way we were before the engine, the flight to the cities, before the loss of the land. It's sentimental nonsense, I know. Stop me. I don't even know the names of the flowers here – what's a weed and what's a plant – or the birds. I only know the white arse from a book. I'm a city boy. But even I feel it, Sarah. I can sit out there and feel the calm of a settled landscape. The soft curves and rounded slopes, as a Victorian poet said. Nothing complicates it. Nothing that sticks, anyway.'

His fingers make two lines in the condensation. 'There's a car coming down that long road from Beachy Head, running alongside the cliff edge. I wonder if he knows how close it is. He'll disappear in a minute and go round the bottom of this hill, past the wood, towards the Gap. If he doesn't turn in there he'll have to head inland again, climbing up towards East Dean. That's when they put their foot down. It's like a racing circuit sometimes. I have seen a million cars in my life, but before I came here I never stopped to watch them. Let them pass through. Like feelings. Mindfulness – the teachers tell you to become aware of your emotions, let them pass through you and go on their way. It's like that. I can sit and watch the cars – it's better out of season – and my mind clears. Never thought of it like that before. Weird. It's the interruptions that show you how peaceful it is.'

'Sorry.'

'I don't mean you. You're . . . welcome. I'm just saying it's simpler here, I can practise gratitude. Even though, you know, I'm on my own. There is electricity, heat and light, water. You'll struggle for a phone signal but it's warm, dry, snug. When the storm comes, it's like a giant cuffing the tower about the ears. You probably heard it. But the tower stands. There is strength. We are on the edge – who knows when the land will slip and the tower will start to go? – but for now it stands, strong. So, there was a sense of refuge here when we came. We thought we'd make a home in this unlikely place. Such beauty. To begin again. I'm sorry, you don't need to hear all this. You can go, you know.'

Gabe looks back at her, and all of a sudden feels exhausted. He's had enough of this talk. More than enough. What's the point? 'Look, can you go? Sorry. I'm not . . . just go.'

Sarah reaches over and puts a hand on his good arm, but he pulls it away quickly, which confuses her. 'Sorry, I did not mean . . . please. Tell me about Maria.'

They are locked into this now, he realizes. She won't tell him anything unless he talks to her. He wants her to go, she seems to want to stay for some reason, but the only way to break the lock is to talk. That's how it works.

'What if I don't want to?' But even as he says this, he realizes it is probably time he did. He wants to. That's a surprise. Why not talk to this stranger, this woman who will go then and leave him alone and never come back? 'Okay. When we came here she was always banging on about how it was a thin place, where the space between this life and whatever happens next is so thin. Do you know what I mean by that? No. I didn't. I know what that means now. She was a therapist. As her job, I mean, not just for me, although that too, probably. That's how we met. I went to interview the mother of a child who had brain damage because of some terrible mistake in

153

the hospital. Rí was there in the kitchen, helping him paint. Big sploshes of colour, it was everywhere, all over the table, the floor. She was laughing, the boy was laughing, the mum was laughing. I felt like an intruder, coming into the room, all that laughter. I was hoping for tears. Isn't that awful? Hoping that the mother would cry and I could write about that, and make the reader cry too. I was a tear-maker, a one-man raincloud, but that day I stepped into a room full of sunshine. Rí didn't notice. I came, I went; she says she didn't even see me . . .'

'That's not what I was expecting.'

'No. I should tidy that bit of the story up really, if I'm going to start telling people. Not that anyone else is interested. Thank God. I should make her fall in love with me at first sight. I still don't know if she . . .'

Yes you do. You really do.

'I saw her again a couple of weeks later, in a bar. By then I had quit. She didn't know who I was, of course. She was singing with a band but we got there late and didn't see that. I was with friends, but they were all talking and I was just sitting there, looking over at her. She had shaved her head since we met – you know, like Sinead O'Connor? She'd hate me for saying that, but there it is. Ironic really, she did it long before she had to, but if anything she looked even more amazing that night. Magnificent. Last orders had gone. There was a guy up at the bar giving her the chat and when she tried to walk away he sort of reached out and scooped her up. I couldn't have that. Weird, isn't it? We had never spoken to each other but I already felt like she was mine. I had been drinking, though! I was worried for her. This guy was big, heavy.' Should he do the voice this time? Ah hell, why not? '"Awright, darlin'? You gonna sing me a song, aintcha?"'

Sarah laughs – that's great, she's laughing – covering her mouth.

'No, I know, it's okay. I'm not great at accents. That was Cockney with a bit of Welsh.'

'Maybe some Italian?'

'Yeah. *EastEnders*, Napoli style. Thing is, Rí didn't need me. That's how she signed her name, with the Irish fada. Rí to rhyme with free. She stood back from him, and his arm fell. Then she stepped back into his space. Right in his face. She looked right into his eyes and began to sing. He didn't know what he was messing with. She did this.'

He stands there with his legs apart in a strong stance, as Maria did, and brings one hand up past his chest, opening the fingers like a flower in front of his face as if drawing something out of himself. 'I didn't have a clue what she was singing, but nor did the guy either.'

The language of the mountains and the hiding places.

'It was Irish. The old way, it's called. You're supposed to call to mind all the people who have sung the song before, over the centuries, so that they are in the room. It was like that, Sarah. Such a sound. I couldn't believe it was coming from her and I've never seen anything like this, as if the song was a sword hovering over this creep and it fell, cutting him in two, right down the middle. He fell apart. Slid off the chair, threw his glass down and got out of there, shouting out: "You're a nutter!" as he ran away. I thought, this is the one, here she is, right here. I mean, wow. She picked up his beer and drank it. Finished it, wiped her mouth. She saw I was looking at her and she said in this really heavy accent, comedy Irish, "Yer man wanted a song!"'

I did recognize you, very well. I just didn't want to show it.

'I was smitten.'

Sarah smiles at him.

'I'll just say this. She saw me. She understood me, more than I thought was possible. She helped me heal. I had been moving around for so long, following the story, being one thing to this person and something else to another, listening and writing, like a mirror, never thinking about who I was beyond the story and never wanting to face it, and she said: "Stop. You've been looking for home. Here I am. This is home."'

Pacing the edge of the circular lantern room, he trails a hand along the window rail. 'She showed me how to see differently, too. We came to the coast and walked for miles at weekends and she would paint and draw, and I would read and sleep and watch her. She taught me how to sit and wait and watch and let the shapes and the colours settle until you see what is there, properly. Then

155

I saw that there was more than suffering. I knew that, but I hadn't stopped to look. So much more. Such beauty.'

They both look beyond the glass, to the landscape that surrounds them in their tower, wrapped in the darkening arms of the Downs.

'You were lucky,' says Sarah, smoothing down a cushion cover and picking at the zip.

'I was,' says Gabe. 'I really was. So I quit work – or rather accepted voluntary redundancy – with a glad heart, and came here with her.'

She waits for him to say what he needs to say next. He doesn't know if he can. The room trembles in the wind. The world outside is turning blue. Sarah thinks of the long, difficult walk to the cottage, where her stuff is waiting. She won't go. But if she is to stay, and be here when it is time to test, when she finds out what to do next, there are things to ask.

'How did she do it?'

'I don't understand.'

'Did she leave you a note? Did she say goodbye?'

He looks at her blankly.

'Was it quick? Did you . . . did you watch?'

He laughs a little, and feels so tired again. What can he say to that? Stupid. Why doesn't she just piss off? 'Okay, that's what you think this is? She just jumped or something? You could not be more wrong. She lived every moment of her life, every single moment, with a passion. Fought for it – no, that's not right – held on to it. Tight. Right to the end. Can you go now? Please, go. I mean it. Go.'

'No!' She panics, wanting to stay here and be safe, even if it is with him, but he means it, she has really upset him. There is no choice. Sarah stands up, and starts for the steps. She is shaking. What has she done that is so bad? Why does she feel silly? Worse than that, she is scared. Really scared. 'Sorry. I don't know . . . can I stay? Please?'

'Just go,' says Gabe with a weird calm that really spooks her. 'That is the safest thing, for both of us.'

Thirty-eight

So to hell with him, that man, that broken, awful man and his creepy tower. Sarah is glad to be out of there, striding hard down the hill away from the lighthouse, wondering if he is watching her, knowing that he is. That bloody man with his stories and his soup and his skin tight on the bones and his blue eyes that never look at you and when they do they see right through you. The late afternoon is absurdly still; she can hear her breathing in time with the crunch and slip of her boots on chalk and grass. The sea is a flat grey snakeskin, sliding into a slightly lighter sky. All the walkers have gone home, there are no cars on the road below. The thud of a farmer's gun echoes over the Downs from a field somewhere, followed by a crack. And the cry of a child . . . no, it's the mocking call of a gull, away out of sight where the nests are, on the sheer cliff edge below the line.

As she walks on the broad green back of the hill, there is a dip to the left where the ground falls, then rises again to the edge like a wave. And in among the bushes a woman dressed in green and black, almost hidden but for a red cloth folded over her arm. It's a sweater, with gold lettering. She's a Guardian. Calling out something to Sarah. What is it? She can't hear. Too late to turn away.

'Hi! Please, I am not a busybody, it is my job. Are you okay?'

'No. Not at all. I'm thinking of throwing myself off.'

'Oh! My name is Magda—'

'I was joking,' says Sarah, walking on. 'But thank you.'

Magda is there in front of her, alongside her. 'Let me help, please. I can. You see.'

Her grip is strong. This Magda is wiry, hard. She has full, flushed cheeks, a button nose, dark-rimmed eyes that dart across the Downs as she takes the lead. Her bright white hair flicks into Sarah's eyes. 'You come. Here. Sit.'

Seriously? It's a mound of grass sheltered by shrub and gorse, out of the wind . . . but right on the edge. Three, four steps away. The drop looms, it's giddying.

'It is safe,' says Magda. 'A quiet place.'

No, thinks Sarah, but she's so tired, so empty, she sits down anyway.

Magda holds out a white paper bag. 'Fudge? I make it myself.'

It tastes good, sweet, rich. There is tea to drink, from a flask. The steam curls straight, there is barely any wind in this moment. Sarah has not seen it like this up here before. Is Gabe still watching, from the tower? He will be thinking she is safe now. Who is this woman?

'Where are you from?'

'London.'

'No, where from?'

Oh please, not that again now. 'London.'

'Yes. Okay. I can help. More tea?'

It's thick, dark, laden with sugar and it makes Sarah feel sick, but she does want more. She's so tired.

'Would you like to lie down?'

Yes, she would. She feels safer that way, with her face to the sky. If this great chalk wave collapses into the sea, then she will go with it. But Sarah feels bonded to the earth.

'Better? More comfortable?'

She could sleep.

She could.

Sleep.

Magda is beside her. Speaking. Slowly. Softly.

'Now that is better. You are very beautiful. I like your hair, it is very special. My mother, she was beautiful. Different to you, of course, she is from Poland, but so beautiful, even when she was old. Full of life, you say, *zywa*.'

Sarah feels breath on her cheek but her eyes are closed.

'That is better. You should rest. We are not to suffer, God does not want that. I know this. He has shown me, through my mother. She got sick. It begins with her fingers. She cannot feel. Then her arm, two arms. Legs. She is a bird in a cage, she is, unable to fly.

158

Pain all day, all night. I cannot stand to see her but I must be in the room, to feed her. Clean her. Everywhere. She cannot speak but she begs me, you know?'

Magda is so close, but Sarah is lost in a light, a blinding light from long ago.

'I saw that it was kind to help her go on, *woli Bozej*, will of God. You are so lovely, like her.' She moves closer still, cheek to cheek. 'I want to help you. There is no shame. It was good for me to come to this country, away from the talking. The priests do not understand. God is peace. Love. Mercy. No more tears. No more suffering. We go to a better place. Perhaps it is better while you are still young and strong and beautiful, while you can choose. Before the pain.'

A gust of wind is like a slap in the face that wakes Sarah, just enough, but Magda's hand is firm on her shoulder, pressing her back down into the earth.

'Hey! Hush, now. Be still.'

'Stop!'

'I am doing nothing. I am a Guardian, I am here to help. Is God's will. He loves you. He tells me, after my mother. You miss your mother, yes? She waits for you.'

Magda stands, and pulls a wobbly Sarah to her feet.

'See, the light shining on the water?'

She does. Far out to sea. As if through a fog.

'Your mother is there. She is happy, she wants you. This is the door. Take a step. Good, now again. You can go through to her. She is waiting—'

'Sarah! Sarah!' The lighthouse man is calling, from far away. 'Magda, is she okay?'

He's running over the slope towards them, approaching fast, barefoot despite the stones. Sarah feels Magda's grip tighten and she is yanked back, away from the edge and down, manhandled like a sickly patient.

'There is something wrong with her,' Magda tells him urgently. 'She is not sensible. She was here by the edge and I saw her, I came across to stop her, I pull her back,' she says, talking fast, wrapping Sarah in the red sweater that smells of heavy, sickly perfume. 'Is this the one who is missing? Jack, the husband, he is in the pub. London today, but we have the booking, so he will return this evening, I think. Shall we take her there, to the pub?' There is desperation in her voice. Whatever this is, whatever it was Gabe saw that made him run, he suddenly doesn't trust Magda like he did.

'The lighthouse is closer. I'll take care of her.'

'Until Jack comes?'

'Yes, okay,' he says reluctantly, stopping himself from saying any more.

Sarah feels fuzzy. Her head is so heavy. Magda whispers in her ear: 'Your mother is waiting.' Then the lighthouse man lifts her up and off the ground and walks with her in his arms. She can smell the sweat on him and something else, darker, stronger. What is that? What is it? Wondering, she sleeps.

Thirty-nine

He waits in the lantern room in the gathering dark, looking out for the blue lights, seeing himself reflected back in the glass. This room was built to look outwards in all directions at once and it holds on to the view until the last embers of the day have gone out. Then it snaps shut. The darkness comes rushing in and wraps around the windows as if there is nothing more worth seeing. This is the still moment, the claustrophobic moment. The moment that makes his pulse rise every time. The panic.

His face looms up in the glass. God, he looks knackered. More than ever. There will be no sleep when the police come and ask what Sarah is doing here and why he didn't tell them. He'll be in trouble for that. Magda was frightened. Should he have called an ambulance? They will be here soon. If Sarah is lucky, she will wake up in a hospital, in a bed with clean white linen, under the care of someone who knows how to treat her properly. That's what she needs, not to be hiding here with him, for reasons he does not understand. It will be over soon anyway. Magda will tell them. She will have done so by now. Why are the police taking so long?

'Please don't let them take me away from here tonight.'

Sarah's in the stairwell, looking up into the room.

'Hey. Come up. Hang on a second. Look at this.' He lights a church candle in a tall metal lantern, then reaches across to switch off the main lamp. Now the infinite darkness outside is revealed and the room appears to be suspended in the black of space. She rises from the stairs as if entering a space station, woozy and weightless. They could be in orbit above a mystery planet, astronauts in some kind of steampunk Victorian command module with metal window frames, and glass that reflects the million stars. There is also the moon, a pale orange disc caught in the glass beside, behind and beyond her. Three moons – it is impossible to say which is real.

'Wow.'

'I know. How are you feeling?'

'I have an elephant on my head. Wow though. Really.'

Sarah slides into the room and he can't help himself: he's wowed by the way she moves. Wrapped in a bottle green blanket, hair wild, eyes bloodshot, chalk on her rusty jeans, it doesn't matter, she's . . . stop this.

'What happened—'

They say it together.

'I thought you'd tell me,' he says.

'I don't remember. Magda, is it? She was being nice, trying to help.'

Gabe sits down beside her on the bench that runs along the curve of half the room, a semi-circular wooden frame of the kind you might find on a ship. He's going to build hot-air heaters underneath it and hide them with the slats that are piled by the top of the stairs, as yet untreated. For now, there is warmth and an orange glow from a stinky old paraffin heater.

'The police will want to know what you took.'

'What do you mean? Nothing.'

'Look at you.' He nods at the black mirror of the window.

She looks, and winces. 'Not good.'

'Oh, I don't know . . . Listen, Sarah, you've got to tell me what this is.'

'There is no time. Unless you promise I can stay here. Until the morning, first thing. When they come, let me hide. Tell them I'm okay.'

'They won't listen. Jack was here. Yesterday. Before I knew you were . . . hiding. I sent him away. We had a bit of a row. A fight.'

'Oh. Gabe.'

She has not said his name before. It snags his breath. Panic rising, he moves away quickly. Rí? Where has she gone?

'I was exhausted, that's all. I think. You don't think . . .'

He's not listening, he's trying to get a grip, focus on what's happening here, what it means. 'Talk to me, Sarah. Tell me. I need to know.'

She will talk. Make a start at least, before they come. She owes him that. Maybe she can still persuade him to give her the time she needs. Just until morning, that is all. Then she will be gone, out of here, either way. But where to start? Four days ago, when she knew she had to get away? When she clicked on the photograph and suddenly knew what to do? Or before that, way back, on the day she became a childless woman? The day the doctor told her it would be impossible to have a baby without spending money, more money than she had or would ever have. Her mind races through the memory, coming out in a daze to a crowded hospital corridor, a waiting room with toys and games and cartoons on the wall and Jack angry. No, not there. In the bedroom? Should she start that way? Lying on the bed in the early morning with her trousers half down, waiting for Jack to crack the ampoules, fill the syringe, make the injection. Bruising her, every time. He cut his thumb and cursed, every time. Not there either. Where?

'Ask me questions,' she says.

Gabe tries to put on a friendly face. 'Okay. So.' He can't be direct. He must take it easy. Let her talk. 'Do you have brothers and sisters?'

A flick of the head says no.

'How about your mum and dad, are they around?'

The silence that follows makes him think he has said completely the wrong thing, again. But then she says, 'My father is alone. He has friends, of course. He is in the south of France this week, staying with someone from church. I envy him the sunshine. I should have gone with him.'

'Why did you come here?'

Too soon. She pulls the blanket tighter.

'Okay. Tell me about Jack . . .'

'Really? You want to do this?'

'I'm sorry,' says Gabe. 'You don't have to.'

'I thought—'

'You asked about Rf. I told you.'

'Yes.'

'So tell me.'

She will not sit still, but wriggles and shifts and tucks her legs up, puts them down again. All the time looking out of the windows, eyes searching west, north and east for the blue lights. She judges the directions from a stained-glass compass point in the centre circle of the roof. How much longer has she got?

'You have to let me stay here,' she says. 'Please. I need this time. I will know what to do in the morning.' Her hands move as if she needs a cigarette. He wishes he smoked. She's chewing her nails now, but tuts and tucks her hand back under the blanket. 'I love my husband. I should say that. He makes me laugh. He is a kind person, who cares about the world. He is a good man. It is not his fault. I am tired. It all hurts too much. I wish I had the energy to love him in the way that he needs, but I do not. It is my fault.'

'Not sure I believe that,' says Gabe too quickly.

'You cannot know. You know nothing about it.'

'No. Okay. Fair enough.'

'Jack has dreams to chase. Demons chase him.'

That he can believe.

'He was a mess when I met him, a bundle of nerves.'

Not much has changed then.

'When I first met Jack, he was always quoting his father. He was so idealistic, there were all these words about changing the world. It was inspiring, to be with someone who cared so much. I would ask when we could meet and Jack was keen for that to happen, but it was never the right time. I should have realized, I suppose, but then one time I was watching the guy on YouTube, to see what he was like—'

'What is he, a preacher?'

'Not quite.' She says his name and Gabe is surprised. He knows the music and used to like some of it, on the right night. Epic, overblown gothic love songs.

'I asked Jack about it when he came home, and he went really quiet on me. I remember that so well, he had never been like it. He was always on the move, fidgeting, drumming, but then he was absolutely still, on the sofa. There was a CD on the coffee table. He picked it up, slipped out the paper inlay and kissed it, like he was kissing his dad on the forehead. Then he ripped the picture up, slowly, into little pieces. All over the floor. Do you know why?'

'It wasn't really his dad?'

'No, he is his father. That's for sure. His mother loved that man, I think, truly. She was young. Very young. Still at school. She went to see him at a gig and he picked her out of the crowd. Kidnapped her, effectively. She wanted to go with him, though, that is true. Nobody noticed, because she was in care; they thought she'd absconded and gave her up as a runaway, which I suppose she was, in a way. Then he left her at a hotel in Vegas, a fortnight later. They all left while she was sleeping. There was no note, or anything. She was pregnant.'

'Bastard,' says Gabe, wondering if it is true.

'You look as if you don't believe me.'

'I believe you. That's not the issue.'

'Well, I know Chana. That's her name now. I admire her. She brought her son up alone, in terrible places. She was a virgin when she met that man, and two weeks later she was a coke user with a baby inside her. In Vegas. With nothing. Can you imagine? Jack was a handful too. As a child he wouldn't speak for hours at a time, but would sit there drumming out rhythms on his own head, or lash out at anyone who came close. Even his mum. They were always fighting but she was in control. She is a survivor. Sometimes she even laughs about him. She told me that he called her Layla.'

'After the Eric Clapton song? God, that's cheesy.'

'Yes, probably, but it is also some kind of woman of the night in Hebrew, Chana told me. Spelt differently, but still. Nice nickname for a little girl. I looked it up and this Leila has to do with conception. How ironic is that? When Jack was old enough to ask questions, she had no answers. So she went to a lawyer, had a DNA test and they sued.'

'Did she win?'

'He paid her off, to keep it out of the papers.'

'That's something.'

'Money always runs out. She paid the lawyer and bought Jack an education, which was a good one, but that was more or less it. Everything else that she has she built up by herself. There was just one other thing that she paid for, with the last of his money . . .'

Sarah pats her knees in a little rhythm, like Jack, underneath the blanket. She inhales and exhales, as if with an invisible cigarette, and it seems to calm her.

'Go on . . .'

'Well. Look. We got this present, just before our wedding. From him. There was a note. Rings, incredibly expensive, Cartier. "Sorry I can't be there. To my son and his bride, love Dad." Love? That was the giveaway.'

'Chana?'

'She sent the rings herself. Jack's father never knew a thing about it.'

'You don't wear a ring.'

'Not now. It is in the drawer at home. But that's a cheaper ring, a more comfortable one to wear in the classroom, you know? The Cartier was in the bank, in the safe. I sold it, to pay for . . . treatment.'

'And Jack?'

'He kept his. Refused to sell. Said it was his only link to his father.'

'But it wasn't from him—'

'Try telling him that. Good luck. He says all these things from his father as if he was told them when they were going fishing or watching a game or something, but you know what? They are all taken from songs and interviews. "Music can change the world, because music can change people," or something like that. Lifted. He learned them off by heart. They've never met. Jack tried once, at the apartment in New York. It was like something from *The Great Gatsby*. He was turned away.'

She feels sorry for him, thinks Gabe. That's how this works.

'Jack came here because he wanted to be someone else, you see? He leant on me and I let him, I liked it. I wanted someone to love. That was okay, then. Now, it's different. I can't help him in the same way, because I need some of that kind of love myself and he doesn't know what to do about that,' she says, shifting again in the chair, stretching out her legs and looking at her boots. 'I think that's a fair, accurate summary. He would shout me down, though. Jack is a hothead, always moving, drumming. Passionate. He always wanted me to tell him that everything would be all

166

right. He still does.' Sarah pats the wood at the back of the sofa bench, then spreads out her palms as if arranging an imaginary table. She has unwound in the telling of the story, her voice is less dislocated now, less abstract.

You're in the room, thinks Gabe. Good.

Suddenly, she turns to look him in the eyes. 'I don't think everything will be all right. Not at all.'

Forty

The stories we tell define us. So do the stories we don't tell and the ones we never finish. When she was a young girl, five or six, Sarah loved to sit on her granny's lap and nuzzle up, and Granny would tell Bible tales in that soft, precise voice of hers from the lowlands around Dumfries. The Good Samaritan, of course. The Pearl of Great Price. Noah and the Ark, Sarah liked that one: there was a song about the animals and they'd be cats and meow or wave their arms like elephants' trunks or Sarah would jump down and hop like a kangaroo. Two by two. 'We two,' said Granny, but wee sometimes meant little and wee sometimes meant wee, like you did sitting down; it could all get a bit confusing. Granny would laugh. 'Shall we two kangaroos have a wee wee-wee?'

She laughed a lot and so did Sarah, even though it sometimes felt as if she was being naughty for being happy. She didn't tell anyone that, though. Then one day Granny got out her little white leather Bible with the silver-edged pages that were as thin as tissue, and she wet her finger and looked through, humming to herself as Sarah lay on the floor playing with an old wooden set of the ark and all the animals and Mr and Mrs Noah and the little white dove that was her favourite. Apart from the tigers.

'Come here, lovely; listen to this one,' said Granny, and Sarah shuffled on her bottom across the floor and leaned against Granny's legs, one arm wrapped around a knee, sucking her thumb. Her daddy would say that she might be getting a bit old for that, but Granny let her do it while she told the story.

'There was a man and a woman and they lived in the desert and they were terribly old, like me . . .' Granny's laugh was like a happy little hiss. 'The man was called Abraham and his wife was called Sarah.'

That caught her attention.

'Yes, like you, my love. She was a special lady.' And Granny told how Sarah and her husband Abraham were both very old, they lived in a caravan – which was not a caravan like the one they stayed in on holiday at Camber Sands, but another name for a lot of tents and camels and a camp fire and servants (they had servants but they must have been very nice to them because they were nice people, because they were the good people in a story), the caravan was what you called all these people and things and animals as they moved through the desert together – and at night the men would sit around the fire and talk while the women stayed in the tent and cooked.

'That's not fair,' said little Sarah, who was used to having her tea cooked by Daddy, and Granny laughed. 'No, it's not. I wish you'd been able to tell your grandad, bless his soul. But anyway . . . these two were old and they had not been able to have any children, which made them very sad. They would have been so jealous of me, sitting here with you like this, it's such a blessing. They prayed about it and God told Abraham they would have children – as many as the stars, would you believe? That's a lot, isn't it? But nothing happened, the stork didn't come and bring them a baby. Have I told you about the stork? Oh, that's for another day then!'

She ruffled Sarah's hair with her free hand, the Bible balanced on a knee but disregarded now that her memory had been refreshed. 'So, one day Abraham was sitting under the shade of a tree they had found, when three men turned up. Mysterious men. Tall, dark and handsome, I like to think. Like your father. Do you know who they were?'

Sarah shook her head.

'No, nor did Abraham. He had never seen them before, but they looked fine. They had nice robes and healthy, fat camels and there was a custom they had in those days – my own granny had it too on the farm: if a stranger came, you had to be nice to them and give them food, maybe even a place to sleep.'

'Even if you didn't know them? Strangers?'

'Aye, pet. The world was different then. You're quite right, you should never take sweets or go with a stranger, that's true, but Abraham was a grown-up and he was just being nice to these men who were on a journey somewhere, so he offered them a cold drink and a bit of lunch, with a scone maybe.'

That made it all right as far as Sarah was concerned, because she had been a bit worried about the strangers, but there could be no harm in a scone.

'Then one of the men asked where Sarah was and Abraham was really surprised, because he didn't know how the man knew Sarah's name. So he looked again and he saw this wasn't any ordinary man, it was God himself.'

'Wow!'

'Ha! Yes, wow indeed.'

'What did he look like?'

'I don't know, pet, the Bible doesn't say. But it was God anyway, and Sarah could hear him talking from where she was in the shade in the tent and she heard him say, "We will come back in a year's time and you will have a child!" And do you know what Sarah did?'

Little Sarah shook her head again, just a tiny bit.

'She laughed. She laughed at God, because she was old and very tired and not able to have babies any more.'

'But it wasn't funny.'

'No, it wasn't funny. It was sad. Sarah laughed at God because she was sad and angry and couldn't have babies, but do you know what happened next? Sarah?'

But Sarah didn't hear what happened next, because she had her hands over her ears and was running fast for the garden, elbows banging into things, tripping over the step and out into the sunshine, confused and upset about this person Sarah who was her, she was named after her, they were the same and Sarah could not have babies, Sarah could not have babies, she would not have babies and she loved babies, she really, really loved babies and she wanted to be a mummy and she wanted her mummy and she wanted her mummy so much it was a nasty, nasty pain that made her cry and she couldn't see for tears and stumbled again and fell down on the grass, by the swing, sobbing and sobbing and sobbing.

Forty-one

Gabe sees something he didn't know he had, half hidden under the flap of a packing box of books. A bottle of bourbon whiskey.

'Wait,' he says and takes off down the stairs.

Sarah examines herself in the reflecting glass. The candle gives a soft, grainy light, easy on the brain. Now that her eyes have adjusted, she can make out the signals of super-tankers in the Channel, but no flashing blue lights inland. Where are the police? It must be nearly time. She wraps herself again in the blanket. It's warming up in here with the heater blaring, even getting toasty, but it's damp too. The windows are heavy with condensation.

'Here,' he says, offering a glass. He's put on a jumper, an old rusty sweater with a fraying V-neck, with an army-green shirt poking out at the cuffs and tails. He's a scruff, but somehow it works. Something to do with the way he carries himself, like a runner. Always balanced but never quite settled. Ready to go. He chews his shirt collar, she can see that.

The bourbon hits the top of her mouth. It is good. She should not drink; it is dangerous if . . . but it does not matter, she is sure. Still, one sip is enough.

'I am not a victim,' she says, although he has not said she is. 'Tell me something, a different subject. Let me ask you something, actually. Where do you think I am from?'

'I don't know. Your voice is . . . well, nice.'

That is a mistake. Sarah looks away and he feels embarrassed.

'London, I guess. There's a bit of something else, though.'

'Birmingham. Brum. Selly Oak. We lived there when I was very small, before Essex. You didn't say Trinidad or Jamaica. I get that a lot, but I'm not from Trinidad. My father is the palest Scotsman you ever saw. I didn't know I was black until big school. Then there was this boy called Gordon, who had a lovely mum with huge bosoms, bountiful. She came to the school gate sometimes. They invited me round for tea and I didn't know why, because Gordon

171

wasn't my boyfriend, although people said he was, even on the first day. I didn't know why, but I do now, of course. Ackee and saltfish was for tea. I'd never seen it before, I didn't like it, but I swallowed all of it because I wanted Gordon's mum to like me and give me a cuddle.' She looks at the swirl of bourbon in the glass. 'Do you think Magda gave me something earlier? Why would she?'

'Don't know.'

'So Gordon was in the playground with the other boys around him in a circle, chanting, "Get back on the boat. Black so-and-so." I don't want to say. The leader wore his collar up and spiked his hair. I had a crush on him, predictably. When Gordon went down, Stevo kicked him in the head. Hard.' She looks across for reassurance. 'I didn't do anything. As he walked away, Stevo put his arm around me. He said, "You're okay."'

'Were you angry?'

'No! I had no idea why he would say that, but I felt like a princess.' She waits for some response. 'Why am I telling you this?'

'I was wondering,' he says, smiling.

'My mother.'

'I see.'

'Do you?'

'No. Not really, to be honest. Please—'

'I wanted her, all the time. I could not have her, because she was not there, Gabe. I have only a passing memory, like a person you see out of the corner of your eye as they leave the room. I was three years old, that is all,' she says, her voice fading away to a whisper. 'She was from Jamaica but I didn't want to know about that or have anything to do with what it all meant. I didn't want to look or speak like her. I couldn't stand to think of her, it hurt so much.'

Gabe wants to reach out and comfort her, because it obviously still hurts now, he can see that, but he stays back. Looks at his untouched bourbon. Waits and wonders how to react if this gets too much.

'I had a letter with me that she wrote to me. I don't know what it said. I didn't want to know until now, Gabe. Is that terrible? Years and years I refused. I thought I would break if I read it. Then I went to my father, last month. He was so surprised, but I need

172

her. I am ready to hear her voice. I needed to hear it – who knows why? Maybe to know what she would say. I came here to be alone and read the letter away from him and to wait and to do this test on my own.'

'Without the pressure?'

'I wish. There's always pressure, but it comes from me. Myself. I'm not a victim, remember? I am my mother's daughter. I've always known that, but I ran away from her. These last few days I have felt it strongly, as if she is calling me to come to her at last. I am ready for her. But Gabe, I lost the letter,' she says, her voice cracking. 'It blew away, I don't know when. I need her. She's not here.'

'Where did you lose it?'

'Out there, on the Downs. I told you. It will have gone over now. Some sailor will pick it up. A sheep will eat it. I've lost the last of her. It is too much. Too much!'

She closes up, as if squeezing out the tears, and Gabe wants to go to her but he can't, he mustn't. He waits as she coughs, hacking, clearing the ways. She sits up straight-backed and flicks with a fingertip at the corners of each eye.

'Sorry. I'm sorry,' she says.

'It's okay.'

'There's something else I remember. A story my granny told me from the Bible. She was often doing that. I'm not sure it was always wise, you know? God tells this woman – her name is Sarah – she will have a baby, but Sarah is old and angry and can't believe it, so she laughs. Disbelief. She laughs because she can't have a baby, it's impossible. That's what I heard when I was little. Granny was saying I would never have babies.'

'She can't have meant it that way, surely?'

'I know. I've read the story many times since then, but I can never get past the laughter. I've always been convinced, deep down, that I won't have kids. Do you think that's why, because of the story? I am Sarah. Sarah is barren. I am barren. Such a cruel word. I never told Granny or anyone else how I felt. I just knew.'

'You took the story very seriously,' he says gently.

'Not until now. Not really. I forgot about it by tea time. It's only lately, these last few days, going over everything, I remember. It

was always there, growing up. Like a curse. Granny cursed me.'
She catches the way he is looking at her and smiles. 'That's a bit
hard on her, isn't it? I don't really believe in curses, but if it was
one, it did come true. We were trying for a baby for three years
before they told me what I already knew, that it could not happen
naturally. I had to have an operation. A little one. Keyhole surgery.
Put a camera in there, have a look at my ovaries and zap the cysts.
Simple.'

'It wasn't?'

'No. Thank you. I remember thrashing about and shivering
a lot when I came out of the anaesthetic, really shivering. I was
scared. I had this big pain right across my stomach, and could not
feel parts of myself. Something terrible had happened. The nurse
said the doctor would be there soon, doing his rounds, but he was
not. He did not come that night. Jack did. He held my hand, and
sorted out the television that was on a swivel arm over the bed, so
that I could watch *EastEnders*. It was a bit of a blur. Then he went
and I lay there and listened to the pipes gargling all night. I was
not sure if it was the pipes – the noises sounded human. I dropped
off about half five in the morning. They woke me at six-thirty for
my medicine. The doctor said they had cut me open, to get at all
the cysts. There were too many. I kept thinking of the blade. Not
the real blade, something like a cutlass.

'I went home to my grandmother, who made me toast and let
me doze on the sofa and helped me up to my old room at night.
Jack was away. He kept his distance anyway, and I do not blame
him because when he did come round I had nothing to say that
was not about how I was never going to have a baby now. Then
the tears, always the tears, every day, several times a day. I was
swimming all day and all night. Floating. The drugs, pain-killers
and anti-depressants, made me sleepy. The tears made me hollow
out. I was not eating. I was getting lighter and lighter, drifting,
looking down from the ceiling. Floating away.'

'For how long?'

'Three months. All that, and the cysts were still there. I was
given a drug to try and shrink them, because that would make it
easier to conceive. It made me feel sick all the time. Like morning

174

sickness. Worse. There was bile in the back of my throat all day. I just wanted to sleep. Jack was not coming anywhere near me, and I just was not interested in him. What was the point anyway? You get like that. You shrivel up.

'I went back to work and tried to carry on, but that first day, Jack does not know this, I put my battle clothes on for school and I got on the Central Line in the morning and there was a pregnant woman who got on at the next stop. She was huge, sweating, it looked like the baby was coming, and I thought, You lucky cow! Nobody would give her their seat, but I did and as I stood up I thought, I am going to go, I am going to faint. So I got off and sat on the bench there with my head between my knees.

'People were milling all around, the service was so bad. I do not know how long I sat afterwards, watching the trains come and go. Floating. The crowds thinned and disappeared. A woman with a baby strapped to her chest came with her hand out for money. I wanted to give her money for the baby, honestly. "I will take the baby." I couldn't say that, though, could I? It was quiet. Drugged maybe, like me. I just sat and sat, feeling everything and nothing – the clouds changing colours were like magic. My body was numb. Then it got busy again, the evening rush hour was starting. Can you believe it? So I got on a train going the other way and went home. Do you know what the nurse said?'

'When?'

'At the hospital. I went for an injection. She said it was cruel. I said, "What is?" She said, "This. Has nobody told you? The best way to cure what you have is to get pregnant."'

Gabe watches her rubbing the palm of one hand with the thumb of the other, reddening the flesh, digging in her nail.

'What kind of teacher are you?'

'History, English, drama.'

'I'm sorry.'

'The school is not so bad.'

'The operation,' he says.

'I know. I was joking too. Do you want to hear all this?'

He indicates that he does and holds out the bottle.

She shakes her head and says, 'I am glad to be saying it. Get it out. Always best. Do you think they're coming?'

'The police? I don't know. Not tonight, maybe.'

'Tomorrow then. First thing. After . . . I had better write something so they know . . . What do I do about Jack?'

'He can't get in here, Sarah. I won't open the door until you're ready.'

'You are a good man.'

'I'm not so sure. Go on.'

'Ah yes, you want the truth, the whole truth and nothing but the truth,' she says, swilling the mostly undrunk whiskey around the glass. 'I don't know the truth. I do know they lied to me, that time and next time. Then again after the second operation. We had artificial insemination. It's as romantic as it sounds. They give you more drugs to regulate the ovaries.'

'I know.'

'Oh.' She pauses. 'You know about the scans then. I did not produce enough eggs the first month. Then the next month there were not enough staff to do the scan. The month after that, the nurse was not around to read it. This went on and on, for a year nearly, Gabe. Then someone new said she was really sorry but the clinic was closing because they didn't have enough staff to cover for the nurse, who was going on sabbatical.'

'On the NHS? That's unlikely.'

'Yes. I heard someone talking about it on the reception desk. They were not allowed to say.'

'What?'

'Catch up! The nurse was pregnant.'

'God—'

'. . . wants nothing to do with this. Clearly.'

She's quick, thinks Gabe, noticing the fine hairs at her temple as she asks him: 'Are you a believer? You have the right name. . .'

'My mum loved *One Hundred Years of Solitude*.' Examining his untouched glass of bourbon, he makes a decision, puffs his cheeks for the sake of marking it, and puts the glass down on the window ledge, undrunk. 'Apt, really. Haven't thought about that until now. I don't know the answer to your question. I was brought up to believe, like you. I lost that faith a long time ago. Saw too much. But living here, I wonder if heaven and hell are the same. This place is beautiful, staggeringly so. Heavenly. If you treat it with respect there is no finer place to be. If not—'

'How far did you get?' she asks.

'With the treatment? Ah. Not far.'

'IVF?'

'What I'm trying to say is that heaven and hell are the same place – the same cliff, the same sea, always changing with the weather but still basically the same – but it can be heavenly or hellish depending on how prepared you are—'

'You don't have to answer,' she says, cutting him off. 'Not sure I care about God just now, to be honest. I am going to tell you how it is for me. You did ask. Nobody else does any more, they have learned not to ask, but as you insist, I will tell you.'

Sarah takes a breath. 'Let me see. You must know about hospitals and clinics, but once you get into the actual treatment, things change. You have to go late at night, when the pubs are closing and all the happy couples are walking arm in arm down the street. It feels furtive. You have an injection, one you cannot give yourself. Profasi.'

'Sounds like a tribe of ancient Greeks who swear a lot.'

Her thin smile says, Please shut up, I am trying to talk; you wanted me to talk and now I am talking, so please listen. That's a lot for a thin smile to say, but he gets the message. Her voice says, 'It ripens the eggs, whatever that means. You go home and you can't sleep, so you watch ice hockey, or whatever is on. Your husband gets up and sits with you and asks why you didn't want him to go with you to the clinic, and he talks some more but you're not listening and you don't want to talk. You can't talk. Shall I go on?'

He says yes. What else can he do?

Forty-two

Miracles never happen, thinks Sarai in the desert, four thousand years away. Or if they do, they hurt. A daughter is born, her cry makes the soul sing, but when she is lifted to the breast there is no sound and her mouth is cold. The soft wind blows on her face but there is no breath. Where is God then? Where? A son comes at last, a great blessing, an answer to prayer, but he is born to a servant girl and the longing remains. It gets worse. It used to hurt so much she doubled over in pain and then she got used to the hurt and forgot to notice that it was still there, but now the old fool has stirred it all up again.

'Abraham, where is your wife, Sarah?'

That is not her name. She is Sarai. It's not even the name of her husband, Abram. But he has been trying to force these different names on her lately, with some crazy idea that their fate will change. He says God told him to do it, but she knows the trouble that comes when men say such things. They are small changes, but in her language the new sounds alter the meanings in a way he seems to find inspiring. She finds it cruel. Abram becomes Abraham, Father of Many. Sarai becomes Sarah, Mother of Nations, which is not funny. It stings. She is ninety years old and has no children and knows she never will.

Sarai watches from the shadows as her wizened husband dips both his aching hands into a bowl, fingers and fists, and rubs his face and eyes with the water. She hears him mutter to the strangers and hopes there will not be trouble. In the days of her great beauty, she was sold as a slave – to the pharaoh, no less – for gold, and animals and food. The man who did that to her so many years ago is still her husband now. He is forgiven. You have to compromise if you want to live. But there is no danger of being sold again, not at her great age.

'She's going to have a baby, wait and see,' says the visitor, wiping meat grease from his fingers with the end of his robe before taking his turn with the bowl. 'I'll be back this way next year and she will be nursing a son.'

Sarai cannot help herself then. She laughs out loud.

'Why are you laughing, Sarah?'

It's a good job you can't see me, she thinks. I am exhausted. If you saw these gnarled fingers, these slack breasts, you would know. I have lost hair in some places and grown it in others I never expected. My beauty blew away like sand years ago. As for that old man who lay down the skins for you, he is losing his mind.

She calls back from the darkness, unwilling to show her face: 'I did not laugh.'

'Oh, you did,' says the stranger. 'No matter. You will see.'

Madness. Utter madness. But later, when she thinks about the voice of the visitor who called her Sarah and her mad old husband Abraham, a question forms within her like a tiny spark that might so easily blow out. 'Do I believe this nonsense? Do I dare?'

Forty-three

'So the happy day arrives. You can't eat breakfast but you must. You feel strong, in your blood, like this is the day you become invincible; but afraid, like you're made of glass. Brittle. You go to the clinic together, but in the car on the way there is nothing to say.'

Sarah goes on, but Gabe is lost in thinking about Rí and wondering if he ever really realized what it was like for her when they were trying for a child. They didn't get far. There wasn't time.

'The clinic is like a bad hotel. There are flowers, and prints on the walls. It isn't like the hospital that failed you, that was knackered and run-down and free. You are in safe hands now. Expensive hands. The anaesthetist is like an uncle, an older man who would pat your knee if that sort of thing was still allowed, and he says, "Everything will go smoothly. We do this every day." But you do not do this every day. You are scared stiff. Do you have a cigarette?'

She's caught him out – listening but not really listening, letting it slide over him – then he realizes she's serious. 'Sorry. I don't any more.'

'Good. I'm glad. Thank you. Right then. Sperm. You may wish to go together, the nurse says. You may not. You may wish him to get it over with on his own, as quickly as possible. Too much information?'

'A bit.' Helping? He doesn't want to think about her doing that. Not to Jack.

'You may then relax. They give you the anaesthetic. You count backwards from ten and drift away. You wake up unsure of where you are, with pains in your shoulders and you feel bloated, but this is normal, says the nurse. They've inflated your abdomen in order to aspirate and flush out the eggs. You're halfway there, she says, but she's wrong.'

Now Sarah is in full flow, transformed by the chance to say all this out loud, and Gabe is listening, properly. As hard as he can.

'You can go home this afternoon, but you want to stay and be safe. You don't want the cold of an empty house. You don't want to go back to work in a couple of days' time. You don't want to walk or do anything at all that might agitate your womb and the contents thereof. You want to be still and sleep,' she says, pushing fingers into her hair and pulling out the curls. Her scent reaches him across the room. Somehow, she smells of oranges. It's getting colder. He switches on a single bar electric heater as a help to the other fire, and the smell of burning dust rises to mingle with that of paraffin.

'You want to be able to believe that it might happen. You want to put all your eggs in that basket. That was a joke.' She doesn't bother to look round. 'So. You will take the pain that burns like acid, you will accept it, for the few sweet moments when you think it might work. You'll do nothing to endanger that possibility. You feed on it. At first.'

She stops and waits, scratching the side of her nose, checking he's listening.

'At first?'

'I saw the cells. I looked into a microscope and saw five cells pulsing. It made me weak. It gave me hope. Jack was there too. Later, when they had been placed inside me, he said, "What shall we call him?"'

She pauses again and Gabe wonders if this is for emotion or to catch her breath.

What should he say? This mesmerizing woman is in his house, in his tower – in their tower – and she should be somewhere else.

'What about Jack? How does he cope?'

'He hits me.' She says it simply, coldly. When he looks confused, she says it again. 'He hits me. Every time we go through this. Beats me, if you like. I fail him. That is what he says. I am useless and I fail him.'

'That's not good,' says Gabe, unsure of himself. Feeling stupid.

'Ha! No. Very much not.' Throwing off the blanket, she turns to sit facing him, leaning forward. 'Thank you for asking me these questions. I've been silent. I realized that, on these hills, walking around, before I met you. I've been silenced by this man and his fists. You want to know about that? I will tell you. Jack is restless,

181

you've seen it for yourself, he is quick to anger. The drumming is a warning. When that starts, watch out. He used to throw tantrums when we first met, but only ever little ones. A glass might get smashed, accidentally. It was never directed at me. I thought it would stop when he calmed down, and it did. But IVF is vicious. The frustration, the helplessness, gets worse and worse. The band around your chest gets tighter. I'm not making excuses for him, although I could make a case. I'm trying to make sense of it, you understand?'

She checks in with him, then goes on. 'We stopped talking, really, about anything, and when we tried, there would be an argument. Everything I did was wrong, and he was just a jerk. The whole time. We were sick of each other. The love gets drowned out. So anyway, on the day of the first test, when I had built my hopes up so much and been so disappointed, I cried and cried. He held me, in the kitchen. I mean really held me. Tight. It was comforting at first, but then I couldn't breathe and I couldn't move. I said, "What are you doing?" I broke away and the tears came again – I had no control over that – and he hit me. I am not sure he even meant to.' She sniffs and shrugs. 'The back of his hand, out of irritation, more of a flick than a slap. It stung. Maybe he was trying to shut me up – you know, like in the movies. Shut the hysterical woman up by slapping her. Maybe that was it. Of course, he was horrified. Good for him. He was so, so sorry. So sorry. "It will never happen again," he said. It did, of course. Every time, after every test. Every failure.'

So that's why she doesn't want to be found, thinks Gabe.

'The first time, I did not see it coming. That seemed to give him permission somehow, he said he was taking control. For a change. As if. I don't know. The second time, I freaked at the thought of what he was going to do and grabbed this knife from the sink top and threw it at him and missed – the handle hit the wall and it clattered into the sink – and he looked at me as if he was pleased. I was like him. I smashed a glass – the knife did – his best pint glass, but now I was down in the dirty place with him. The next time I was crying, he just hit me properly. Flat of the hand that time, like it was what I deserved, or even wanted.'

Gabe closes his eyes, and hears her tell him off.

'I'm not a victim. I told you. No sympathy, please. It doesn't help.'

Why does she stand it? The question is unspoken but she hears it anyway.

'I love him, Gabe. I loved him.' It sounds, even to her, as if she is repeating those words from memory. 'I knew in my head that what he was doing was wrong, of course; it hurt like hell, but I was so numb, I couldn't feel anything. Even when we went to the Long Man, he had this ridiculous idea that we would – you know – have sex on the hillside, by this fertility symbol—'

'I thought it was graffiti. Civil war.'

'Who knows? I said no, of course I said no, but he got angry, really angry. He pushed me down on the ground and winded me, then . . . well.'

'Seriously?' Gabe puts his hand up, realizing what she is telling him.

'He got his way.'

The bastard.

'You think that is horrifying, do you? Your face says so. Yes, it is. I think so, now. I thought so then, but I didn't feel anything, or see a way out. It was what it was. That's the hell you're in, the madness, you think it will stop if you can just get pregnant. Everything will be made right and you'll be okay then. Back in love. So you push the feelings away and try again. You wait. After the procedure there is nothing else you can do. You can't eat much, or sleep much. You have two weeks to wait. This is where we are now, Gabriel, with hours to go before I can find out if it has worked, although I know the answer. I've always known, but still the hope won't quite die, so the hours feel like days. You dread the test but you want it to come. Time moves so slowly. You close up then. You feel the hope subside and it's a relief. You know before the test that the life inside you, if there ever was one, has died. You know but you dare not say so. Only I just did. I know it, right now.'

She retrieves her glass and drains the bourbon in one gulp, and winces. Then holds it out to be topped up again. 'So you have the first drink in a very, very long time.'

He stops halfway out of his seat, bottle held towards her, sitting back down. 'No more. Just in case.'

'In case of what? A baby? No chance. There is nothing. Why should you care?'

He shouldn't. That's the truth. He feels guilty, although he has done nothing to feel guilty about. Who is he accountable to now – a voice in his head? Rí, where are you?

'I had to come here,' says Sarah, putting the glass down. 'To get away from him. I took a train to Seaford, then a bus to Cuckmere Haven – you know the Coastguard Cottages by the sea where the river comes out? We went there once when I was young, but I never told him about that, for some reason. That's where my bags are.'

That makes sense. The other end of the Seven Sisters, half a dozen miles away over the hills without roads. There are no patrols there. You can hide if you want to.

'Jack was convinced you were at Beachy Head.'

'Good. I was never going there. We stayed at a farm once, back over the other side of the Head towards town; he will have asked there. The Seven Sisters are even more beautiful and almost as high. I didn't mean to come this far, but I was walking and the tower drew me. Then the storm came down, so suddenly. How can it do that? I had to take shelter. I'm sorry.'

'I don't mind. I'm glad.'

'Why?'

He doesn't know. Or doesn't want to say.

'Me too,' she says, with surprising warmth. 'I knew he would come looking for me but I need this time, this space. I want to do the next bit on my own. My life. My choice.'

'Someone should say this, Sarah, so I will. You don't have to do it.'

'Thank you, I do know that.'

This can't happen, thinks Gabe with rising panic. This astonishing woman, filling his lighthouse with her presence, cannot be allowed to take her own life. 'You can't—'

'Yes I can, if I want to. That is the point. All my life I have done what other people want. My father, always telling me to be a brave girl. The Bible, saying marry or burn. Do you know that

184

saying? Marry or give in to the flesh and burn in hell. So I did. The doctors, saying no babies for you. You are barren. You are worthless, you are not a woman, but a husk of a body—'

'They don't say that.'

'A shell. A dry skin left on the dirt by a snake—'

'Stop it—'

'An empty tin can rattling in the bin. Why, Gabriel? Do you not like me saying these things? This is me. This is what I am. Nothing, nobody.'

'That's not true.'

She's getting worked up. 'This is me. The real me. You want to see me? Here I am. Come on! You want more? Get ready for it.' She looks at him strangely, suddenly suspicious, and her voice changes. 'What is your game anyway? What are you doing, keeping me here? Do you think you are going to have me? Is that it? You want me?'

He turns away, not wanting her to see his face and not wanting to accept what he knows he feels but can't feel, not now, it's impossible and wrong and it hurts. For God's sake. What is she doing here?

Looking out of the window is the answer, with her hands and forehead pressed to the glass.

'We might as well get that out in the open, Gabe, if that is your intention. Is that what it takes to stay here for the night?'

'No.'

'Say now if it is.'

'Sarah . . .'

'You are a man, Gabe. You are alone.'

'You are out of order. You hear me? Shut it. Shut up. I didn't ask you in here—'

'Yes, you did.'

'That's—'

'Come back to the house, you said. For a nice cup of tea. Cheer yourself up. Well, mister lighthouse keeper, is that all you had in mind? Tea? You got more than you asked for. So, you want it?'

Gabe is at a loss. If only this were for real. No, don't think like that. If only, he would . . . no. Rí, for God's sake, where are you?

He throws his hands up to say please, stop it, just give it a rest. He has to calm her down.

Say her name.

'Sarah . . .'

'Oh, you don't want me, I'm not enough, okay. Empty husk. Useless. Worthless,' she says, mumbling, sliding down the window, down to the floor like a coiling rope, head down and all closed up.

'You're not,' he says, going across and kneeling beside her but being careful. 'You shouldn't say those things, they are not true. You're amazing, Sarah. You're incredible.'

'You are full of crap.'

'Maybe. Most of the time. Not now.' He softens his voice, gets right down on the cold stone floor there, but doesn't touch. Mustn't touch. 'You need to know something, Sarah. You are safe here.'

She looks up at him, hair in her wet, wide eyes.

'You can stay. I promise.'

'I am tired, Gabe. I need a place, just for now.'

'Sarah, stay. Alive, I mean. Not here. Wherever your life is. Oh, I don't know what I'm saying. Yes I do. Live, Sarah. Please.'

She hangs her head again and is still for a long, long time. So long that he lets her be and moves around the room, putting things back into order, waiting. For what, he is not sure.

'You don't understand,' she says quietly, on her feet again.

'I must confess I don't.'

'I have not been myself for so long. I've been what they wanted me to be. My father, the church, the doctors. Jack. I told you that. I am repeating myself. I lost sight of who I was, but coming here – not to you, no offence, but to this place, this sea and sky – I remember. I have denied my real identity, my self, my mother . . . all of it. I am Sarah Hallelujah Jones, the daughter of Jasmine who has gone, so long ago, but has never left. I want to be able to see her again, Gabe. I only remember the light. I can't see her face, only a light.'

'You are going to have a child, Sarah. Maybe.'

'Ha! You think? There is no child. That won't happen.'

'It might—'

'Do you know my body? Are you inside me?'

He can't help his reaction – a flashing thought, no more – and she notices.

'Ah. We are back to that again! I'm sorry. I needed to know.'

'The doors are locked, but the keys are on the table. Take them. You can go at any time.'

'Out there? I would go the wrong way in the dark.'

'I can take you anywhere. The car—'

'Is a death trap, by the look of it.'

'Sarah—'

'I know. You said. It must seem strange. You can't understand. It's simple, in my mind. If there is a line, there will be a child. I will stay with him, with my life. If there is no line, and this is what I know will happen, then my decision is made. The life I have must end. I have known this for a long time. This pain must stop.'

'The pain will pass . . .'

'Seven years, Gabe. Prodding. Poking. Knives. Drugs. Hope, despair, hope, despair, hope, that is the worst of it. Hope rising when you wish it would not, because you know it will die, more painfully every time. It is a kind of torture. Now it will end, all that. Either way. I am too tired for anything else. What you're talking about would only be a step from one state to another, anyway. Step outside the capsule of the lantern room and float free, like a space walk. Like ashes in the wind. Like gravity. It's natural.'

'How can you talk about it like that?'

'I've thought about it more often than you.'

'How do you know? I have seen what is left behind.'

She smiles to herself, strangely. 'But anyway, no need to worry. It's not your fault. What will be will be. Tomorrow.' Sarah looks at her watch. 'Today, in fact. When the sun comes up. Will you let me stay here until then?'

He can't. His heart is breaking again. It is obscene. She's so young, so lovely, how dare she do this? How can he help her?

You must, Gabe. You must.

You had no choice, Rí. She has a choice.

Help her make one. Help her.

187

Saying nothing, he moves to the seat where Sarah has sat down again, and puts his arm along the wooden curve behind her. She shifts up into him, and leans so that her head is resting on him and she can feel his breath on her forehead and his arm around her, close.

'I will,' he says. 'God help us both.'

Forty-four

They can't sit like that for ever. Perhaps it would be better if they could, now that a balance has been reached between them, but the balance cannot last. There must be a tipping point, after which things begin to slide, one way or another. Sometimes in life it is a kiss, but not now. Sarah needs more than a physical gesture to rescue her. Gabe is sitting there with her scent in his nostrils, her hair almost in his mouth, the softness of a breast against his arm, a nod away from kissing her forehead then her face then her lips, but he knows that would be a betrayal. He is not about to risk Rí's wrath, even as he knows very well that there is no wrath. There is no Rí except in his heart, his mind, on his skin. The sadness is always there – he wades through it waist deep every moment of every day, lies down with it lapping at his mouth at night. He wants to be furious with Sarah for being ready to throw everything she has away, and all the hurt it will cause, but what is the point? He feels for her. He knows what grief can do, even if it is grief for a life that has not yet begun. So he offers her the one thing he can. His only love.

'She went away on a summer's day,' he says quietly, hoping Sarah's slow and deep breathing means she is asleep. 'It was quick, at least. We knew it was coming some time, but not when. They said it could be years, a whole lifetime. It was inoperable, sitting in her brain, waiting. No need to shave her head then. Live every day as if it is your last. We had three years, eight months, four days and eleven hours together, from the moment outside the bar when she kissed me to the moment in the garden here when she turned to say the honeysuckle was in bloom and she fell . . .'

Turning, like a dancer. Falling, like a sleeper.

'I went to her and held her and she was warm, breathing. I shook her and hugged her and kissed her, but she would not speak and she lay there in the chalk with dust on her clothes. I couldn't phone. There was no signal. I pulled her into the car and drove down to the town, to the hospital, as fast as I could. Took the wing off on a bollard. The police stopped me and I said help me, there is something wrong, and they did and she was gone and the ambulance came, but she was gone, there was nothing they could do they said, she was gone, just gone . . .'

Always and for ever.

The noise he makes is pitiful. The anger left him long ago. Regret is all, now. The keeper of the light with no light left to keep. The man who cannot leave, however much it hurts to stay. This is home, she said, and he has had no other. This tower on a windy hill is where she wanted to be with him and where she is now. This is where he let her go on a sharpening day in late summer, raising a fist and opening his fingers, because he had to. Letting go of the ashes that vanished in a moment like a twist of smoke. Now she hangs in the air between the sky and the sea, like the spirit woman in the song she used to sing, and she leaves her lover grounded, unable to lift his feet from the earth, always sensing her just out of reach, seeing her face in the shifting clouds.

Always. And for ever.

Sarah is not asleep, she heard it all. Reaching up above her head, she finds his jaw with her cool fingers and without turning around, says, 'I'm sorry.'

Of course. That's what they all say, when they say anything at all. At first there was astonishment among the friends they had left in London, and endlessly painful discussions about how awful it was, how she had never been ill, how cruel it was to take somebody like that so unexpectedly. They had not known. That was her plan. There was a lot of sympathy, a crushing weight of goodwill, but one man's grief is another man's boredom in the end. So after the memorial service, after the weeping, drunken friends, he came back here to hide himself away in the tower, with only Maria.

'Really, I am sorry,' says Sarah. 'You must think me selfish.'

'You have a choice. That's all. She didn't.'

'Would you be angry with me if I did what you think I want to do?'

'Yes.'

'What's that over there?' Sarah's looking at a pile of white feathers on the floor, beside the end of the semi-circular sofa bench. There's another by the pile of wood and another a few feet away and they are all connected somehow, like someone has rolled up wings and put them away for another day. 'Is it all the same thing?'

Now Gabe knows he is encircled. There are three of them in this room. 'It's an angel,' he says, and Sarah laughs. 'Really. She made it. The last thing. For in here. An installation. It hung from there . . .' He looks to the circle at the centre of the ceiling, where a hook hangs from the lead cross in the middle of the stained-glass compass. 'It was beautiful. He or she, you never know with angels, was going to fly.'

Sarah shifts on the sofa, pulls herself away, sits up. 'How?'

'Like a kite. I'm not sure. There is no weight to it. She made it to fly away on the thermals and to be biodegradable, so that it could do no harm.'

'Can I see?' Sarah is up and moving towards the feathers.

'*No! Don't touch it!*'

'Wow. I'm sorry.' She backs away.

Okay, Gabe. Okay. Easy. Empty. His eyes close. She says nothing. Good. So that's it. She'll go. No point even apologizing. Stupid, but what does she expect, coming in here? Who the hell is she anyway?

Then he feels a hand on his head, in his hair, running through his hair, and the other on his cheek again. He's so tired. Her touch is refreshing, water in the desert. He opens his eyes to her but Sarah is nowhere near him; it wasn't her, she's on the other side of the room, bending down, lifting the angel. Carefully. She does it so carefully, as if lifting a child. Feathers cascade over her arm. She's having difficulty. Gabe is afraid she will tear the wing, so he goes to her and takes the next part and the next, until the soft, weightless silk and paper and feather angel is in both their arms. And without saying anything, without even saying how she knows what to do, Sarah finds the head of the angel with golden eyes looking upwards and moves a chair across with her foot and stands on the chair and lifts the angel up towards the hook and tries to put him back where he – or she – belongs.

'I tore it down,' says Gabe, swallowing the pain in his throat. 'I fixed the hook when . . . but I didn't put it back up. Why are you doing this?'

'I don't know. Help me.'

He finds the long pole they bought for opening higher windows, with a boat hook and spike on the end. She offers a loop of thread at the back of the angel's head and he lifts it into place on the ceiling hook.

'Where do these go?'

Together they unfold the wings and the arms that run through them and fix the frame of the featherweight angel so that he or she is in the room, filling the room, the angel of the south with arms wide open. The uplights illuminate the wings. The man and the woman caught in the shimmering light of the angel's embrace. Sarah's legs shake and the chair wobbles and she seems about to fall, but Gabe grabs her waist and holds her there steady and safe, his head against her belly.

That is what Magda sees, as she stands outside the tower in the half-dark, looking up at the lantern room. A shimmering light and the Keeper and the beautiful stranger in a loving embrace. Now she knows why the Lord made her sleepless, why she was called from her bed to climb the hill in the moonlight. She had thought it was to make a deal, silence for silence – no police, no accusations on either side – but instead it was to do this, to be a witness, which is God's work. Magda takes a photograph with the camera on her phone. Then she hurries away through the cold, waking dawn, back to the pub and Jack.

Forty-five

The day is coming. The moon has slid away but there are stars above, around and beneath them still, falling through time and bouncing upwards again on the mirror of the sea. Far away to the east there is a low glow, a promise. The air is unusually calm, the almost-morning wind feathers their faces as they stand on the balcony outside the lantern room, with their backs to the glass and the angel inside. Shoulder to shoulder, hands side by side on the rail, not quite touching, when he speaks.

'I don't blame you. I've thought about it many times. Of course I have, living here. It would be so easy, look.'

They are somewhere between twenty and thirty feet from the ground, although it feels like more, and below them on this side of the tower is only a precariously narrow ledge, pockmarked and filled in with pools of builder's gravel to make a way around the building for those who dare, but no more than eight feet wide before it falls away to the rocks. It looks narrower. Much narrower. Four seconds on from there, the outcome would be certain.

'I'm not trying to tell you what to do.'

'Are you sure?'

'Well, okay.'

'You don't understand,' she says.

'I get that. I'm trying to stay calm, Sarah, doing my best. Will you let me try and say something? I need to get this off my chest. For my own sake. I could have gone over that day, when I let her ashes go. I wanted to. I understand that desire to be with your mum – you can't know how much. I'm a coward, maybe. It's a long way down. I have seen the bodies, I know what happens to them. That's not it, though. Rí didn't want me to go. She didn't want that.'

The wind hides Sarah's face in a wrap of hair.

'I heard her voice that day. She said no. Don't do it. Maybe I'm mad. I hear voices. Her voice. No others, just Rí. She talks

193

to me. I don't know what it is, Sarah, but it sounds like her. She says the things she used to say, and that day she said no. Live. Breathe. Seize the day, bite the head off life – that was one of her favourites – and chew it until the juices run down your chin. Be alive!'

'Did you talk back?'

'I do. I told her: "That's easy to say when you're dead!"'

Sarah's hand goes to her mouth to stifle a laugh through her hair. He puts his hand on hers and returns it to the rail. 'Hold on. It's okay, I was trying to be funny. You're different, you know that?'

'To her? Thanks for that.'

'No. I mean different to when you came here. You would not have laughed. You would have given me that face.'

'What face?'

'This one.' He tries to do a deadpan stare, and turns down the corners of his mouth with his fingers, but cracks up.

'Are you laughing at me?'

'No, no. Yes. Maybe. A bit. Sorry. I don't get much company up here.'

'I can see why.'

'You don't have to go. Did I just say that? Oh God. Sorry.'

'I do, Gabe. One way or another. Not long now.' She looks towards the dawn. A crowbar of light is pushing a space between the weight of dark clouds and black sea. 'Almost time.'

'For God's sake, Sarah!' His voice flies out over the edge, dying into the drop. 'Look, hang on, I'm sorry, Rí is right. There is too much beauty to see, too much to enjoy, too much life to live; you can't just throw it away. You have to swallow the bitter and taste the sweet. You have to go on because there is no choice, this is what we have. This is what we do. It's a privilege, Sarah, a privilege. You've made me see that, coming in here where nobody asked you, filling the place up with yourself. I didn't want you here, but you came anyway and you're waking me up, making me feel. I don't want to feel, I want it to stop. I want to sleep, but you won't let me and Rí won't let me and you're both bloody right. This life is a wonderful thing. Look. The sea never stops shifting, shining even in the night; that sun coming up over there won't be stopped whether I'm here or not, but I want to be here because even when it hurts, so much, the pain is life and life is right. Live every moment. She had it stolen from her. She had no choice, do you see that? No choice. You have. You're making the wrong one! Come on, Sarah . . . get a grip!'

He's gone way too far. Sarah recoils, he can see her pained face in the light from the room, and now she is moving towards him with a weird, open smile, and maybe this is it, maybe he can stop her, because Rí would want that, because it would matter. Sarah's hand is on his neck, she is leaning in close and her lips brush his cheek in a kiss and she whispers something in his ear. He feels the warmth of her breath and the shudder of arousal before he realizes what she has said.

'You know nothing.'

Nothing, she thinks, running down the stairs. Nothing, she thinks, striding down the big steps and over the gravel on the land side of the tower.

'Nothing!'

Nothing about the grief, the pain that never goes away, the throbbing, constant pain in her head, in her body – the doctors say it does not exist, but it is everywhere, always, now and all the time – he knows nothing about that or the coldness, the chill, the emptiness in her like a dead thing. 'You don't know,' she says, stumbling over the ground beyond the lighthouse wall, where there is only deeper shadow and her feet are unsure. The ground is blue, her feet are blue, her clothes and hands are blue, the sea is blue and the sky is a deep, dark, mournful, moody black and blue. He knows nothing about her, nothing about the way Jack comes at her, nothing about the way he leaves her when he has done what he needs to do, nothing about the nothingness inside her. There is nothing. No feeling, no hope, no humour, no laughter, no light. She is all shut down. So let it stop now, this morning. Let it cease. Let there be an end to all this and let her go.

She feels her way along the wall to where it breaks down, to where she knows there is a little wooden stake driven into the

195

ground, near the edge. Here it is. She plants her feet wide and opens her arms as if to plead for mercy, but it is far too late for that. The test will be negative, she knows that. She looks down and sees the blue ground give way to the rumpled blue sea just in front of her feet and knows she need only take a step to end her life now. You don't jump, you walk. One step at a time. Just one. The little fire in the east makes her think of her mother in the hospital and the blinding white light. She opens her arms wide and feels the wind take her. This is the way they go. She is going.

She is dying for a wee.

Forty-six

A wing blocks his way into the room at the top of the tower and Gabe realizes the absurdity of it all: his name and this mythical thing, this creation of Rí's. An angel for you, Gabriel. Her joke. Her last laugh. Her gift. Looking out for him. Always and for ever.

'I want to live,' he says and feels a hand inside him, moving in his guts, sliding behind the back of his lungs, pushing on up through his oesophagus, filling his throat, cramming his mouth, spilling out of his mouth and into the room, the lantern room in the sky in the cold morning: a laugh. A bloody laugh. A big, fat, unexpected shoulder-heaving bubble of a laugh, full of transparent joy, glistening with a surface sheen that is all the colours of the rainbow, floating upwards above him and bursting all over his face with a bloody great pop.

Forty-seven

Magda pours coffee in the breakfast room at the Gap, having given Jack a laminated menu of items she knows he will not want once he has heard what she has to say.

'This is not so good maybe, but I have something to show you. I have not long come from the hill.' The dish of fruit salad and the individual selection boxes of Rice Krispies, Frosties and Coco Pops remain untouched as she speaks quietly and calmly. 'I was on patrol with the Guardians and I saw her.'

Jack shifts around in his chair, knocking the coffee.

'She was in the lighthouse. I saw something in the tower and I took a picture on my phone, but I did not realize until just now. I think it is her. Look . . .'

She offers the black Samsung, already open at the image. Jack's hands shake. What is this? What is he looking at? A blurred, grainy photo, barely lit. Some kind of weird canopy, spread out like wings. The guy . . . with Sarah. Is it Sarah, with her arms tied up above her head? As Magda coos, he curses and questions her and demands that she call the police and tell them he is right and Sarah has been kidnapped and she is in the lighthouse and he is going there and they should come with the dogs and helicopter and whatever they need to stop him because he is going to get his wife and kill that son of a bitch.

And he goes. Angry, way beyond anger. The chalk explodes under his feet. The shush of the sea is a loud shut up, get on with it, get there and find her; the tang of the ozone is tear gas to his mouth and nose. Streaming, weeping, oozing, he climbs the steep, stony steps at the bottom of the hill with his calves screaming and his chest on fire. The sun is up and in his eyes, the dawn is unexpectedly hot now. The world is against him. The gull stretching black-tipped wings on a wall and laughing. The morning chorus squealing and squalling. The buttercups and daisies, the purple clusters and those little studs of vivid orange set against the grass and the grass itself all jewelled with dew and burning green – all these are insults. The fat bee boozing on a bright yellow celandine, the butterflies doing their stupid little dance, the buzzing, whirring things he can hardly see. The whole of creation laughing in his face, teasing. So rich, so fucking fecund. All this was made or meant or just happened by accident – who cares how? – life bursting out from every pore of the planet but from him, the dead, lost, useless boy with the empty seed, lying to everybody the whole time. This is not just her problem, whatever he says. It is him as well, with his hopeless sperm, his lazy boys, his blanks, his squirt of nothing. Useless, pointless Jack, drumming on his thigh with his fingers as he climbs the hill, all clatter but no bang, all noise but no melody.

Behind him, the faces of the Seven Sisters are veiled in shadow, ashamed. The sea sound is harsher up here, nastier. Get on with it, you creep, the waves say. Get her. Ahead on the broad back of the hill the bright white tails of rabbits twitch and scatter. Rabbits everywhere: prolific little bunnies who drop more little bunnies as easily as breathing, a countless crowd parting before him, nearly under his feet. So hot already, breathing hurts. He climbs the hill, seeming to step upwards into the sky. Then there it is.

The tower, with the sun behind.

Jack stops, gasping for breath. Through the binoculars Magda gave him, squinting against the brilliant light, he sees the figure of a man in the lantern room, arms outstretched as if on a cross. Holding that pose. Sarah must be up there somewhere . . . A smoker's cough rips his lungs, twists his ribs, and he hacks out phlegm on to the flinty chalk and grass.

For a moment, it all pauses. Up here where the scale is vast, where you can see for twenty miles or more, everything is still. The sea is utterly calm, a swathe of iris blue. Then a hare tears across the grass in front of him – a hare now, for Christ's sake – the ears trailing, flying for the cover of the gorse. A fox appears from nowhere, caught between chasing the hare and glaring at Jack, and settles for the glare. What are you doing up here so early, loser?

This climb is taking longer than Jack bargained for, it is further than it seemed. Hands on his knees, he heaves in air to his lungs and feels his heart thump. Then he goes again, onwards and upwards towards the tower, like a flaming arrow to end a siege. Picking up time again. Sarah, a march in his head. One-two, one-two. Sarah, Sarah. Somebody has drawn in chalk all over the bench up ahead in a language and symbols he does not understand – what the hell is this? – and a crisp packet snagged in the gorse, a Coke can rammed down a rabbit hole. These filthy bastards, these human vermin spewing their junk-food guts all over the beautiful earth, and Jack is raging against them now as he strides up the hill and then runs full pelt towards the tower, where the strange figure still stands in the lantern room like a beast in a cage looking down on him. A beast in a cage – Sarah in a cage. He will find her, he will rescue her from the beast.

He throws himself against the wall, feels a sharp dig at his ribs, swings his leg over and he is in now, beyond the barricade and up to the wall, banging on the wall, useless, soundless slapping on the stone wall, banging on the window – loud resounding claps into the dark room – but where is the door, where is the door? He finds the door and pounds the frosted glass with his fists, shouting, 'Let me in! I know you've got her. Let me in! Sarah, I love you. I am coming for you. I love you. Let me in . . .'

Forty-eight

Sarah is thinking of her father. On the other side of the wall beyond the lighthouse, oblivious to Jack's approach, summoned back from the edge by the burning in her bladder, burning through the numbness, she remembers a walk with her dad on these cliffs one early morning just like this. It was one of their summer holidays. He held her hand and told her the names of the birds they were seeing, but he made them all up. The Squirly Bird. The Great Black-tipped Mugger Bird. The Tiny Tit. That made her laugh; she was thirteen and conscious of her growing body. When she wanted the loo he made her go behind a bush, the last time she ever did that. A wild wee, he called it. She should do that now, have a wild wee here, because what does it matter if she does not do the test?

'Every day brings a fresh miracle,' her father said from the other side of the bush, where he had turned right away from her, to keep a lookout for anyone who might see. There was nobody about at all. 'Today's miracle is your presence with me here on this walk, my splendidly moody daughter.' She hated him. She did not want to be there. She got up at that insane hour and went out with him that morning because he made her do it, by wanting it so much. Now she remembers it as one of the great walks of her life, one of the precious times. Apart from the wee. Funny how things turn out.

That same man, older now but still her father, said he was gob-smacked when she went to him a month ago. She let herself into the rectory – more like a council flat – with his spare key and stood there looking at him for a while on the edge of the room, away from the flickering blue light of the television screen. He looked older and heavier, with silver at his temples and his black hair in need of a cut. The belly of his black clerical shirt was spilling over his black clerical trousers. His shirt was open at the throat, his dog collar on the floor. The mole on his cheek had swollen

201

and sprouted hairs, his face was set with shadows. Resting, weary. Then he sensed her.

'My love!' he said, jumping up in his slippers, hastily brushing crumbs off his chest. 'This is brilliant. Wow. I'm gobsmacked. How are you?'

There was no need to answer that, but he was even more surprised when she asked to read the letter from her mother.

'I'm ready for it, Dad.'

'Why now?'

'The treatment. I need her. And you. We would like to take up your offer, thank you. We could not do it without that money, whatever Jack says.'

'I'm glad. I'll pray. I was praying,' said her father.

'I know. I thought you might be.'

'There you are. It's my job to worry, my nature to pray.'

'Good line. You should make a note of it.'

The eyebrows of the Reverend Robert Jones were raised. 'I seem to remember using it once or twice already, over the years, but thank you.'

'I'm sorry he lost his temper.'

'Are you two okay?'

She nodded, but he did not know what to make of his daughter's expression or what to say. They held each other's gaze, blaze to blaze in the semi-darkness, Sarah standing and her father sitting again, his fork halfway to his mouth, until he spoke again.

'You have taken your time.'

'You let me,' she said.

He put down his fork and held his arms out.

She knelt down and snuggled in tight to her daddy.

He stroked her hair. 'Oh Sarah.'

They let the grandfather clock tick and the church bells ring on the quarter hour before they moved. Then the clock went on ticking, as Sarah and her father knelt on the floor or laid on a cushion or stood to adjust the light for a better look at the photographs and keepsakes and letters of a woman called Jasmine, who had been born and raised in the mountains in the blue sky and warm rain, and come a long way to fall in love

202

with a silly, stubborn, strong Scotsman who could not believe his good fortune.

'I loved her so much,' he said, but Sarah had always known that; how could she not have done? How could she not have noticed the way he looked at his daughter when there was a christening or somebody was having their banns read? How could she not have noticed the hour he always spent on his own between the morning service and the big lunch on Christmas Day, in his bedroom with the door locked? Now she could hold the same fragile, yellowed papers, and read the words her mother had written to him. There were not many, because they were seldom apart. Just a note here, an airmail slip there, when she went home to visit. 'Do not worry, my darling Bobby,' she wrote, in large, looping letters, and signed off with three big, loose cross-kisses. There was one more letter, but this one had her name on it. To have opened it as a child would have been to let all the hurt and longing overwhelm her, and she could not have stood it. Not then, nor for so many years after; but she was ready now. She was strong enough. It was what she had come for. But she would do it on her own, in private, not with her father. Away from him, to spare them both. So instead Sarah touched a photograph of them both laughing on their wedding day, the bride trying to cover her mouth with a cupped hand but the sunlight of her smile spilling out anyway.

It was late that night when Sarah smoothed the tissue paper of the wedding album and closed the last page, and her father tucked the last loose photographs back into their case. White, no bigger than a hat box and lined with pink silk with a mirror set inside. 'She bought this for the honeymoon. It was not even big enough for her underwear.' He was tired. She felt her father tremble when she held him again, and she stayed there with him for as long as she could, steady and still.

But now she is here on the edge of this cliff in the startling beauty of the morning, no longer as sure about what to do as she was in the dark. And somehow, on the wind or in her imagination, at this weary, wobbly moment, she hears a voice.

'Mum?'

'Sarah? Where are you? I'm coming for you!'

That's not her mum, that's Jack. He's back. She has to run, get back into the house before he sees her. Not easy with a full bladder. Sarah waddles as fast as she can over the gravel and sees him up at the door, but he has not seen her. Good. She can duck in through the window, like she did when she first came here, to get out of the storm, when the window was flapping in the wind. It is still loose. She hauls herself over the ledge and into the room with the bed covered in plastic, and there is the letter. There is the letter she lost. There it is on the bed. The letter from her mother. Of all the times. How can that be? What is it doing here? It should be floating on the waves, caught up in some fishing net or broken into pieces by now, but here it is intact, inside the blank white envelope her father gave her. The letter from her mother that she could have read at any time over the years but refused, but this is here and now, with her bladder bursting and her maniac of a husband about to break down the door.

'Oh Mum, your timing is terrible.'

But she opens the envelope carefully and finds another, old and worn and lilac, with her name on. The sight of her mother's writing causes a flutter of panic. The paper inside is thin and fragile, and as she reads it, the paper trembles.

Forty-nine

Dearest Sarah, my love,

All mothers are proud. One day you will know that for yourself. Every one of us believes that our child is the most beautiful there has ever been. That does not mean that it is not true. When I first saw you, nearly three years ago now, my heart leapt. You were perfect. I was so thankful for you, and I have been thankful every day since. You can be moody, of course; I expected that from my little girl! You have the gift of a charming nature, though, my darling. You can make anyone do anything when you choose to smile. When you are playing, all I want to do is sit and watch you, for ever.

[The ink is smudged on the lilac paper. The writing is shaky.]

When you read this, you will know that was not possible. I am sorry, my angel – more sorry than I can say here – that I will not be with you as you grow. At least, not in this body that I occupy now. It hurts, Sarah, this body, but the pain is nothing compared to the pain I feel now as I think about my little one getting bigger without me.

I am afraid, my precious. I am afraid to die, although I know I am going to a place without pain. There will be no more crying. I will hold the hand of my Lord. Is it so wrong to say that I would rather hold the hand of my child?

I am not afraid for you. I know you are strong and clever and resourceful, and you will look life in the eye and rise to every challenge. I have faith in you, my Sarah. Wherever you are, whatever you do, I will be watching over you, praying for you. Delighting in you. I know that your father will give you all that he can, all that he has. Be patient with him, he loves you as passionately as I do. You were born from the love we shared: you came out of the bright burning love that was between us from the moment we met, and that will not die even though I must, apparently. Take care of my man for me, please. Woman to the woman you will be. He will need you. I am with you both.

As you grow, Sarah, you will be challenged by the world. You will make mistakes and feel like a failure. You will feel sad and lonely. Have faith, my darling. Never give up. Trust in the Lord, but trust in yourself. You are enough. You have all that you need inside you. Remember that, above all. Your life is a miracle to me, a gift more precious than I can say. May it be the same to you. You are my daughter and always will be, Sarah Hallelujah Jones, beautiful and proud and strong.

Love, for ever,
Mummy xxx

Fifty

They pass at the foot of the stairs, as Gabe leaps down to see about the banging and Sarah flees upwards to escape it.

'Don't let him in,' she says fiercely, urgently, waving the pregnancy test. 'Let me do this.'

Gabe gestures to the Keeper's Cabin. 'Take the key here, lock it. Do what you need to do.' And he's away down through the kitchen, through the reception to the frosted door that Jack is pounding with his fist as he yells and bellows to be let in.

'Calm down,' Gabe yells through the door. 'You're not getting in here until—'

But Jack is smashing something hefty and grey against the glass, a cornerstone from the garden wall, flaking the toughened glass on the other side. It might not hold – can it hold? Now he's jumping up against the door with his shoulder. Right. Deep breath.

Gabe grabs the door handle tightly. One, two and open . . . and he times it right. Jack falls through the door that is not there any more, and flies past Gabe and lands hard on the floor and rolls over and pulls himself up against the wall, snarling, 'You bastard.' He's in the house now, prowling and roaring and calling her name and opening rooms, tearing open the doors, turning over desks, ripping off covers, pulling over wardrobes.

'Sarah!'

Gabe tries to restrain him and gets the back of a hand across his face, cutting his brow, filling his eye with blood. Jack is wild, searching, screaming for her.

'Sarah!'

Gabe blocks the doorway to the tower and Jack comes at him with a broken chair, stabbing with the splintered wood, lashing out at his head and missing. Gabe grabs Jack's waist, swings him down to the floor and pins him there, but pain rips into his hand and he sees bite marks. Jack is through the door, up the stairs, into the tower kitchen, turning over the table with a heave, clattering the pans, smashing the dirty crockery.

'She's here! That's her scarf. Where is she? Sarah!'

'She's safe. Calm down, for God's sake, just let me talk . . .'

But there's no talking to be done, no space left for words in Jack's bushfire mind, and he's getting closer. She can hear him coming, hear the crash and bang and the shouts. Is the door locked? Yes, it won't give. It's thick and strong. Sarah is fit to bursting, but what the hell is she supposed to pee in? There's a wash basin without a plug, a wide-mouthed bottle as a tooth mug, with gunk in the bottom. A razor with hairs in the blade. Books, lined up tightly on the shelf. Broken spines, frayed pages. Can't pee in those. The bed's unmade, the shape of Gabe's head in the pillow. Another book on the floor: Tommy Cooper. Unexpected, reminds her of a clip she saw once, he was funny. But a pint glass, there is a pint glass with an inch of vodka in it – she sniffs, no, it's water – that will do. Ridiculous bloody situation. Bottle or glass? Glass, bottle? Glass. Sarah pulls her jeans down to her ankles, puts her back up against the wall and slides down into a crouching position. If that door opens, she will die. The thought makes her shudder. She holds the pint glass between her legs to catch the first urine of the day, and feels a warm splash on her hand. The glass warms too, as it fills. Such relief. Then the sound of a miss. Overflow. Never mind, it is done. That will stink, but he can clean the carpet later, if they get out of this. The pregnancy test is like a pen with a little window on the side where the result will show. She dips one end into the wee and starts to count, under her breath, backwards from thirty. 'Twenty-nine, twenty-eight . . .'

How blue is a blue line? She does not dare to straighten up or pull her jeans up. How clear does it have to be? There won't be one anyway. Never is. Something smashes in the kitchen, a mug perhaps. The shouts get louder.

'Fifteen, fourteen . . .'

The door of the cabin booms under the weight of Jack's hand, then again. It is solid in the frame, locked hard. The keepers must have put good locks on when they were all going mad with each other. Concentrate.

'Ten, nine . . .'

Jack has gone, it sounds like. Upstairs. Sarah is still crouching over the glass, her jeans still down, her elbows on her haunches.

'Five, four . . .'

I can cope, she thinks. I can do this. I'm strong. I am not barren. I am not this or that or anything else they say. I am enough, I am myself. The daughter of my mother and my father. *Sarah Hallelujah Jones, beautiful and proud and strong.* I can do this. Please God. Half blinded by tears now, she blinks them back to look down at the test pen in her hand and sees the result, which is in this moment truly a matter of life or death.

Fifty-one

'Upstairs,' says Gabe, to stop Jack hammering on the cabin door. 'She's up there, right at the top. Go to her.'

Jack isn't sure, but a mighty crash comes from above, like someone falling over, smashing things. He leaps the first three steps, skittering upwards through the tight turn, imagining himself going to Sarah's rescue. A low beam catches his head with a glancing blow. Jack staggers into Maria's artroom, and feathers cling to his face, pricking his eyes. He feels his way out and up the last few stairs to the big, circular lantern room, with its views of the Downs and the sea wrapping around him, only to find a wing in his way, a white billowing thing blocking the room. Jack curses, feeling trapped and tricked, and pushes through it looking for her. 'What have you done?'

'She isn't here, I lied. Calm down, she's on the Downs,' says Gabe, coming up behind and trying to put his arms around Jack to pin him down, but Jack spins away, tripping over the long boat hook with the spike on the end and scooping it up as he falls.

So now he is on his back, jabbing away with it. 'Get off me!'

A jab catches Gabe in the ribs and Jack scrambles away through the door of the lantern room out to the balcony that encircles it, calling for her as he goes. The breathtaking morning air floods back towards Gabe in the room, with a swirl that lifts feathers and papers and scraps of material, and whirls them around. As he steps outside on to the narrow balcony, with its curved red iron rail, Jack rams into his stomach with one bony shoulder, winding him, jamming his spine against the metal. There's a terrible, apocalyptic noise, and they both look up to see the police helicopter come low overhead. Very low, huge in the sky, the rotor thundering and the skis reaching down like claws. The downdraught tornado blinds them with grit and gets right into the lantern room, sending the angel spinning, stretching and snapping the cord and pulling the wings and the body, then the head back out through the door with a rush of air, but one of the wings snags on the window frame. The angel is plastered against the glass, arms spread out like the keeper who was left for dead, only this time trapped on the inside. Ripped silk and torn feathers are tumbling, now settling.

Gabe is groggy, his head somehow jammed against the hard metal rail, forcing him back to look at the ground thirty feet below, and he realizes Jack's hands are on his throat. He's not a fighter, he's never been a fighter, but he has lived with fighters and seen their ways and his hand forms a blade that pushes up inside Jack's open leather jacket, through his T-shirt and under his ribs, right to where some vital organs ought to be. Jack yelps and falls off him backwards along the narrow balcony, but kicks out. Gabe feels nothing, but he knows some teeth have gone. He tastes blood.

The police are coming up the long hill towards the tower, a dozen on foot moving like overweight toddlers in their bulky black body armour and a four-by-four patrol car with the blue lights on, and an ambulance too. They look like the vanguard of an invading army, the black-clad shock troops of a modern Roman legion with demonic metallic beasts that have wild, flashing eyes. Behind him and below, creeping up the steeper side of the hill from the lay-by, the Guardians are in their Land Rover. The police, the Guardians, the helicopter swooping in again.

'They're coming for you, bastard! What have you done with her?' screams Jack. He is bleeding heavily from his head, blood purpling his hair, a line running down the side of his face like a scar. He's holding something out to Gabe. What is it? Focus. The pole. The spike, coming at him fast. Catching him in the side of his neck, going in. There is no pain, only the feeling of something hard and strange tugging at his skin from the inside. He's buckling, fading.

'Stop,' says a calm, strong voice amid all the noise. Sarah is in the doorway, one foot on the balcony. 'Stop it, Jack. Put it down. Stop.' The handle of the pole clatters on the wooden floor, between Gabe's feet. The sharp end has blood from his neck on it. He's weak and on the floor now, holding his wound, looking up at Sarah.

'No more, Jack. You have done enough.'

'Aw, honey, are you okay? I'm so glad to see you. What did he do, did he hurt you? Come here, baby . . .'

But Sarah steps back, away from his advance, shrugging off his embrace.

'What's the matter, love? Are you hurt?'

'I am fine,' she says, standing straight and tall, fully out on the balcony now, one hand on the rail, keeping her distance from him. The light from the rising sun sets her skin to glow, sparks fly in her copper hair. 'Nothing has happened here.'

'I knew I would find you. I knew you were here, Sarah. I haven't stopped looking for you. I was scared, baby, you made me so scared – how could you do that? I found you. Are you okay?'

'Listen to me, Jack.' She speaks slowly, clearly. 'I am fine. I am not scared. I am here by choice. Do you understand?'

But Jack is talking, not listening. 'The police are here now, baby, they will take him away; he can't hurt you any more. You can come with me. We'll go home, it will be okay. I'll look after you, everything will be like it was. Only better. Not the same, it will be great. I'm here for you, Saz. I'm here.'

Jack takes her hand, smearing blood across it from his own. She pulls away.

'I won't be coming home, Jack. I'm not coming back. I've had enough.'

'I know. It has been hard, but listen, it can get better—'

'Jack.'

Gabe sees that she is holding the letter, close to her chest.

'I've had enough of you, Jack.'

'Saz! You're just saying that. The test didn't work. I get it. That's okay. I know it's hard, but we will be okay. I will make it okay, Saz. I will. Somehow—'

'Thank you. For everything. I've made a decision.'

Jack realizes what she is saying. 'You're not serious?' He laughs, nervously, hoping she will laugh too and ruffle his hair and put the kettle on.

'You keep complaining you have lost me, Jack. It turns out you're right.'

'Why? Come on, Saz, why now?'

'I can make it. Whatever happens.'

'You're being strange, you're frightening me. This is the drugs, right? The hormones?' She says nothing. 'Oh, come on. Just like that? You think you can just click your fucking fingers after all this time and I walk away? You're mad.'

'It is what you want.' Those sea-green eyes look at him and Jack flinches, visibly, unable to deny that which is true, deep down. Deeper than he knew until this moment. 'Go,' she says. 'I'm giving you the chance. You have no more obligation.'

'What if there is a child?'

'There is no child.'

'You've done the test?'

'Yes.'

Oh no, thinks Gabe in his wounded weakness. No, Sarah.

'Go, Jack,' she says. 'You don't believe in a child.'

'I do! I don't know how, but I do believe it can happen. Liar!'

'I have the test here,' she says, holding up a clenched fist.

'Show me. *Show me!*'

He makes a lunge but Sarah is too quick. She steps back and calls out to Gabe, who now has blood all over his shirt. It is comfortingly warm, in this wind. He could sleep.

'Gabe! Stay awake! The ambulance is coming.' There's a commotion down below, inside the tower. 'Stay with us.'

'You too,' says Gabe, breathless.

'Is it fucking his?' The hatred and violence in Jack's voice shocks her, but Sarah is not going to do his bidding any more.

'How could it be his? Now listen to me. I'm talking. You are in trouble. Whatever you have told the police, they will see it's not true. And there is something else you need to know before they come. I have done the test, yes. Here it is, in my hand. I thought it would give me the answer, Jack, but I already knew what to do, before I looked.'

'Don't do it, Sarah. Don't go. I'll take care of you. I will—'

'You idiot. You have no idea, either of you,' she says, looking from Jack to where Gabe is slumped against the balcony rail, trying to stand. 'I was never going to jump off this cliff. You said I was.

Both of you. Your fears. Your words. You put that all on me. You decided what was going to happen, just like people always do. Have you even thought about it, seriously? There is no jumping. You walk, one step then another. But not now. I came here to get away from you, Jack, to remember myself. Not to end my life. To get the strength to start again. I thought I would stay with you if the test was positive, for the sake of the child, but that would be wrong. The test does not decide. I decide. I'll tell them what you did to me. We are through. You are not going to hurt me any more.'

I am in control, she tells herself, not quite believing it. Feeling fizzy, faint. I am in control. I can choose. *Beautiful and proud and strong.* 'Go,' she says. There are policemen coming up the stairs. 'Jack, tell them what this is.'

He's making odd noises, holding his hands to his face to cover his tears, smearing his eyes and cheeks with blood. Gabe's blood and his own. Jack's on his knees, but then he leaps forward towards her, grabbing her arm hard and wrenching her wrist, trying for the pregnancy test pen but sending it clattering on to the balcony and over the edge, lost. Jack tries to pull her back into the room with him and comes through the doorway first, but the police have seen the fight and in the same moment a twenty-stone officer comes up and out of the stairwell like a diving flanker and slams hard sideways into Jack, knocking him away from the door on to the floor so he has to let go of Sarah. Her Jack, brittle Jack, tiny Jack, scratchy, vicious Jack, the Jack she loves and has loved. The boy in the park, the boy with the dreams, the boy with the broken heart and the wicked hands.

'Don't hurt him!'

Jack twists away, scrambles up and throws something behind him: the pole. It bounces off the policeman's shoulder and trips a second officer coming up to help. The falling officer kicks out for balance, knocking over the paraffin heater. A spray of flame flashes out just for a moment, but it catches the heap of silk and feathers, the broken tip of an angel's wing. The officer tries to stamp it out but the fire grows fast around his boot and spreads to a cushion on the floor that becomes a ball of fire. 'Get out!' he shouts to his colleague, who backs off down the stairwell. Now the pile of slats

214

is burning too, and setting fire to the new wall panels. None of the wood has yet been treated, it is all going up like matchsticks. Windows crack. The downdraught from the helicopter outside creates a vortex in the room again, sucking feathers, scraps of silk and smoke upwards in spirals. Jack is dragged through the burning room and down the stairs by the huge officer, who has him in an arm lock, growling as Jack struggles: 'Stop it, you ungrateful little bastard.' Out on the balcony, there is no escape for Sarah and Gabe. The lantern room has become a ring of fire behind them, pumping out choking black smoke with the flames, blocking their way to the stairs.

'What do we do?'

'What can we do?' says Gabe weakly, pulling himself fully to his feet. The heat is intense. They can't move around the balcony. Above them is the vast sky. Ahead of them is the glittering sea. Below them is the void, the long way down. A four-hundred-foot drop. Their only chance is to jump and somehow hit the narrow strip of chalk and gravel that wraps around the bottom of the building thirty feet below, but it's barely more than eight feet wide from the tower to the edge. It looks much narrower from up here, impossibly so. Even if they land on the ledge and survive, the momentum of their bodies could carry them over anyway. But there is no other way and their backs are burning.

'We have to risk it,' says Gabe, one leg over the railing. 'Quick, I can't hold on.'

'Too far,' she says, but there is no choice and she is over too now, backside on the railing, her arms hooked into it, head swimming. 'This is mad. Hold my hand.'

'Will that help?'

'For your sake. On my count of three . . .'

'Sarah, I just want to say—'

'*One, two . . .*'

So they jump. Gabe and Sarah – the lighthouse keeper and the stranger, the lost and the found, and the found and the lost – holding hands, leaping into the void. Sometimes you just have to jump. And for a moment they are suspended between sea, land and sky like creatures of the air . . .

215

Fifty-two

The Chief reacts first. Sarah hits the narrow strip of land at the foot of the tower and folds into the ground, but she bounces and rolls in the dust to the lip of the ledge, right on the edge of the void. The police officers shout, but the veteran Guardian is the one who acts, hauling himself forward, heaving that cannonball belly, ignoring the twist of pain in his back and the sharp, shooting agony in his knees. He scrambles out along the ledge, skidding on the gravel but planting his boots and somehow grabbing a handful of Sarah's shirt and yanking her with all his might. She ends up on her back between his legs, dazed and moaning, and he tells her not to move, for fear they will both go over.

They don't. Still got it, he thinks, gulping for air. Still got it!

'That was stupid,' says the coastguard, who comes more carefully with ropes anchored to the ground and moves them both back, slowly, to safety. 'And brave too.'

'I know,' says the Chief, but he's thinking that Sarah is the brave one. They had to jump – what other choice was there? But still . . . So later he finds himself going to Waitrose to buy a bouquet of white and yellow flowers, roses and other things he doesn't know the names of, to take to Sarah in her hospital ward, just to check she's okay.

'Thank you,' she says softly, surprised and pleased, allowing him to kiss her on the cheek. 'There is something I wanted to tell you.' But in her fuzzy state, still full of morphine, she can't for the moment remember what it is.

For seven days, she rests: at first in the hospital, then in the lighthouse. It's handy for the follow-up appointments. There's no money for a proper bed and breakfast, and anyway the big sky, the horizon and the company help her feel calm. Jack is in custody. But Sarah has to go back; the neighbour is sick of looking after the cat.

'Wait a moment,' she says, pausing for breath about a third of the way up the narrow, winding stairs to the lantern room, nursing her broken heel in a cast. Gabe is going up ahead of her because he is weaker and his healing will take longer. They are close together, her hand on his elbow and her breath on his neck; but in these days of sitting and talking and walking – or hobbling – just a little on the hills and taking the air and laughing sometimes and crying, they have come no closer than this, physically. Neither is ready. One day, perhaps. They go on to the top and each takes a moment to be steady and look around the partially burnt-out room.

'This may not be so bad,' he says, running a hand along a blackened sill. The windows are cracked or missing, but the metal frames remain. 'The structure is still good, somehow.' The wind calls them both out to the balcony, where the South Downs and the Channel encircle them. The day is wide and bright. 'I can put it all back together.'

'I know how that feels,' says Sarah.

'You do. Are you ready?'

'I think so. Whatever comes next.'

They turn to look west and miss what is happening to the east, where the long slope rises again towards Beachy Head. The Chief is climbing the hillside, as fast as he can manage, with a police officer on either side. They look up ahead to the cliff edge, where a slight young woman sits in silhouette with her legs hanging over. That's dangerous, but the person beside her is the one they have come for, come to arrest, dressed in red with her long white hair streaming in the wind. She's a Guardian. Her name is Magda and she's there to help.

Sarah and Gabe look west beyond the Gap to those Seven lovely Sisters, each waiting for a bonny boy to come home in a sailing ship. Seven hills looking out to sea, each with a blank white face, shining in the sun. It's a beautiful day, with powder clouds thrown across a wide, pure, deep blue sky and just a breath of wind to move them.

'Perfect weather to fly,' she says.

'Shall we?'

They move back inside, lift down an angel's head from where it hangs on a new hook under the ceiling, and take hold of the frame to ease those wide, fragile wings out of the door on to the balcony, taking care not to snag the feathers or the silk. They have assembled it together, carefully, from the pieces of a second angel stored in Rí's room on the next floor down, out of reach of the fire.

'To you,' says Sarah, shifting her balance.

'To me,' says Gabe, shuffling along the balcony, and they both smile at a shared joke. They lift the angel together and put their arms out straight above their heads to hold the wings. Sarah has to stand on tiptoes. Gabriel is thinking of his love, his angel-maker. No response will come, he knows that now, but still he says to Rí under his breath: 'Thank you.' She will always be there as the sun rises and as it fades and as the seasons turn. Always and for ever, but not in the same way now. For everything there is a season, in every ending a beginning.

'After three,' he says, his arm aching. 'I'm counting this time. Don't go early again. One, two, three . . .'

They let the angel go with a push, both afraid that it will fall to the ground, but it doesn't. Not today. There is warmth enough. This featherlight creature catches the gentle wind and is lifted above them for a moment, sliding this way and that like a giant cloud-white gull with tissue-thin wings that ripple as it flies. The sky breathes and blows under those wings and now it soars away from them towards the sea.

'Will I see you again?'

'Nah. Shouldn't think so.'

'Gabe, I know where you live.'

'Come and stay then. Any time. Both of you.'

The hope-white angel with the wide embracing wings and happy wide golden eyes flies fast as they watch, towards the drop and the rocks, heading out over the waves to soar above the fishing boats, the tankers and the liners, way out to where the sky meets the sea. And as it goes away from them, it passes over a twist of flower stalks tied by green twine to a wooden post at the edge of the cliff. Caught up among them is a fragment of white plastic that looks like a pen but is not a pen. It has been there for a while. Just about still visible, in a little window on the side, is the trace of a thin blue line.

Author's note

The places described in the story do exist and are well worth a visit, but Birling Gap is now run by the National Trust. The awful pub has closed, and there is a café with cakes instead. The lighthouse at Belle Tout is portrayed here as semi-derelict, as it used to be, before it was moved safely back from the edge. The current owners, David and Barbara Shaw, have renovated the place beautifully. Go there for bed and breakfast; it is very comfortable and the views are stunning.

As for the people, nobody in the story is based on a living person. Any resemblance is a coincidence. There are volunteers who patrol the cliff edge in real life, but the Beachy Head chaplains are not the Guardians. The chaplains are skilled, dedicated, courageous people who save lives every day and deserve your support and your prayers, if you are the praying kind.

Thank you to Rachel Moreton, Elizabeth Sheinkman and Alison Barr for believing in and helping to nurture *The Light Keeper*.

Finally, if any of this has brought up issues and you need to talk to someone, the Samaritans are ready to listen on 116 123. Please call them. It is always better to talk. Thanks for reading. Do get in touch and let me know what you think, via <www.thelightkeeper. org>.

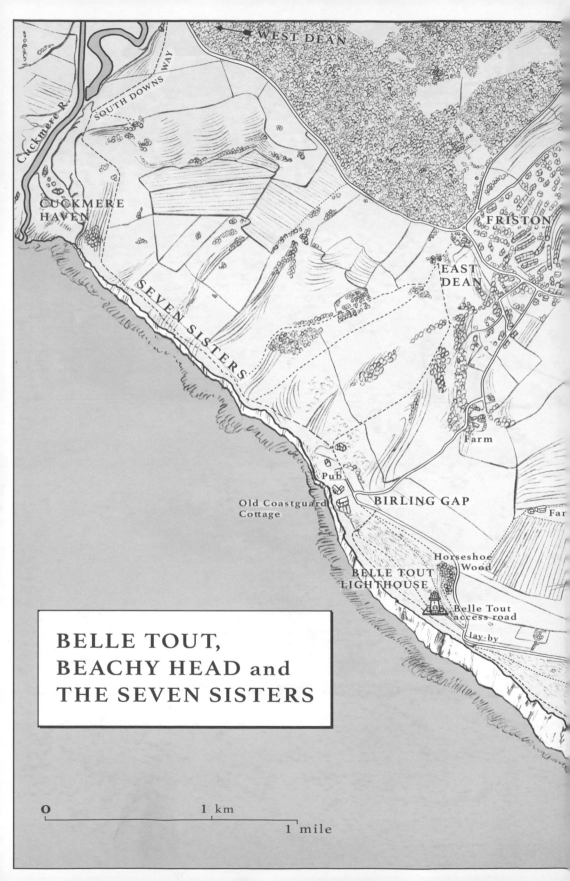

WEST DEAN

SOUTH DOWNS WAY

Cuckmere R.

CUCKMERE
HAVEN

FRISTON

EAST
DEAN

SEVEN SISTERS

Farm

Pub

Old Coastguard
Cottage

BIRLING GAP

Far

Horseshoe
Wood

BELLE TOUT
LIGHTHOUSE

Belle Tout
access road

lay-by

BELLE TOUT,
BEACHY HEAD and
THE SEVEN SISTERS

O   1 km

1 mile

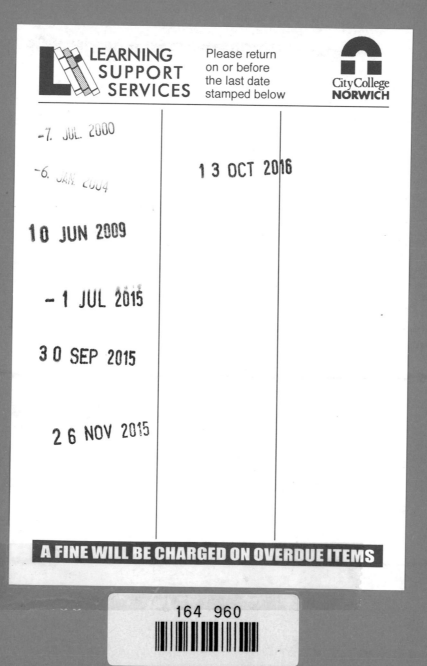

COUNTRY INSIGHTS

KENYA

Máiréad Dunne, Wambui Kairi
& Eric Nyanjom

WAYLAND

COUNTRY INSIGHTS

BRAZIL • CHINA • CUBA • CZECH REPUBLIC • DENMARK • INDIA
FRANCE • JAMAICA • JAPAN • KENYA • MEXICO • PAKISTAN

GUIDE TO THIS BOOK

As well as telling you about the whole of Kenya, this book looks closely at the city of Mombasa and the village of Matinyani.

Each time the book looks at Mombasa, this city symbol will appear at the top of the page and information boxes.

 This rural symbol will appear each time the book looks at Matinyani.

Cover photograph: Children in the playground of Matinyani Primary School.

Title page: Schoolchildren from Bomu School, in Mombasa, hold up the leaves they are studying in their nature lesson.

Contents page: Mount Kenya (*Kirinyaga),* rising above the clouds in central Kenya.

Series editor: Polly Goodman
Book editor: Penny McDowell
Series and book designer: Tim Mayer

First published in 1997 by
Wayland Publishers Ltd
61 Western Road, Hove
East Sussex, BN3 1JD, England

British Library Cataloguing in Publication Data
Dunne, Máiréad
  Kenya. – (Country insights)
  1. Kenya – Juvenile literature
  I. Title
  967.6'2'04

ISBN 0 7502 1777 4

Typeset by Tim Mayer, England
Printed and bound in Italy by LEGO S.p.A., Vicenza

Picture acknowledgements:
All photographs are by Paul Kenward.
All map artwork is by Hardlines.
Border artwork is by Catherine Davenport.

Contents

Introducing Kenya

People have lived in Kenya for over 3 million years. But the ancestors of the people who live in Kenya today came from the surrounding countries over the last 1,000 years.

From AD 1500, many traders visited the Kenyan coast for spices and slaves. Eventually, in 1895, British explorers formed a colony. In 1920, Kenya was named after its highest mountain, the snow-capped Mount Kenya, or *Kirinyaga*, which means 'Mountain of God'.

While the British were in charge, many Africans worked on farms run by British settlers. They were paid very little and lived hard lives while the British took the profits. In the late 1950s, a rebellion against British rule took place, known as the Mau Mau Uprising. The rebellion was crushed by 1959, but four years later Kenya gained its independence and the British left.

Far left: The Kenyan national flag. The spears, shield and colours represent the right of Kenyans to be able to farm in peace.

Left: Children playing in the warm waters of the Indian Ocean, on a Mombasa beach.

4

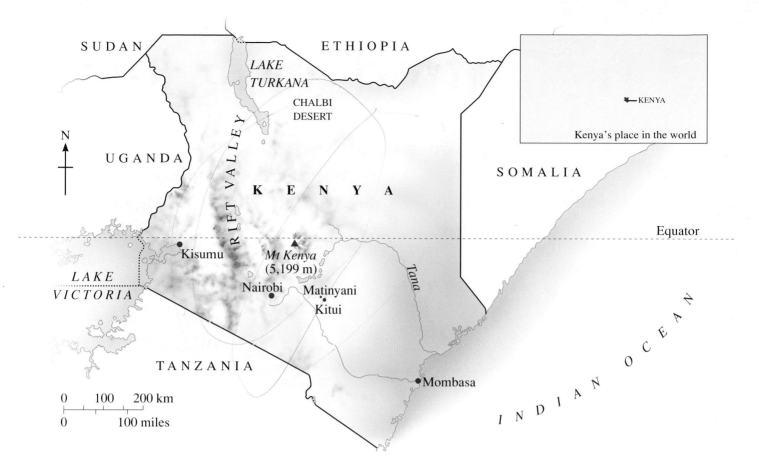

Today, Kenya is divided into eight provinces, each with many districts and forty different ethnic groups. Agriculture provides most of the jobs, and the food and goods produced are sold for export. Tourism is also very important and manufacturing industries are on the increase.

Kenya's soldiers have often served the United Nations. Kenya has friendly relations and good communications with many countries, especially Britain. This has allowed Nairobi, the capital, to become an important centre for large companies such as Shell Oil.

▲ **This book will take you to the city of Mombasa and the village of Matinyani, as well as the rest of Kenya. You can find these places on the map.**

KENYA FACTS	
Population:	27 million
Area:	580,400 km²
Capital:	Nairobi (1.7 million people)
Currency:	Kenya Shilling (K Shs)
Languages:	National: Kiswahili Official: English
National motto:	*Harambee!* ('Let us pull together')

Source: *Republic of Kenya (Statistical Abstract, 1990)*

5

The city of Mombasa

Mombasa is Kenya's second-largest city after Nairobi. It is a port and harbour city, and is divided into mainland and island Mombasa. The city was founded by the Greeks in the seventh century AD. It has a long history of wars and conquest, and has always been a major trading centre. During British rule in Kenya, Mombasa was such an important port that it was made the country's capital.

Goods pass through the harbour to and from Kenya, Uganda, Rwanda and other neighbouring countries. The city is home to monuments and beaches, and Kenya's national parks are nearby. This makes it a popular destination for tourists. Travellers to Kenya can arrive in Nairobi first, or fly directly to Mombasa. There are many different ways to travel between Nairobi and Mombasa, but many people find that the twelve-hour, overnight train journey is an exciting experience.

Looking over Mombasa island. As the city grows in importance, skyscrapers replace the old office blocks.

MOMBASA FACTS

Area:	District: 275 km²
	Island: 15 km²
Population:	700,000
Languages:	Kiswahili; Miji Kenda

Source: *Mombasa District Development Plan, 1989*

Unlike many Kenyan towns, Mombasa does not belong to any single ethnic group. Its inhabitants are a mixture of many different peoples, from all over Kenya and the world.

The city also has a mixture of the old and the new. The Old Town is filled with ancient Arabic buildings, and the Old Harbour is often busy with traditional sailing boats, called *dhows*, carrying tourists. In contrast, barely three kilometres away is the modern Kilindini Harbour, which handles many big cargo liners and oil tankers.

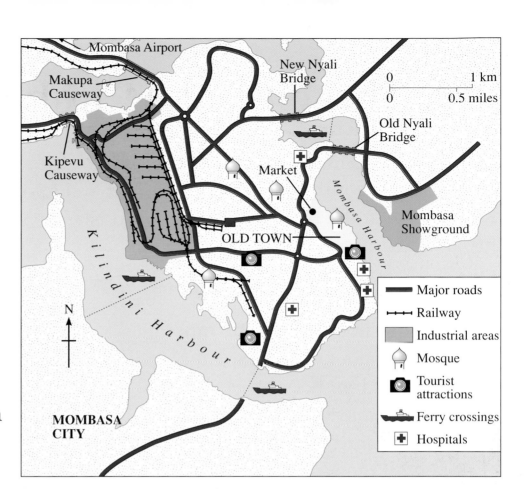

Mombasa Airport

Makupa Causeway

New Nyali Bridge

Old Nyali Bridge

Kipevu Causeway

Market

Mombasa Harbour

OLD TOWN

Mombasa Showground

Kilindini Harbour

N

MOMBASA CITY

0   1 km
0   0.5 miles

━━━ Major roads
┝┿┿┥ Railway
▨ Industrial areas
🕌 Mosque
📷 Tourist attractions
⛴ Ferry crossings
✚ Hospitals

▼ *On the way to the beach, people can buy roasted corn and coconuts from this roadside stall.*

The village of Matinyani

Matinyani is a small village in the Kitui district, south-east of Nairobi. Kitui is one of the two districts of the Akamba people. Homes in the village are simple and are shared by many people.

Most of the men in Matinyani work as farmers or herders. The climate is so dry and water is in such short supply that everyone has to work hard to make a living.

Many of the women in the village have joined projects where they learn to make rugs, baskets and other handicrafts. They use the fibres of sisal plants that grow around the village. The handicrafts are then sold to shops in Europe.

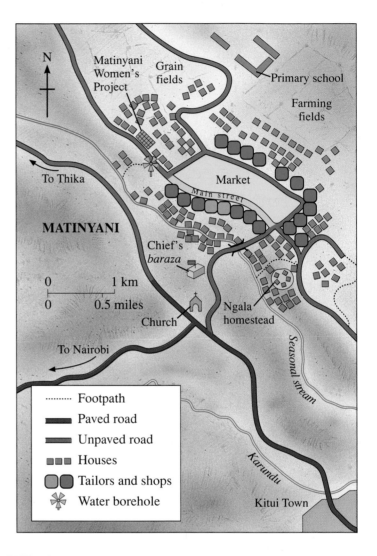

The village hotel and bus stop in the main street of Matinyani.

MATINYANI FACTS

Population:	5,000
Number of houses:	500
Languages:	Kamba; Kiswahili

Matinyani's main street has a hotel, three butchers' shops, four pubs and several second-hand clothes and tailors' shops. There is also a marketplace, where a market is held every Friday.

Young people often move away from the village to Mombasa or Nairobi when they are older to look for work. The government is trying to make improvements in Matinyani to reduce poverty and encourage people not to leave. Trees are being planted to stop the soil eroding, roads are being built and water supplies improved.

Women from the Matinyani Women's Weaving Project with a basket they are making. Baskets are made in many different colours, designs and sizes.

9

Landscape and climate

Kenya lies on the equator, so the sun is very hot and shines for twelve hours a day. The rivers are poor for travel, but their water is used to produce electricity, and dams have been built to create reservoirs for fishing and irrigation. From April to June, heavy rains cause serious floods on the shores of Lake Victoria in the west and the Indian Ocean in the east.

The climate in different parts of Kenya is affected by the height of the land and its distance from the sea. The coast is hot and wet all year round, which is ideal for growing coconuts. But the coconut plantations leave little room for other farming. Mangrove swamps and white sandy beaches line the shores.

Picking tea on a plantation in the highlands west of the Rift Valley.

KENYA'S LAND AND CLIMATE

Hottest temperature:	above 35 °C (deserts)
Coldest temperature:	below 5 °C (slopes of Mount Kenya)
Hottest months:	November–February
Coldest months:	July–August
Heavy rains:	April–June
Highest point:	5,200 m (Mount Kenya)
Longest river:	700 km (Tana river)

Source: *Republic of Kenya (Statistical Abstract, 1991)*

▼ *Tourists on safari in one of Kenya's wildlife parks. Tourism is an important source of income in Kenya.*

▼ *Good roads mean that the fertile central highlands can now be easily reached.*

The north and east sit on a plateau 1,000 metres high. This means that the rainfall, soil and vegetation are poor. In these regions, animal herders have to keep moving to find water and fresh pasture for their animals to graze. Although the days are hot, the nights can be very cold.

In the south of Kenya are the grasslands, home to the country's famous wild animals. Here, national parks protect wildlife such as antelope, elephants, giraffes, rhinoceroses and zebras.

From the grasslands, the land climbs into the highlands, where Kenya's coffee, tea and flower farming takes place. These 'White Highlands' (named after the former European settlers) have a temperate climate. Finally, the Lake Victoria Plateau has good soils and rains, but it is very hot.

11

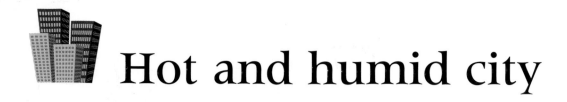

Hot and humid city

▲ *Likoni Ferry takes passengers from the island to the southern mainland of Mombasa.*

Mombasa island fits neatly into a horse-shoe-shaped creek. A forty-metre-deep channel leads to Kilindini Harbour and a ferry crossing connects the island with mainland Mombasa to the south. To the west is a causeway, and to the north, the two, old and new Nyali bridges.

Mombasa's climate is typically humid, hot and wet, and houses are designed to allow as much air through them as possible. In April and May, there are big downpours of rain. Between October and December there are shorter rains. The climate is good for coconut palms and mangrove trees, which dot the coastline. Tropical fruits, including mangoes, oranges, lemons and papaws are abundant, some growing wild.

◀ *Camels come from the dry north of Kenya, but some are brought to Mombasa for pleasure rides on the beaches.*

Mombasa island is mainly a business area, and office rents are quite costly because of limited space and high demand. This has sometimes meant that new, high-rise office blocks have replaced old historic houses. In the crowded Old Town, the streets are so narrow in places that people on upper floors can reach across to each other across the street.

Most wealthy people in Mombasa live on the northern mainland. Tourist hotels stretch along the shoreline and their private beaches merge into the 40–100 metre-wide coral reefs. South of the city there are fishing villages surrounded by small farms.

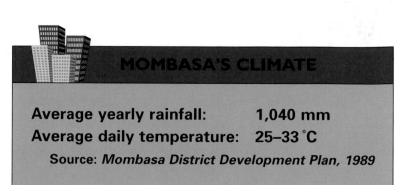

MOMBASA'S CLIMATE

Average yearly rainfall: 1,040 mm
Average daily temperature: 25–33 °C
Source: *Mombasa District Development Plan, 1989*

The view across Nyali creek from the mainland to Mombasa island.

Dry plateau

Matinyani sits on a dry plateau area, 1,000 metres above sea-level. During the wet season, the winds that bring rain from the Indian Ocean bypass this region and take heavy rain to Mount Kenya instead. The heavy water run-off from the mountains, causes injury and death to people and animals. It also damages property, crops, trees and roads. Many projects are underway to restore tree cover to help reduce soil erosion and the loss of rainwater. This would also improve the supply of safe water all year round.

MATINYANI'S CLIMATE

Average yearly rainfall: 700 mm
Average daily temperature: 16–28 °C

Source: *Kitui District Development Plan, 1989*

A typical roadside goat market near Matinyani. Almost nothing can grow on this dry soil.

▼ *A villager carries homemade brooms to the market. People walk distances of up to 20 kilometres to get to the market in Matinyani.*

▲ *This land is green after the rains, but the short mango trees show that crops will not grow well here.*

During the dry season, there is so little rain that water shortages and drought are common. Crops wilt, and pastures and dams disappear. Only the sisal plant thrives. People have to travel far to find water, which is carried in containers by people on foot, or by using ox-drawn carts.

Without the help of food brought in from outside the village, drought kills many animals and brings famine to the villagers. The climate of flooding and drought is too extreme for farmers to make a living. Much research is being done on seeds that can grow quickly and be used for food under such low rainfall conditions.

Home life

There are many different ethnic groups and religions in Kenya. Each has its own culture and way of life, but the family is important to all groups.

Kenya's population is growing fast, and the majority of people are under fifteen years old. The average Kenyan family has four children. But there are often more than six people in each home because in rural areas, it is common for one man to have two wives, and relatives often live together.

In the countryside, many families live in homesteads with more than one house. The parents, young children and girls live in the main house, while older boys live in smaller houses on the compound. Grandparents are looked after by their children and grandchildren.

Inside a basic rural home. The radio and the thermos flasks are the only signs of modern life.

MAJOR ETHNIC GROUPS IN KENYA	
	POPULATION
Gikuyu:	6 million
Abaluhya:	4.5 million
Jo-Luo:	4 million
Akamba:	3.5 million
Kalenjin:	3.5 million
Non-Kenyans:	0.25 million

Source: Adapted from *The Courier,* May–June, 1996

Life in the towns and cities is different. Housing is limited, so many people live in overcrowded flats or houses made from makeshift shelters. In contrast, wealthy Kenyans live in large villas, own many cars and are waited upon by servants.

Many men leave their village to live and work in a town. To save money, their family will stay in the village, where the children go to school.

Different ethnic groups have their own traditional dishes. Meat, *ugali* (a porridge of maize flour that is boiled until it hardens), beans and vegetables are eaten most. On the coast, spiced rice, *chapatti* and fish are common. In the cities, a great variety of foods are eaten, including Western and Indian dishes.

▲ **These narrow streets of Mombasa's Old Town have many small flats in them.**

▲ **Wealthy Kenyans enjoy the luxuries of carpets, electricity and television in their homes.**

Home life in Mombasa

During festivities, children and adults wear their best clothes.

Mombasa is dominated by the Swahili and Muslim cultures. Most people live in bungalows with open patios, where families relax and eat their meals in the hot weather.

Saidi comes from a typical Muslim family. He lives with his sister, Fatuma, and their parents on an estate called Majengo. Their home is thatched with palm leaves called *makuti*. It has a living room, two bedrooms and a bathroom. At the end of the long corridor there is a cooking area for preparing food. Saidi's house has electricity, but there is no running water. His family has to buy water from a tap connected to a pipe near their house.

Saidi's family eat *ugali* and beans. Fish is also popular, but their favourite food is rice, which is saved for special occasions because it is so expensive.

RAMADAN

During the Muslim holy month of Ramadan, every Muslim fasts from dawn until dusk. At the end of the month, the festival of Eid-ul-Fitr celebrates the end of the fasting, and people spill out into the streets at night in carnival mood.

The full variety of food in Mombasa is cooked during the festivals of Eid-ul-Nabi (Prophet Muhammad's birthday) and Eid-ul-Fitr, which celebrates the end of the Muslim month of fasting.

Every Friday at midday, Muslim men in Mombasa go to pray at one of the mosques in the city. Women are not allowed into the mosques, so they pray at home instead.

▲ *Rich and spicy beef is a favourite festival food in Mombasa.*

When Saidi goes out, he puts on a white, full-length outfit, called a *kanzu*, and a cap. Fatuma wears a black, full-length outfit called a *bui-bui* when she leaves the house.

Saidi and his friends often walk into the wealthy areas of Mombasa. They walk past large houses surrounded by fences and protected by guards. Huge dogs bark at the boys as they pass by.

The boys admire all the expensive cars, and sometimes they glimpse swimming pools and tennis courts at the backs of the houses.

◄ *The rent for flats like these in Mombasa are cheap, but they are often overcrowded and in poor condition.*

Home life in Matinyani

Typical village homes with well-trimmed thatched roofs.

Ngala and his wife Mwende live in a homestead of nine houses in Matinyani. They have three children, aged two, four and seven. They share the homestead with Ngala's elderly parents, his brothers and their families. Each main house has earth-brick walls, thatched roofs and a cement floor. A separate hut acts as a kitchen and store room, and there is an outside toilet and a bathroom, which are shared by everyone.

Ngala's sisters are married and have moved to their own homes. The younger children sleep in their mothers' houses. As the girls get older, they move to a grandmother's house to be educated into womanhood. The older boys have their own rooms within the homestead.

◀ *Mweni Kimanzi, aged seven, eats a bowl of beans beside the kitchen fire. Above her, corn cobs are hung above the fire to dry.*

'I will soon pay to have electricity, especially now that I am about to finish building my new, big house.' – Ngala Kimanzi, store manager.

Although the nearby market has electricity, not all families can afford the connection fee. So they use paraffin lamps for lighting and cook on open hearths using firewood.

Many people own radios, but very few have televisions. However, some of the bars in the main street have televisions, where villagers can catch up on national and international news. The local chief's *baraza* (meeting place), the Friday market and Sunday worship are all times for catching up on local news.

Visitors are always made welcome in the village and they stay wherever there is room for them. Traditionally, it is considered rude for a visitor to refuse food that is offered to them.

▲ *Donkeys make fetching water faster and lighter work.*

21

Kenya at work

Kenyans are a hard-working people. They have a saying, *'kula jasho'*, which means 'eat from your own sweat'. Since there is little paid employment in Kenya, most people work for themselves. In the countryside, many people simply tend their own farms. Others work on the large coffee, tea or sisal plantations, or on cattle ranches.

In the towns and cities, there is employed work in offices, or in factories that produce goods to sell abroad. There is also professional work for qualified graduates, such as engineering, medicine, law and teaching.

But many rely on informal work, known as *jua kali*, where any available scraps are used to make products that can be sold, such as using timber crates to make furniture.

WORKING VISITORS

A popular traditional song says that on the first day a visitor must be waited upon, but by the fourth day they must be given a share of the work to do.

A young girl does her share of the work by herding the donkeys.

22

▲ *Coconuts and chips are sold at a roadside stall. Work like this is very common in Kenya, where there is little paid employment.*

Since Kenya attracts many tourists, the tourist industry provides different types of work. Hotels near the wildlife parks and along the coast employ people as tour guides, chefs or general hotel staff. Kenya's two international airports provide jobs as pilots, air stewards and tour operators. Tourism also provides work to villagers, who sell handicrafts and souvenirs.

Small-scale farmers in the countryside produce enough food for their families and a little extra to sell.

TYPE OF WORK IN KENYA	
	Percentage of population
Small-scale farming:	62%
Informal work:	24%
Employed work:	14%
Source: *National Development Plan, 1994*	

Many women in towns and cities make money by selling crafts and other goods on the street. Younger girls often do paid housework and many children work after school. Some pupils even leave school to work full-time. Employment for women in towns and cities is usually in catering or secretarial work, but these jobs are just for women who have been to school.

▲ *Building work is increasing as the demand for new offices rises.*

23

Work in Mombasa

There are many different types of work in Mombasa. Since the city is also a port, there is much work in Kilindini harbour, where ships bring in goods from other parts of the world. Saidi's father works in the busy warehouses at the shipyard. There is also work in the cement factory, the oil refinery and smaller factories, which make goods such as soap, matches and corrugated-iron sheets.

'I work at the docks unloading goods from cargo ships. We get a two-hour lunch break every day.' – Benson Karisa, dock worker.

Saidi's Uncle Abedi is a taxi driver and owns his own car. He earns good money, but he has to work long hours so his children see very little of him.

Many people work in tourism in Mombasa, in hotels, night-clubs or casinos, or as tourist guides around the city. These jobs are well-paid, and many children leave school early to earn money from tourism.

Tourists are taken out on a traditional fishing boat.

▲ Rajesh Patel helps in his father's office after school. Children start work in family businesses at an early age.

Saidi's mother is a housewife. She also takes in other people's laundry to earn extra money because Saidi's father's income is not enough. Other mothers do the same, selling snacks or cutting people's hair to add to their family's income.

Fishing is important work to older men in the city, who sell their catch in the markets. But they earn very little money because as the town grows, the fish do not come so close to the shore.

▼ This boy is increasing his family's income by selling peanuts on the side of the road.

TYPE OF WORK IN MOMBASA	
	Percentage of workers
Industry	47%
Self-employed	39%
Finance	14%

Source: *Mombasa District Development Plan, 1989*

Work in Matinyani

There is very little paid employment in Matinyani because there are no businesses there. So many people work in Mombasa, Nairobi or other towns. They send money home to their families and return briefly for weekends and holidays.

Most people in Matinyani work as farmers growing maize, millet and beans. They also keep cattle, goats and donkeys, and everybody in the family shares the workload. A few people work as tailors, shopkeepers or butchers.

Ngala is lucky to have a job as a store manager for the Matinyani Women's Weaving Project. The project has six people who train women in

▲ *An ox-drawn cart delivers blocks to a building site near the village.*

'In *harambee* (fund-raising) work, everyone must chip in. So for a house, the men will build and the women will make bricks and fetch water. The children will gather pebbles and stones, and run errands. In this way the house is really ours!' – Ngala Kimanzi, store manager.

handicraft, weaving and pottery skills. Their colourful rugs and baskets are sold locally and to Europe. Other women's groups keep bees, chickens and goats.

Ngala's brother grows and sells tree and flower seedlings. These are important to the area because they save water and keep the soil from eroding.

Friday is market day and men and women bring their cows, goats and farm produce on ox-carts, donkeys, bicycles and on their backs. Some people walk long distances of up to 20 kilometres to get to the market. Afterwards, the bars and shops on the main street do a little business, before the villagers return to their quiet lives.

Elephants are woven into a colourful rug made by the Matinyani Women's Weaving Project.

Going to school

Although primary education in Kenya is free, secondary school is very expensive. So many children, especially girls, leave at the end of primary school to work.

Most schools are built through contributions of money and voluntary help from the community. Where there are not enough classrooms, children learn outdoors or classes take turns to use the available rooms. Every child is supposed to wear school uniform and buy their own books, but many families cannot afford these needs.

School is hard work, especially for girls and children from poorer families, who have to do jobs at home as well. At the end of primary and secondary school, students take national exams. To prepare for these exams, they have to go to extra lessons at the weekends and miss their eight-week school holiday.

Fourteen subjects are studied in primary school, including maths, Kiswahili and English (the language children are taught in). Nine are studied at secondary school. Teachers are trained in the skills needed for teaching children with special needs.

Lunchtime in a secondary-school playground in Kenya.

SCHOOL IN KENYA

	Age
Primary school	7–14 years
Secondary school	14–18 years
University	18–22 years

Source: *National Development Plan, 1994*

▶ *The high fees of this nursery school mean that the children have all they need.*

Outside the classroom, students can enjoy drama, music, and a variety of sports and after-school courses are popular. Since Kenya only has eight universities, many students leave the country to go to university abroad.

▼ *Schoolchildren play a game with a homemade ball in their lunch break.*

School in Mombasa

There are many schools in Mombasa, including both state and private schools. Saidi's school is near his home on Mombasa island, so he can walk home for lunch. Older children, who go to mainland schools, take packed lunches, or money to buy snacks.

Most children walk to school, but if they want to catch the bus, their school uniform allows them a student fare. Children from wealthier families are sometimes driven to school.

A schoolgirl waits for the school bus, while a matatu driver tries to attract passengers to ride in his minibus.

Saidi is ten years old. He enjoys maths and is planning on studying engineering at college. Saidi wants to be able to build a bridge like the Nyali, which crosses Mombasa harbour.

His sister, Fatuma, is fourteen and is studying for her national exams at the end of primary school. Fatuma leaves home for school at 6 am to study for twelve hours each day. Fatuma and Saidi's father wants her to pass her exams so that she can be the first girl in the family to go to secondary school. At least her housework duties have been stopped for the year!

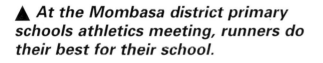

▲ **At the Mombasa district primary schools athletics meeting, runners do their best for their school.**

Sports are important in all Mombasa schools and annual school competitions are a big event. Sports include athletics, swimming, football, rugby and netball. Many children learn to swim in the ocean because few schools have swimming pools.

'I am hoping that if I train hard, I will be able to join the **Olympics** running team for Kenya in a few years.' – Ruth Mutinda, aged 14, Kamodya School (above right).

The winners of the 110-metre hurdle race are presented with their prizes.

31

School in Matinyani

Mweni and Kyalo go to Matinyani Primary School, which is about two kilometres from their home. The rest of the 800 pupils come from up to five kilometres away. Each class has about thirty students. Unlike schools in Mombasa, the children do not have to wear shoes and socks as part of their uniform because many parents cannot afford them.

There are no lockers at their school, so Mweni and Kyalo have to carry all their books, as well as their lunch, to school and back each day. They don't mind carrying sports, music or drama equipment, because the best students travel to other villages and towns for competitions.

▲ *Barefoot on the football pitch. The ball is made out of paper, plastic and string.*

▲ *The school in Matinyani is neat and simple.*

'I like it when the rains come because we don't have to go so far to fetch water.' – Mweni Kimanzi, 7 years old.

The children of Matinyani Primary School have to keep their school clean. They wash the classrooms and weed the flowerbeds in the school compound. Sometimes they have to do these chores as punishment for being late or getting into trouble, but they prefer to work rather than receive the cane.

During the rains, the children enjoy working on the school farm. It is very different from their home farms and produces much more food. The children enjoy pushing or digging out the vehicles that get stuck in the mud outside the school. The rains also mean that less time is spent fetching water because the tanks and nearby dams are full.

There is no secondary school in Matinyani, so students who pass their national exams have to go to school in Kitui town.

Mweni and her friends looking out of their classroom window.

33

Kenya at play

Evenings, weekends and holidays in Kenya are spent on favourite pastimes such as sport, meeting with friends and family, or simply catching up on jobs around the home.

Kenya is famous for producing some of the world's best athletes, especially long-distance runners. Olympic champions are an inspiration to young Kenyans, many of whom have to run long distances to and from school every day, and who hope to become Olympic gold medalists themselves one day. Football is another popular sport, which is played almost everywhere in the country since it does not require expensive equipment.

Other sports and big events are boxing, swimming, tennis, golf, rugby, hockey, horse riding, cycling and volleyball. However, only a small percentage of Kenyans have access to these sports because they are expensive and are concentrated in the big towns and cities.

Children play games such as 'hide-and-seek' or 'hula-hoops', and use playthings that usually come from scrap heaps rather than toy shops.

Children play on a makeshift roundabout in a city park.

A traditional Kenyan pastime is a type of fund-raising called *harambee*. This is a way of getting jobs done, while also having fun, and includes singing, dancing and feasting. Public holidays are a good excuse for Kenyans to treat themselves and enjoy time with relatives and friends.

▲ *Football is a very popular pastime among Kenyan boys.*

OLYMPIC CHAMPIONS

Since 1968, Kenya's runners have won the 3,000-metre steeplechase in every Olympics and World Cup!

KENYAN PUBLIC HOLIDAYS

1 January:	New Year's Day
March/April:	Good Friday and Easter Monday
1 May:	Labour Day
1 June:	Madaraka Day
10 October:	Moi Day
20 October:	Kenyatta Day (all heroes day)
12 December:	Jamhuri Day (independence day)
25–26 December:	Christmas Day and Boxing Day

The Muslim festival of Eid-ul-Fitr is also a public holiday. Its date varies according to the month of Ramadan each year.

◀ *A hurdle race in a sports festival between schools at Mombasa Stadium.*

Leisure time in Mombasa

There are lots of ways to relax and have fun in Mombasa. In the daytime there are beaches for swimmers and sun-bathers, and at night there is both modern and more traditional dancing.

Families can visit the crocodile farm, meat-roasting dens called *Nyama Choma*, or ancient monuments such as Fort Jesus. Schoolchildren are often taken on trips to the national parks outside the city, to see the wild elephants, giraffes and zebras.

Football is very popular in the city, as it is all over the country. Kenya's third-largest football stadium, Mombasa Stadium, attracts many fans and players. Athletics meetings are often a big family occasion and the annual, International Mombasa Marathon is a very colourful event.

> '**I have been saving money so that I can enjoy more of the stands at the Mombasa Show this year.**'
> **– Salama Karisa, 10 years old.**

Relaxing in the warm sea. On the horizon you can see waves breaking on the coral reef that fringes the coastline.

◀ *A Muslim family in their best clothes browse for festival goodies at Eid-ul-Fitr.*

▼ *Giving a friend a lift along the beach.*

The annual Muslim festival of Eid-ul-Fitr is a special occasion for families. People wear bright, new clothes and the festivities flow out on to the streets. Other festivities include the Mombasa Agricultural Show, which attracts visitors from all over the country and provides a week of continuous fun for everyone to enjoy. Many Kenyans also flock to Mombasa for their Easter and Christmas holidays.

For tourists and wealthier families there is plenty to do. Many go on guided tours into the surrounding national parks. Or they take part in watersports such as water-skiing, scuba-diving or deep-sea fishing. At night, there are many restaurants to choose from and the evening breeze draws people to the seafront gardens.

Leisure time in Matinyani

Matinyani, like other villages in Kenya, has far fewer leisure facilities than in the towns and cities. So people have to be creative and make their own fun.

Children make toys from local materials such as clay, straw, beans and sand. They also use cardboard boxes and leftover cloth from the tailors' shops.

Singing is very important in the village because it cheers people up while they work. Since there are no books or comics available to read, singing is a good way of entertaining the children. Many of the songs also teach children about the history of their family or community.

Women hardly ever rest during the day because there is so much work to be done. Instead, they make the most of being with their friends while they work and swap news and stories.

Joseph Kilonzo and his friends with their football in the street.

'We play football whenever we get the chance. We've got our own ball and we've marked out a pitch with piles of stones.' – Joseph Kilonzo, 14 years old (right).

38

The men have an easier time because their work, such as herding cattle, means that they can sit and chat together during the day. In the evenings, they go to the local pub and watch television.

The chief of the village is elected by the government and remains chief until he dies. His *baraza* is a good place for the villagers to meet and discuss important matters about Matinyani. The elected leaders also have meetings which often become heated with noisy discussions.

Everyone looks forward to the Friday market and Sunday church, when they can wear their best clothes and see their friends. Weddings and funerals are also big occasions and become festivals for everyone to enjoy.

▲ *This toy car has been made out of scrap tin, wood and string.*

▼ *Stallholders sell vegetables and fruit on market day in Matinyani.*

The future

The future for most Kenyans is in farming, since eight-out-of-ten people in Kenya rely on farming to make a living. However, most farmers only have small areas of poor-quality land, while a few wealthy farmers own huge plantations.

The growth of Kenya's population is adding to this problem. Poor people usually have large families so that their children can help on the farm. But as the number of farmers grows, the quality of the land and produce gets worse. If the government can share out more of the high-quality land, and the larger farms can offer work to some of the smaller farmers, it would give people in the countryside a better future.

Kenya's population is still growing, and all these children will need more jobs and better healthcare in the future.

POPULATION GROWTH	
	Millions
1989	23.513
1990	24.397
1991	25.308
1992	26.247
1993	27.214

Source: *National Development Plan, 1994*

As the population grows, more young people will be looking for jobs, and could face unemployment. So self-employment is being encouraged, especially in the towns and cities.

Kenya's stunning landscapes continue to attract many tourists every year, and the tourist industry should provide more jobs and money in the future. But tourism also causes problems, such as encouraging children to leave school early, which will have to be looked at in the future alongside the industry's growth.

If Kenya can make good use of its large, young population and other natural resources, as well as relying less on other countries for help, Kenyans should be able to feel proud of their independence and successes.

▲ *This guide drives tourists through a wildlife park. He knows the best places to watch the animals.*

▶ *The entrance to a national wildlife park. This kind of tourism is essential to Kenya's future income.*

The future of Mombasa

These beautiful beaches could be threatened by pollution from the growth of the city.

Mombasa's future must be carefully planned. It is important that the city's growth in industry and population is balanced against pollution, shortage of fresh water and overcrowding that growth may cause.

The demand for more office space could mean that historic buildings, which can never be replaced, will be knocked down. People in Mombasa are also worried that parkland in the city will be lost as land is taken for housing and business. These could all mean that fewer tourists would come to Mombasa. But the city and its people cannot afford to lose the money that is made from tourism.

On the other hand, it is important that the many visitors to Mombasa do not destroy local cultural values. The Muslims do not want their culture to be affected and the traditions of the original nine peoples of the area, the Miji Kenda, should be respected. For example, it is essential to them that their *kaya* – sacred prayer forests – are not damaged in any way.

'The new office building is beautiful, but it has been built on our football pitch. Where will we play now?' – Hamisi Omar, 10 years old.

At present, school results in Mombasa are among the worst in Kenya. Many children leave school early to take jobs in tourism and girls often leave school to get married. This is partly because of the need to earn money, but also because of tradition. If children are encouraged to stay at school, they stand a better chance of getting higher-paid jobs at the end of their education. This would mean a better quality of life for themselves and their families.

◄ *New, high-rise blocks help the demand for more offices, but overcrowding may create new problems.*

▼*Improving education is one of Mombasa's most important tasks in the future.*

The future of Matinyani

Despite their hardships, the people of Matinyani are full of hope for the future. They hope that their lives will improve and that financial help will be offered by well-wishers. For example, the heavy floods can cause terrible damage, but with financial help, dams could be built upstream. This would protect the village from flooding and create a supply of water for irrigation and drinking.

The village is also hopeful that the arrival of electricity nearby will attract new businesses and new jobs. This might bring the young, who have left to find work in the city, back to Matinyani. More importantly, it may stop young people from leaving their friends and families in years to come.

The famous Matinyani rugs will bring much-needed money to the village in the future.

▲ *Tree cover is essential to protect the soil from erosion. If projects to restore tree cover are successful in Matinyani, crops will be more successful.*

It is hoped that the growth of women's projects will mean more money for education and healthcare in the village. As the groups become stronger, it will be possible to get better prices for their crafts.

As research on new seeds for crops in this dry land continues, it should mean that more money will be made from farming and there will be more food to go around. More money should make it possible for the villagers to improve their homes. They should be able to pay for electricity to be connected to their homes, and to buy other items to make their lives easier.

'The primary school has been built through *harambee*. I hope to become a leader so that I can build a secondary school for Matinyani.' – Joseph Kilonzo, 14 years old.

▶ *Small businesses, such as this tailor's shop, do not rely on the success of crops, so they are safer than farming in Matinyani.*

Glossary

Baraza A central meeting place in a community where members discuss serious matters or simply chat.

Causeway A raised road built over a stretch of water.

Colony A territory or country which is controlled by another country.

Compound A group of houses with shared facilities, such as toilets.

Crops Plants grown on a farm for food.

Dhows Large Arabian wind-driven boats.

Equator An imaginary line around the earth, which is an equal distance from the North and South poles.

Eroding The wearing away of a substance, such as soil.

Ethnic groups Groups of people identified by their language or culture.

Export A country's produce that is sold to other countries.

Harambee A type of fund-raising in Kenya where people contribute work and money to gain a need, such as building a school.

Homestead A house, especially on a farm, and outbuildings.

Humid Air that is full of moisture.

Independence When a colony gains the right to control its own affairs.

Irrigation The artificial watering of the land to grow crops, using channels, sprinklers or pipes.

Maize Corn.

Makeshift Temporary.

Makuti The leaves or branches of the coconut tree, used for roofing.

Matatu A type of taxi, usually a minibus. Matatu drivers are renowned for overloading and overspeeding.

Monuments Historic remains, such as buildings or statues.

Paraffin An oil used for fuel.

Plantation An area of land planted with a single crop or type of tree.

Plateau An area of fairly flat land, raised above the surrounding area.

Rent To pay money to live in a house or flat.

Sisal plant A plant with large, fleshy leaves. The plant has tough fibres that are used to make rope and handicrafts.

Settlers People who move from their original home or country to live elsewhere, often to farm.

Slums Dirt-filled areas in towns where people live in poor, makeshift housing. Usually there is no proper water supply, lighting or even streets.

Temperate climate A mild climate that is never very hot or very cold.

Ugali A preparation of maize flour that is boiled until it hardens.

Voluntary Actions done from free will rather than being paid or forced to do them.

Further information

Books to Read

Continents: Africa by P. Cremin and C. Regan (Wayland, 1996)

Focus On Kenya by Fleur Ng'weno (Evans, 1994)

Eyewitness Guide: Africa by Yvonne Ayo (Dorling Kindersley, 1995)

World Focus: Kenya by David Marshall and Geoff Sayer (Heinemann, 1994)

Useful Addresses

Kenya High Commission
45 Portland Place,
London W1N 4AS
Tel: 0171 636 2371

Kenya Tourist Office
25 Brooks Mews,
London W1Y 1LF
Tel: 0171 355 3144

Photopacks

A Week with a Family in Kenya (Warwickshire World Studies Centre, 1993)

Barichao: A Village in Kenya (Warwickshire World Studies Centre, 1993)

Feeling Good About Far-away Friends: Daily life of a Maasai family in Kenya by Leeds Development Education Centre (1995)

Kapsokwony: Rural Kenya: A Locality in an Economically Developing Country by Steve Brace (Actionaid, 1992)

Nairobi: Kenyan City Life: A Locality in an Economically Developing Country by Steve Brace (Actionaid, 1992)

New Journeys: Learning from Kenya and Tanzania (Birmingham Development Education Centre, 1991)

Speaking for Ourselves, Listening to Others (Leeds Development Education Centre, 1996)

Index

Page numbers in **bold** refer to photographs.